HALI
and
COLLECTED STORIES

Also by G.V. Desani

All About H. Hatterr
Definitive Edition
McPherson & Company

G. V. DESANI

HALI

AND

COLLECTED
STORIES

McPherson and Company

Published by McPherson & Company, Post Office Box 1126, Kingston, New York 12401. No part of this publication may be reproduced by any means, electronic or mechanical including photocopy, recording or any information storage and retrieval system without the written permission of the publishers. This first printing has been assisted by grants from the literature programs of the New York State Council on the Arts and the National Endowment for the Arts, a federal agency. Design by Bruce McPherson. Typeset in Times Roman by Delmas Typographers. Manufactured in the United States of America. First edition.
1 3 5 7 9 10 8 6 4 2   1991   1992   1993   1994   1995   1996

Library of Congress Cataloging-in-Publication Data

Desani, G.V. (Govindas Vishnoodas), 1909–
   Hali and collected stories / G.V. Desani.
     p.   cm.
   ISBN 0–929701–12–7
   I. Title.
PR9499.3.D472H35   1990
823—dc20   90–46599

Hali was first published in Britain in 1950 by Saturn Press; revised editions followed in 1952 in *The Illustrated Weekly of India* (Bombay) and in 1953 again in Great Britain. The present text is the fourth revised and definitive edition, considerably enlarged and published here for the first time, and supercedes the Watergate Theatre stage version (London, 1950), the broadcast versions by All India Radio (1950 and '51), and the 1967 edition which was not authorized by the author. The following stories were first published in *The Illustrated Weekly of India:* "Mephisto's Daughter," "The Lama Arupa," "A New Bridge of Plenty," "Sutta Abandoned," "The Fiend Screams 'Kyā Chāhate Ho?'," "With Malice Aforethought," "The Last Long Letter," "A Border Incident," "The Barber of Sāhibsarāi," "The Pansārī's Account of the Incident," "The Second Mrs. Was Wed in a Nightmare," "Abdullāh Haii," "Gypsy Jim Brazil to Kumari Kishino" (in considerably different form), and "In Memorium." "Rudyard Kipling's Evaluation of His Mother" first appeared in the *ACLAS Bulletin,* University of Mysore, 1976, and ". . . Down with Philosophy" in *Boston University Journal,* XXVI, 1979. "The Merchant of Kisingarh" was first published by *Westerly Magazine,* University of Western Australia. "The Valley of Lions," "This Shrub, This Child of God," "Correspondence with Sister Jay," "Country Life, Country Folk, Cobras, *Thok!,*" "The Mandatory Interview with the Dean," and "Since a Nation Must Export, Smithers!" are original to this volume.

C O N T E N T S

PREFACE

Had the ancient sage Mārkandeya, the author of the *Durgāsaptashatī,* hired an apologist, he might have argued that the two, three or more faces of the divinity named Durgā are necessary metaphors: those being the facets and aspects of her personality. A face of hers is gentle and beautiful; that is the face which is venerated and grants the supplicant beauty, victory, honor—thus the *Argalā,* the hymn to Durgā. The great Goddess' other face is cruel: that face exacts sacrifice. Mounted on her charger, the frantic lion, tearing up the fleeing clouds with his flashing claws, and leading a legion of nineteen million furies, that face is Durgā's, too, the celestial presence, with limbs of gold, her crowned head ringed by the halo of blinding light, descending from the sky upon the green hills of Vindhyā, India, to destroy the thousand-armed, the as yet invincible demon and his audacious horde. In seven of her hands, the sage records, she carried weapons of dreadful power; of flames, venom, slaughter and death. In her eighth hand, she bore a mountain lily. Whoever heard of a general, lodged on a lion, racing to wage the war of all time, herself merrily certain of overcoming the enemy with a mountain lily? The gentle and the beautiful face, and the lily, say the devout, were seen only by those who were blessed by Durgā. They had sighted the radiant Lady, moreover, upon the throne of sunlighted emerald, its glowing canopy of green and gold exalting the glittering array of clouds arched above the earth, and they had cried to the sky, "Sky, sweet sky, let kindly clouds shower pearls and jasmines on holy Durgā!" To them, the divine Mother was everything: the merciful deity thus manifested, thus revealed, thus named, thus declared Durgā! the adored Shri Durgā! the victorious Shri Shri Durgā!—the keeper of all creatures, the giver of all life, and the taker, too, if she so willed. The many-headed and many-armed ancient images and icons of Durgā, therefore, the apologist would insist, are legitimate representations of Mārkandeya's avenger-Durgā: to say nothing of this writer's personal, very own imagined, beautiful and beloved angel Durgā, herewith with feelings described. The spinning sphere, the earth, too, is perceived variously and has formidable and contradicting aspects. Her great belly is stark and dark and fiery and kindled and crimson and on her surface are the splendid seas—their spirited waves surging to be with the moon. Yet, settled on this very wet and very ignited thing, we read! write! marry! make history! and in this disorganized household there are plans yet to raise roses—indeed raise a gem of a rose, a unique, precious, frost-white felicity, to shame the moon!

This book has been many years in the making—the experience and the shaping of it. Its publication may be justified as so many faces or facets of a contemporary person. Besides, if the makers of images and icons matter at all, as do the images and icons themselves, then the faces and the facets of the makers might be indulged with a measure of sympathy?

G.V. Desani
Austin, Texas
April, 1991

HALI

I, DWĀRKĀ

I WAS NAMED after a *nātha,* an immortal lord, whose love for the Lord and his creatures was unbounded. I have not loved. Unknowingly, I have been cruel. I pray that I may be endowed with resource to narrate this story of love: the story of HĀLĪ, of his life and death, of his love for ROOH: from as much I, DWĀRKĀ, knew of this lore, and gathered from the voices: the voices of ĪSHA, the Lord, of Hālī's mother MĪRĀ, of his dearly loved Rooh, the Adversary RĀHŪ, MĀYĀ, who befriended him, the MAGICIAN and Hālī's own uttered thought and feeling, as he spoke with the voices he heard.

THUS DWĀRKĀ

HĀLĪ'S MOTHER USED to graze deer in the northern hills of India. Since he was eight, he did not know of a more beautiful being than his mother. The second most beautiful and beloved creature to him was their fawn. He called her Shā and Hālī loved Shā as dearly as his mother loved him.

Then the gods conspired and made him beautiful. The hill women used to cast glances at him, as he passed them by, hungering for a boy who had the likeness of a god. Mīrā, his mother, gave him a girl's name, "Girijā" (Mountain-born): then called

3

him Hālī, after a Dargāh, the shrine of a Muslim saint. She could not believe that her son would be so beautiful but for the saint's grace.

He had long hair like a girl's, and she used to deck it with flowers, and she gave him bangles for his wrists and anklets for his feet. Mīrā, the artless woman of the hills, fell in love with her son again and again. How wonderful it is to have a child whom both the gods and the mortals envy!

She would gaze at his face and like the child that she was, impulsively, gather him in her arms and embrace him. There would be tears in her eyes as her forehead would be against his. And he would cling to her, and close his eyes, afraid he might die, because his mother loved him so!

Then the gods decreed an ordeal for Hālī.

From the foot of a hill he saw his mother climb the rocks. Her pale face seemed to him like a flower of the hills and her lips the color of lighted gold. As he looked up, her yellow robe appeared gilded, for behind her was the setting sun. He saw the wending sunbeams mold a crown of coralline mist around her, and he thought she was divine, deathless, and made of love.

Then he saw her fall from a rock and saw the highlands Indus make her a grave. The bright water of the river churned, the reeds shook, there was foam, then the river was still.

Lost, from hill to hill, forest to forest, Hālī searched for his mother, and he cried for his Shā, till the gods in their mercy took away his strength.

Then Māyā, a good woman from the plains, saw him, and carried him to her home. She nursed him, healed his eyes, plucked thorns from his feet, and called him son. And he grew to be a man.

Then he found a beloved being, the most beloved being God ever made. Rooh was her name. And Rooh is dead.

THUS ĪSHA, THE LORD

I AM ĪSHA, the Lord and Keeper of all!

Long before time was made, the sky was the sky, the earth the earth, I was alone, sufficient, neither living, nor dead, neither asleep nor awake: the great, the least, the first, the last!

Know ye, then, not East, not West, not South, not North were, nor the sun, the moon, the stars!

Nothing, Naught!

No love, no hate, none father, none child, and no will, no desire, no pain, no pleasure.

Void was I, fulfillment I, I of no shape, no form!

In me, at a moment unnamed, breath was born. And I became a form, a form of a seeing Eye, a mystic magic Eye of blood and blue, a quivering melting and a breathing Eye, a seeing Eye, set upon the void of the sky, framed in no frame and such was I!

Then a shape I saw. The shape of a lotus, a lotus of sun and gold, glowing gold, a flower of threadlike flame, of sun and gold, glowing gold, a smouldering kindling flower wrought in enchantment unseen, of radiance unseen!

Then the Eye was not, was a sea, a stilled sea, of blue and pearl, precious pearl, mirroring the flower of enchantment unseen, of radiance unseen. Thus, know ye, beauty and love were born, and by me known!

And the earth came to be, the sky, the moon, the stars, and all shapes and forms. And I, Īsha, thus lured, thus formed, became the Will, the Creator and the Keeper of all!

In me, then, sadness was born!

For know ye, I, the Lord Keeper of all, am the Great Will Accurst, the Eternal Insatiable, the Immeasurable Abandoned, and I will and hunger to die, not be, if be, be what I was, be Naught! when time too was not, ere I became an Eye, a sea, a silent sea, the sea of pearl and blue, bearing beauty, bearing love, and die, I cannot!

And I will, I will, and I will to die!

Curst am I, curst am I!

O hear ye, all mortals, all shapes, all forms! curst am I! curst am I!

THUS MĪRĀ TO HĀLĪ

I AM MĪRĀ, thy mother, my son, canst hear?

Thou wast a little one, my little one, thy palms no bigger than the bud of a rose, bigger, true, but not to me, and so dear!

The fates raged, thou knowest, and I was gone into darkness, and I did hear my little one cry, cry for me. And I could not come to my little one!

I did call, call to thee, my child. I and my little one apart!

I did pray to the Lord for mercy, son. Prayed to the Lord to keep thee, son. My little one, calling for me!

I cannot linger, for the Lord so wills. May he, of many mercies, protect you! May the lords of the earth honor thee as master, may it be so!

When thou art man, and master, wouldst thou remember thy mother? Thy humble loving mother, and wouldst thou, son, forgive? Forgive the Lord-ordained parting, too soon, my little one not grown man, canst hear me! canst hear me! wouldst thou forgive?

THUS ROOH TO HĀLĪ

I AM ROOH, HĀLĪ!

Thy Rooh, beloved!

Yet no limbs have I to be thy slaves, no arms, no hands, to sacrifice to thee, yet thine, thine ever!

Were I flower, at thy feet would I be. Were I earth, at thy feet would I be.

Dead, destroyed of limb, not even a shadow, but thine, thine ever, beloved!

I know of thy pain. Yet no eyes have I to weep. Oh, thine, thine ever, yet not of the earth, blind of eye, in pain for thee, thine, yet not to be!

If I had lips! I will say, here I am! Come to me! Do not cry, beloved! Here I am!

THUS DWĀRKĀ
A past of Hālī

THE SUM OF creatures, the masters say, is nothing.

The sum of creatures, others say, is the mortal soul that is formless, desireless, and steadfastly awake. When she tires, she seeks and yearns, and falls into a snare of dreams. Every such dream in a snare, they say, is the birth of a shape, a form, a being. This earth is a snare of dreams. Beyond the earth are more earths and more snares of dreams.

In a dream now past, Hālī was made of fire. Flames raged around him and he yearned for the sky.

Nymphs from the sea used to drift to his home and be burned and be dead. There were mournings in the sea, their mothers weeping and beating their breasts, and the sea used to rage and roar. He would watch the waves, his eyes streaming fire. The shades of the sea feared him, for he was Lohitah, the terrible, born of a lusting, thirsting fire.

And once a sea nymph, a nymph of a sacred starlike beauty, strayed to the fire. Though of the sea, she had the scent of the sky. She was aflame, and her ashes were upon his feet.

A nymph of the sea, yet not of the sea, a nymph of the sky, dead, burned, and he was sad.

THUS DWĀRKĀ
Rāhū's prophecy

THEN HĀLĪ FELL into another snare of dreams. He was a mortal youth and he was in a wood. Upon the wood shone the moon, silver upon silent shapes.

And he saw a brook. And he saw a whirl. In the whirl stirred a lily, and as a mother her babe, happy, it bore on its petals a petal of the rose.

Then the moon hid behind a cloud. The reeds rustled. Silence became sound. The trees shook and the shadows swelled and he heard savage laughter and he saw light die and he saw darkness fall.

Into the wood then came Rāhū, dread Spirit, to utter a prophecy. Said the Spirit: "The years will now pass as the tides of the sea. Then, one winter night, near the second fall of the snow, Īsha, the Lord, will grant thee all the flowers of the earth. While beholding with wonder and pride thy treasure, wretched youth! thou shalt be lured into the mass and become a yellow rose.

"Then, sudden, as a flash in a moonless sky, thy nymph, not of the sea, not of the sky, but chosen of Īsha, in keeping of Īsha, shall dream and seek of that rose.

"Harried, she shall seek the earth, seek thy earth, maimed, stabbed by a pain not known to thy mortal soul. Stricken with grief, panting from sorrow, she shall be possessed of a dread not known to thy mortal soul.

"And thou shalt sigh but once, and die, die, wretch! thy leaf and petal scattered to the sea, lost, lost, and she, the once chosen of Īsha, shall be abandoned, and be smitten for ever, by the sea, and the snows, seeking, seeking, mourning, murmuring, weeping, weeping, cursed, stricken, stricken for ever and evermore."

And he cried, "Shall she sob like a child, O Spirit? Shall her hair sway in the snow? Oh, would she be seeking for ever, weeping, and murmuring to the snow? Would the curse upon her head be lifted by my anguish, so be it, let it be! Thy curse upon my head, Spirit! let me be stricken, for ever, for ever, and ever-more! Wouldst thou strike thy servant and grant thy mercy to the chosen? Wouldst thou grant me this boon? Thy wrath upon my head, let me be stricken, for ever, for ever, and evermore!"

THUS DWĀRKĀ
Hālī heard a voice

ON THE PYRE, covered with flowers, was Rooh, once the burned nymph of the sea, then the chosen, and now his bride, his child, his all.

He did not go to the ghāts where they burned her. Instead, he wandered. It was a pleasant day and he wandered in the sun. He returned home after the evening prayers.

In the garden, the moonlight made glad patterns. He did not weep. Then he got up and went to say farewell.

The ghāts were silent. The clang of the cymbals was soft. The shrine of Ambā, too, was silent, but for the chant inside the copper dome. A gentle wind rustled the leaves of the Bilva tree.

Hālī went into the temple of Shiva. The temple walls were red from the glare of a burning pyre. In the glare, he saw a Brahmin, squatting on a prayer-mat, and facing the image of Shiva. In front of him lay the unwrapped corpse of a child. It lay on the edge of the altar stone. Upon it were the marigolds fallen from the image of Shiva.

The Brahmin was in meditation, his head and face covered with an orange veil, and he held in his hands the hands of the child.

In the glare, Hālī saw his solemn veiled face, the shadow of Shiva's image etched upon the ochre-tinted walls, and he saw the glowing brightening corpse of the child.

Then he saw the Brahmin uncover his head, bend over the child, and breathe into the open mouth of the corpse, as if to give it breath.

Soon came the wind carrying the smoke from the smouldering pyre. Into the smoke-filled temple then came a beggar. Hālī heard her weep and call upon the lord of the dead to carry her hence.

Then he saw the Brahmin strike his head on the altar. The weeping of the beggar was the omen from Shiva. His child was in keeping of Yama, the lord of the dead, and he must return home, his rites in vain, and grieve and mourn.

Hālī went out of the temple and sat by the pyre of Rooh. He looked into the embers, for his Rooh was dead, charred, her face burnt to ash.

And he felt at peace with the makers of his fate and with things seen and unseen. Then he picked up some ash in his hand and wondered why she, of all, had been his love and his Rooh.

Would she were the queen of the earth, he would be a wanderer, a minstrel, and live to sing the praises of his queen. He would beg from no god, seek mercy from none, but Rooh, his queen.

Why would he let his destiny be linked with a clan, a country, a faith, and a place of birth? Nay, he would be free, free, and know no loves, no hates, for all his cares would belong to his queen.

But he was afflicted by the will of the Lord who made him. He did not long to die, for death might deny him peace.

Thus he spent the night, till the dawn came to the ghāts, and he heard a voice, a gentle voice, a voice like his Rooh's: "Oh, do not dream, but watch the East and see the gates of heaven open, so softly, so sweetly, as the eyes of a waking angel. I go on this strange pilgrimage with eternal sadness. I pray at every sunset for the end of this journey. But the Lord in heaven pities me this dawn and lets me dream of a joyous end.

"But you do not move! Oh, listen to the laughter of the sea! Listen to the whispers of the angels of the East! The stream of joy flows from the heavens, and let it be thine! Do not weep, my friend! Why, the dawn will soon be gone, and this glory, too, shall pass away!"

THUS DWĀRKĀ
Thus the magician

TEN DAYS NOW, since his Rooh died, and Hālī has no peace.

"Tell me, how will it be? How will it be with me?"

And Māyā, his second mother, caressed his head and again bade him sleep.

"Māyā, how will it be?"

"Thou art feverish, child," she said. "Go to sleep. If thou wilt not sleep, Māyā will die!"

"Wilt thou take me to the healer?"

"Yes," and she took his head in her lap and sobbed.

The next day, they went to see the healer.

They walked across a dry sandy river. The sun hurt his eyes and Māyā led him by the hand.

And Hālī saw the magician.

His bare body, so like a skeleton, was smeared with ash, and his hair was matted, and his gaze was fixed, rigid.

"He is like my own little one," Māyā said to him humbly. "I have brought him to thee. Heal him."

She bade Hālī look into the healer's eyes and listen. "Go thou to Gauhati! Go thou to Gauhati! Go thou in a boat! Thou art in Gauhati! Thou art lost in a wood! Thou seest the blue hill!"

And Hālī saw a ridge. A red ridge. Upon the ridge, he saw a man. His face was pierced, fissured, full of holes. Holes, sweating wax. Adhering wax. There was no blood in him, but oozing wax. Adhering wax. His hair was like spikes. And he was panting, panting from pain. His eyes were orange, rust-like, and half-seeing through torn and swollen lids. Upon his chest were the letters "Hālī," written in wounds. And he cried. He cried like an infant in pain. "Thou seest the hill! Thou seest a fire!"

He saw the ridge become a pyre. Flames, purple of color, fierce, palpitating. And, in the fire, he saw a procession of shapes, the shapes of terror, with udder-like chests, their skin bleached, of the color of ash. "Thou seest a cave! Thou goest into the cave! Thou art in the temple of *Ambā Enchantress!*"

And Hālī saw a temple. Of moonstone. Of magic, spiral stone. "Thou Seest the image of the Goddess! Thou seest the holy one at the *feet of the image!*"

And, at the feet of the image of the Goddess, he saw a priestess. And she cried, her cry like the frenzied howl of a wolf, "Victory to Kālī! Victory to Ambā!" "Thou seest the image of the Goddess! Thou adorest Kālī-Ambā! She is the Mother of the earth, the stars, the sun!"

And Hālī saw the sun rise, rise out of a chasm, and rise high into the sky. A sun, terrible of shape, crimson of color, with horns of fire. Beneath it was a mouth, of mashed flesh, eyeless, headless, in a copper burner, praying, praying for mercy. "She is the Mother of the Universe! She is the Great Illusion!"

And, in the temple, under a canopy of silver, Hālī saw Rooh. She wore the ochre robes of a bride. Surrounding her were cauldrons. Cauldrons full of pollen. Lotus-pollen. And he saw the priests. One marked her forehead with sandal and saffron paste. Another gave her the vermillion bridal bracelet to wear on her wrist.

And Hālī was wedded to Rooh. With her, he took the seven vows. And he said, "I am thine, beloved. I am the sky, thou art the earth. I am the stalk, thou the flower. Mayst thou never know sorrow!" Then they faced the polar star. And Hālī said, "Pillar of stars! firm art thou! Protect us, thou! O Arundhatī! as thou art true, so may my love be, for this my bride!"

And he led his Rooh by the hand, away from the temple, to his home, to love, to cherish. "She is the Refuge! She is the Healer! Pray unto Ambā! Pray unto *Kālī-Ambā!*"

Then he saw the shape, the shape of Kālī all-destroying. Her purple tongue stretched to her knees, on her crushed breasts a chain of eyes, human eyes, penitent eyes, eyes filled with tears, and in her hands the torn head and limbs of Shā, the fawn adored. And he cried, "Away! Away, Evil! Thou art a thing of evil, evil, evil!"

And he woke hearing Māyā cry, cry from pity, cry from pain.

I, DWĀRKĀ

AND, SEEING MĀYĀ thus, I, Dwārkā, pleaded with the guardian lords, the *nāthas*, to please intercede and comfort this woman: or, I pleaded, may the gentle forgiving God, in his mercy, grant me strength to dare, to defy and deter death, and so undo this sorry scheme of things.

THUS DWĀRKĀ
(Thus Rāhū to Hālī
Thus phantom to Rooh)

SAID THE SPIRIT: "Anon shadows shall fall upon the earth as fear upon fallen things. Thy night shall come, and thy night shall be, till its hideous head is torn by the lance of day. And her blood shall spout and make the horizon red. Anon, Hālī, shall I, Rāhū, possess thee, and be many-shaped, scarlet, blue, and cling to thee like moss to a hollow tree. And anon shalt thou dream, and meet thy woman, and anon shalt thou deny, deny thy love of the woman." And Rāhū became the phantom Hālī, to taunt Hālī. *To the conjured shape of the weeping, sorrowing Rooh, thus did he speak:* "Do you feel the fear of this night, Rooh? The terror of this darkness?

"Such is the end of our day. We are on the summit at last. This summit, where the highest aspirations reach. But the lights have gone whence they came. The streets are deserted. All roads are quiet. All doors closed.

"My life was a never-ending need. My heart was seized by the yearnings of love. My days were a thirst. My nights a burning. You, my only love, were the breath without which I could not live.

"This night you have come to bring me my reward. The reward of your love. But the spells that fascinated me are no more.

"All desire is dead. My dreams gone. The night has come. The singers are gone, and Hālī is dead! and Hālī is dead!

"Whence the pain of your love? Where the play I planned with you? Where the trees that blossom at dawn? Where my flowers? Where my friends?

"I have this hurt, Rooh. I feel this burning in my soul. This journey has led me to a path unknown. And I have to travel beyond, farther than this summit, seeking still.

"Go back! Go back to gaiety, to music, to the things of love, to flowers, to the lights, and live and be, while I to a land beyond, to the land of the lost, to the land of the shades, in search of a healer of my aching soul."

THUS HĀLĪ TO ROOH

I OF THE HILLS, as a child, knew the lore of the hills. I knew our earth was ruled, ruled by kings, tyrant kings, not of the earth, but from far beyond, I knew not where. Human of limb, clad as kings, the dread snake-kings, hoods of snakes upon human form, smiting the earth, and those of the earth.

I, Hālī, as a child, often dreamed I would free the earth of tyrants, and of this earth, make a garden. Would I seek renown, riches, honor? Nay, I would free the earth of tyrants, and of this earth, make a garden will I!

Yonder, in the plains, is the desert. Sand, blinding, flying sand, and the sun burns, and there is the lurid, lurid light, and none to tend the flaming, flashing earth, no rivers, but desert, vibrant, fierce, kindled. Yonder, beyond the desert, is the sea. Pearl and blue, the surrounding reefs and rocks, and the setting sun and the trail of gold upon the sea, and waves high as the hills, oh, a thing of beauty! a thing of beauty! And the sea will I see, and watch, watch deep, deep as I could see!

Would I tend my garden, once the earth is the garden? Would I love the sea which I will some day see? Nay, I will seek, seek still, seek a thing of glory, of glory undreamed, and wonder, and wonder, and die, for I would see what no mortal ever saw before. Oh, a vision, a vision of such enchanting awful beauty, that a mortal would die! Would my vision be on the earth, upon the sea, or would it be by a star? Nay, I knew not. But seek, seek will I!

No longer child, I ever sought, sought my vision. Sought it in secret, inmost secret, searching, seeking, the earth, the sea and star.

Then, thee, Rooh, I found. Found by the temple. Garlanded with jasmine, thy white raiment! thy brow stained with the temple red, a thing of the earth, but upon thy brow! radiant, holy! And I called thee not Rohini that thou wert, but Rooh! And I knew the God I prayed to was not holier than thou, none holier, none! And I called thee Mala, Garland! Ah, garland wert thou! the garland of beauty! the garland of love! the garland of God! God, to seek which I sought the temple, and thee I found! Oh, would my vision be by a temple, a temple still and a'peace under the stars? The reeds sprung from the parting in the temple stone, upon them the snow, the midnight mist veiling the yonder willow, and the flute faintly heard! And thou, Rooh, in the temple, midst incense, thy temple casting a shadow upon the snow!

I had wept, beloved, when thou didst once avow love to me, to Hālī, whose dreams for ever shall be barren. Despairing am I of ever making the earth garden, despairing am I of ever loving the sea, oh, despairing am I of my vision!

A PROPHECY OF WAR

SAID THE SPIRIT: "Hearken, Hālī! Hearken to the footsteps! The dread footsteps! The perilous footsteps! Affliction approaches! Awed, frenzied, thy brothers and sisters shall war upon one another, and they shall shed their skins, and be drained of blood.

And their ribs shall break, and their bones shall point to the sky, point like fingers to the sky. Ants shall nest in thy brothers' jaws and flies shall feed upon thy sisters' breasts. Mothers shall make their wombs the flesh tombs of their young, a sea of blood shall be upon the burnt purple earth, and thou, stricken from grief shalt cry, cry from pain, thy mouth broken, and it shall be as a gory vent, and thy hair shall bleed. And thou shalt seek flesh, Hālī, seek and violate the flesh of thy chosen, thy chosen sister, thy chosen maid, and thy forehead shall be upon her forehead and thy lips upon her lips. Then thou shalt burn, burn from desire, the desire for her flesh, and comfortless, in anguish, thou shalt be like a beast of prey, thirsting for blood, the blood of thy chosen, thy chosen sister, thy chosen maid, and she shall die of terror! terror! her horrored heart torn, torn of terror!"

"Nay, O Rāhū! None but Rooh will I seek. And my Rooh shall be an angel, the savior angel of the earth and the sky. Know, her feet shall be in the womb of the earth where the fiery minerals glow, and she shall calm the fires, calm the fires, and her tresses shall be upon the roof of the earth, and her breasts, her noble virgin breasts, her great great breasts, her sheened sheened breasts, her scintillant breasts! shall be the refuge of clouds. Oh, unattainable she shall be, unattainable, and I, for ever seeking!"

"Nay, wretch. Thou shalt be upon the earth and live, and thou shalt see the corpse of thy chosen, thy chosen sister, laid upon the earth, and in her reddened mouth shall be ulcers, hungry ulcers, hungering for her flesh.

"Hereafter, Hālī, thy days shall be nights and thy nights pain. And thine eyes shall not tell thee the truth, and thou shalt see thy Rooh ravished, and thou shalt see thy Rooh slain, whenever a sister of thine shall be ravished, whenever a sister of thine shall be slain. Thy heart shall no longer be the cradle of love, as agone, as afore, and thou shalt live in hate, and bear, bear the sins of thy brother, thy curséd curséd brother, and thy sister, thy curséd curséd sister, and thou shalt despise thy brother, despise thy sister, and thy curséd curséd earth!"

THUS HĀLĪ TO ĪSHA

WILT THOU HEED, Lord? Wilt thou heed?

Ensnared in a sea of evil, I despair of reaching thy celestial Court to wail and cry out my sorrows.

It is a sea of blood, Lord! and dead art thou to me and I to thee.

The stars I cannot see, but blood, and headless beasts in agony, limbs, limbs, rising with the tides of the sea, and a rain of blood!

Behold the vulture, the vulture of evil, her carrion beak! and behold the face of thy servant torn, of human shape no more, mass of rent flesh, in a sea of blood! Behold the things of evil, crouching curling things of evil, feast upon the flesh of thy servant, flesh no more! blood, blood, in a sea of blood!

Should I despair of thy grace, Lord? Should I despair of thy grace?

Ah, enflamed, enflamed will I be, and soar, my wings burning the ends of the earth, and the earths beyond, to the twilight horizons where thou rulest, and smite thy peace and thy lofty calm!

Command thee I will to the sunless depths of the sea and the earth! And if thou wouldst not heed, with claws, claws! would I rend thy eyes, thy jaws, and thy fragrant face! Then will I descend, descend upon thy majesty, and bewitch thee, Lord! and wound and gore thy fabled face, thy fabled face, and erst! erst! thy crown asunder, thy countenance in vain, eyeless, headless, lost, now lost upon the sea of blood, of tepid tepid blood, and so shatter the ends of the earth and the earths beyond!

When the dismal light of the darkened sun shall sink deep into the depths abysmal of the eternal night, verily: when the sleep of terror shall fall upon all creation, verily: when the sound shall no longer echo, aye: when thou art lost upon the sea of blood, of tepid tepid blood, verily! verily! then will I be awake, awake anew! and ascend, ascend over ocean, rock, mountain,

continent, away away, covered in scarlet wings, and seek me a
sea of burning gold, and drink and devour the sea will I, oh, drink
and devour the sea will I!

Thus shall I be the Supreme! the Triumph! human no more,
god no more, highest not, fallen not, beyond hope, beyond call,
no rock of beauty with summit of sapphire for my court, Sire!
no sky of emerald and the heart of emerald for my roof, Sire! nor
will I be the bestower of scent and hue upon saffron, the lily and
the rose, but tremulous tempestuous Lord will I be, bereft! bereft!
beyond the ken of mortal precept, naught! naught! the mystic
Mask upon all creation! the magic Mist upon all time! and ever,
ever the legend devourer of seething gold, the sea of gold! burning gold! the Lord sheathed in glowing wings, burning wings!
once mortal, ensnared in a sea of evil, a sea of blood, of tepid
tepid blood, smitten of torture, despair, of agony, wailing to God
unheeding, dead he to me and I to him!

THUS HĀLĪ TO DEATHLESS ROOH

OF EARTHLY MOLD, yet divine, thou too wert changeable, as Īsha,
as Rāhū, as I, and all shapes, all forms. Thou wert a thing of
time, once child, a beautiful child, once maid, a beautiful maid.

No longer of the earth, Rooh, wilt thou be a thing apart, a
thing apart, not the Rooh thou wert, but be eternal changeless
Love, and thus be other than the Rooh thou wert?

Oh, deny, deny thee I will, and my sorrow, my home,
people, faith, the land of my birth, every dear thing, and all I
found, all I loved, if thou wilt no more be Rooh the queen I
mourn, but be eternal changeless Love, and thus be guide light
and star to all changeable things and beings!

Wilt thou be such Love? and no more parting, all things and
beings part of thee, thou deathless changeless Spirit! ever of
mercy! ever beloved! all shapes and forms merged unto thee,
thus Īsha, thus Rāhū, thus Ambā, all unto thy infinite tenderness,
O ever friend! ever child! ever light! and I, Hālī, once of fear,

remorse, agony, despair, abandoned no more, rested, in life, in death, desireless, yet loving thee, and things thine, causing, causing love! sowing, sowing love! and thus for ever be blest, blest, and blest!

THUS RĀHŪ, THUS HĀLĪ

SAID THE SPIRIT: "Hālī, rejoice! Thou hast known Īsha. Thou hast known Rāhū. Hereafter, thou shalt be free, free of pain, and thy days shall be thy days and thy nights thine!"

"Seest thou this steel, O Rāhū? Seest thou this mirror of silver? Know, soon will I slay, slay Hālī, and the mirror shall be my witness that I know no fear and will betray no pain."

"Nay, Hālī! Thou shouldst live, live as master, fearless of Īsha, fearless of Rāhū!"

"Nay, Rāhū."

"Seekest thou redress for thy sorrow? Seekest thou rewards?"

"Rewards? Aye. If thou shouldst see Mīrā, my mother, be of my form, be as Hālī, and count the wounds on her poor head, and tend her, as she tended me. If thou shouldst see Māyā, be of my form, be as Hālī, and comfort her, as she comforted me. And if thou shouldst see my Rooh! she shall be by a sea, a sea of sable pearls, a soundless surging sea of pearls, in each, the image of a brilliant blue star! Go soft, oh, go soft, Rāhū! for she sleeps!"

"Thou hast triumphed, Hālī! Thou art free! Free of Īsha, free of Rāhū! Thou shouldst live, live thy years!"

"Nay, Rāhū. I wish to be gone. I seek no love of the living. I seek no commerce with the dead. But I wish to be nigh, I wish to be nigh, as air, as air bearing love."

"Thou dreamest!"

"Aye. If this too be a dream, soon shall I wake. No drums, no dirge for Hālī, for if there be things of love, and things of beauty, I seek them, I seek them still, but for Hālī no longer.

Oh, be of my form, Rāhū! forbearing friend! and say to my brothers, and say to my sisters, all things of love and all things of beauty are theirs, theirs to be! And say, I shall be nigh, I shall be nigh, as air, as air bearing love!"

"Wouldst be barren, too?"

"Aye. If that is being void, nothing farther of me, nothing nigh of me, no memory of the days gone by, none of the days to come, it is well. I am content. I am at peace, so to be!"

"Hālī, Hālī, I will not be beholden to thee! the lord of the dreaded domain will not be beholden to thee! Remember, thou didst seek of me pain for the ease of thy Rooh?—she, a child, not yet twenty, and thy own years, no more than two and twenty! Remember, thy Rooh, on a pyre, cloaked in a cotton shroud, carried by the priests to the flames? Remember, thyself gathering her ashes in the inlaid box, thy mother's gift, the keepsake, and entrusting it to Nandā, the sacred stream, to be in her keeping, with her children, the blossoming lilies spread upon her? Even so, even so, know, for my content, for my peace, I will rise from the depths, my domain, my braided hair still smoldering, and fly forth to the earth, my great hair behind me as torches, and pour fire upon the Nandā, aye, the unyielding undying fire, till her waters burn, her lilies burn, the greens burn, and all creatures, in and by her burn, and the singers and flyers upon the trees burn, until all the flames become one flame, one with me, Rāhū! Rāhū! Rāhū! Rāhū! and so the remains of Rooh, so the keepsake! Thus, Hālī, the second cremation of Rooh granted thee, and so to be upon the Nandā, but for a prophecy, a prophecy yet to be fulfilled.

THUS THE PROPHECY

"Now, HĀLĪ, HEAR the words of the prophecy: *The Nandā would meander, veering towards the sun. At rising and setting, she would be radiant as the sun, her lilies glittering as glories hallowed by the sun.*

"The prophecy is fulfilled, Hālī, and witnessed, and I am weary of the earth. Anon, I will dive into the crusts, and the rocks, away into the depths, to my domain, forgetful of thee, and thou forgetful of Rāhū, and there would not be an echo heard of this deed for thee to ponder, or a cinder left for any to mourn."

THUS DWĀRKĀ
Thus the end

AND MĀYĀ FOUND him laid upon the prayer-mat, his lifeless eyes set upon their image in the mirror upon the wall, and she pulled the dagger, wedged deep into his heart, and from unwonted anguish, she swayed, his bloodied body in her arms, rocking him, as if to ease his hurt—and she grieved for Hālī, and she grieved for Rooh, thus, *"O children! O children!"*

I, DWĀRKĀ
A postscript

THE HONORED ELDER, the *nātha*, told us to devote ourselves wholly to God. When our souls are purified by our love, our deeds would be purified too. Then the just God would give us the sight to see. That would be fulfillment.

Over the years, I have tried to follow the *nātha*. I have struggled to dedicate my wishes and ventures to God. And I have prayed; when in need, and when not in need, and trusted and confided in God. The nātha told us to do this.

I had the need once to narrate the story of Hālī. It ended with the gentle Māyā, sorrowing, desolate, destined to mourn for the dead. Indeed, all God's created are destined to die. Yet, longing for the sight of those summoned sooner, the living must grieve and mourn. The *nātha* told us not to fear death.

I have the need now to speak assuredly of a gift granted to Dwārkā, to recall the memory of a vision vouchsafed to this servant, and so confess myself a witness of the Lord's untold mercies, of which the good *nātha* spoke so often, as he shared his beautiful faith with us.

I saw the hallowed bell and was healed.

THE BELL

HIGH UP, IN the sky, I saw a bell tolling, and with the waves of the solemn sound, the clouds trembled, and the silences between the tolling of the bell filled me with awe and waiting, and those two, the tolling of the bell and the silences between, filled me with echoes such as I had never known, and made me remember sights such as I had never seen, and it seemed to me that it was the will of God that it should be so, and his will that I be content and question no more, and wait by, for his grace to come upon me, as the gentle twilight came upon me at the end of this autumn's day, as sleep would to soothe an aching heart.

I waited by the river, and saw the light fall on her, and it was by grace. I looked at the sky, and saw a cloud, and that was by grace. I saw a creature look at me, and I looked upon it with love, and that, too, was a deed by grace. The Majesty is near, and not far, and most near. That faith is a deed by grace. In all things whatever that have beauty, a creature human, too, and in the heart of the diamond and the rose, is grace, and thus have I comfort that I never knew, and knew it now, by grace and grace alone.

His way is the way to mystery. They that walk on it have no pain. And past all the lights, and all the sights, and all things whatever, the way is to be trodden still, till the soul aches and is lonely from want, in need, and it is then, by grace, she forgets her aches and pains, and is in God, of God, in his grace, and so touched by the Majesty, the crest and the crown of all the worlds, the sword and the sheath of all things, the love in all things whatever, and thus by grace is she healed.

There is to be no haste and no tears. Ahead is the rain of the petals of the rose, and joy, and rejoicing, that a creature soul never knew, and this remembrance will last till the end of time, for such as have seen and heard, and been in the grace of the

Lord, and no remembrance other than this will be, and that would be by grace and grace alone.

No earthly kings and deeds and things will be, nor hills, mountains and the seas. There is joy so intense that a soul needs the grace to live in it, for such is the joy of God that is come, and I have seen the fall of the petals of the rose, and seen it alone, and seen the mother of waters carry the petals hence, on her crowns and crests, dancing, leaping, running towards the sea, in love, and such is her joy in God, and such is the grace that I have known, seen with the eyes the Majesty bequeathed upon me, to see his glory, and he bequeathed upon me the telling of it, the will and the words, so that his creatures may rejoice, such as have not seen, and not rejoiced, and so call upon themselves the grace of God, and thus will all the winds be scented, all cedar be green, all waters made sweet, and beauty bestowed upon all things whatever, and such are the things that in awe have I seen, and the remembrance of them will be as a pillar, upon which to rest a weary head, when the day comes for me to go, whence I came, and thus will I walk, and thus will I pass, to the glory I never knew, but such as I remember, a thing everlasting, as long as the soul would last, before she is gathered to God, to rest in God, and be of God, and be as a benediction upon other souls, shining as a star, above the stars, and all held by the sky, and the sky over the earth, and the whole to other such, but in secret, naught, not the sword nor the sheath, for of all things, and creatures, the Majesty alone is, and that is the secret not given to creatures and things, unless it be otherwise, and so be by his grace and his grace alone.

I came hither to seek, to solicit, and was come a destitute, and the Majesty heard me, and spoke to me, and such ache and pain that I had is gone, is consumed, and I need to sit by, to sit by whatever is near, any resting place whatever, any pillar, any place, to sing of the glory of God, and remain in joy, for this is not the end of the day, but the dawn, and of such loveliness, and never to be gone, each moment of equal joy, that if I will, the Majesty would be to me as a servant bid, and play upon this heart

as bid, to make this dawn even more of a heaven, and such as
was never known, but I seek no such servant, and no assurance,
and no sound, no word, but to stay, to stay awhile, and in love
be as a thing bid, as a thing owned, a creature slave, for so great
is the grace of him come upon me, and so sweet is become this
giving, this dying of the erstwhile creature, that was in ache and
pain, a creature that trod a road for glory and gain, not knowing
it, not knowing glory and gain, and then found one truly worthy
of such, the Majesty himself, and it is to be his glory and gain,
no other's, and such is the meaning of the signs I have seen, of
the tolling of the bell, and the silences between, both happenings
of mystery and grace, the grace that is come upon me, and so
upon the petals of the rose, and upon the mother of waters, and
I must bear the grace bequeathed, with love, and the memory of
which too is a thing of grace, the grace of the Majesty, and it is
with humility and in joy that I carry it, as would the mother of
waters carry to the sea, so I, carry to the Lord, to the Fount, for
all other deeds are naught, and all other meanings are naught, so
the creatures, so the things, and such is the praise of the grace
that is come upon me, such indeed is the praise of the peace that
is come upon me, and there will now be no thunder, and no
lightning, no aches, no pains, and such is the grace of my God
that is come upon me, such indeed is the praise of the grace that
is come upon me.

A ROSE AND LILAC LIGHT

A ROSE AND lilac light has passed me by, as might a cloud, and
it sailed past from the left to the right of me, and as I turn my
head, I still see the trail of fire, a cool rose and lilac fire, as if all
the diamonds of the purest rose and lilac were awake, and from
their heart came this rose and lilac fire, of such beauty, and the
wonder of it has made me lose all yearning, all need whatever,
and it has bequeathed upon me a joy as true, as sure, as this rose
and lilac light, that passed me by, and this joy is as a treasure
entrusted. This day the Lord's Majesty is in joy, and his joy is
reflected in the mirror of the risen Sun, and the Moon to come

by, with the early gentle dew, and it is reflected in the calmness of the sea, too, in the still water, in the stars above the sea, in the young snow, and the ice laid upon the farther mountain, and in this heart, too, stilled by a peace, past all yearning whatsoever, all need whatsoever, all wanting whatever, all thirst whatsoever, all hunger whatsoever, and if there are clouds, they sail silently by, and they do not come between me and the Majesty's joy, and the clouds frame it, never obscuring it, and this joy came upon me as a shower, as a shower of mercy, as love upon the lily on the stalk, and upon the rose, upon the scarlet velvet of the rose, and upon the streams, the brooks, on such that know of this treasure entrusted.

Once yesterday, whenever such mercy had come upon the earth, it had passed me by, for my heart was of fear, lost, and whenever I saw the Sun setting, with it set the universe, and I was lost, in darkness, and there were but faint lights, lights awed, farther, far, overpowered, so I thought, and it was darkness fathoms deep, that fell upon the earth, and I lost all peace whatever, all love of things whatever, and I was lost in a sea, a sea of darkness, but today, after the trail of light had passed me by, darkness did come hither, but I knew blessedness, heard blessedness, heard the gentlest of sounds, drops of rain falling upon the recent fallen snow, and I heard those sounds sailing through the leaves of the pine, and the poplar, and it was as the song of praises, the praises of Lord God, and thus the darkness passed me by, in peace, in joy, in worship of the worthiest of worship, nowise the erstwhile creature's night, of pain, fear, the creature that I was, and as the sounds and the song blended, it was a stream, then a river of sound, then a sea of sound, untouched of shore, unheard of by the erstwhile creature, but known and heard this instant, this splendid instant, this august sea of sound, such as is by God bequeathed, from mercy bequeathed, from love bequeathed, by the Will uncaused, and, presently, it will bring in its wake the dawn, and in its wake the night, and so will these pass me by, and I shall again see the rose and lilac light, that I saw, not long ago, and it would be another awakening, awaken-

ing of the spirit of all the diamonds flashing the purest rose, and
the lilac luster, bequeathed, as a treasure entrusted.

It would again be the awakening of the spirit of the diamonds, such as were asleep, and such as would awake, and the
wonder of it will have again given me the peace bequeathed, that
I knew not this long past, and the tolling of the bell, and seeing
the moon bathing the seas with her lighted silver, the earth too,
and the clouds too, precious silver, all with joy abounding, then
I, too, will pass by, as did the rose and lilac light, and the trail
of it, that did pass me by, knowing blessedness, such as caresses
the soul, and in such blessedness, there will still be the dew, and
the sea, and the pearls of the sea, and in the midst of this blessedness will God bequeath mercy upon the creatures, and beauty
absolute, and peace absolute, even upon such as do not know of
such a treasure to me entrusted: and such certain passing makes
me want to cry of joy, for today the rose, the lily, the diamond
and the dew, and the sea, all things whatever, are content, at
peace, as am I, and the mercy of God is come upon us, and all
other mercies are become as shadows, as shadows, so happy the
rose, so happy the lily, so content the sea, that naught I know,
but to sing the praises of God, and to rouse the earth, and the
creatures, in one cry, of joy, and with it reach out to the sky, and
the star, the cry of triumph absolute, of triumph absolute, and I
would brook no delay, and I must sing, and cry of joy unbearing,
for this utter grace is come upon me, bequeathed upon me, as a
treasure entrusted.

Bid the singer, the poet, the maker of images, the painter
of images, bid them praise, and praise again, in love as true! for
I can no longer bear this joy, this all, this joy entire, this joy
absolute, and nor can I brook silence, or this soul would be lost,
be as a thing of no substance, no matter, for the Master is now,
this instant, reflected in the center of her, the center of her flame,
and it burns the brightest, the purest, and I must away, knock
on doors, and speak to the trees, to the creatures, and tell them
of it, of joy, such as I cannot bear, without a wanton cry, and I
must speak of this, of this blessedness, such as the erstwhile

creature never knew, he that lived in the dark of the day, and past the setting of the Sun, in the dark of the night, and here am I, in this blessedness, and I must hurry, I must haste, and tell of it, to the pine, the poplar, the lily and the rose, that this blessing by mercy is come, and we must hurry, and we must haste, and we must away, and each give thanks, so the pine, so the poplar, so the lily, so the rose, and so I, too, and pray that the soul of the erstwhile creature may now be the lamp, of the light of him, and in the center of its flame, burn the brightest, and so let's pray, and naught I know now, no word, no thought, just joy, the mercy and the blessing of God, such as would brook no delay, and no word, or silence, for this joy is abounding, and unbounded, and the soul, unused to this blessedness, these gifts that have come, is as one struck and incapable, but let me wait by, let me stay by, and wonder, only to still my heart, and let me wonder, but the tears cloud my sight, and so intense is this joy, and so frail this limb, this tongue, and from all corners of the earth, behind the pillars, behind the arches, the domes, and beneath the earth, the arches, the domes, under the seas, farther than the sky, the stars, come waves of joy, of mercy everlasting, that my heart knows no ease, and I must away, I must away, and tell of it, to the trees, to the leaves, such as would hear, and hearken, for the sky echoes, the sea echoes, the earth echoes, this instant, now, a sound most sacred, the august sound, the unknown, unheard sound, heard and known of those on whom it is bequeathed, as a treasure entrusted.

And I must away, I must away, linger no longer, no more, and I must away, I must hurry, for all the buds do now flower, all beauty asleep is now awake, and there is such love, such adoration, but I must away, I must away! and go talk to the trees, to the leaves, to the lily, the rose, for such is this blessedness, this joy, that I can contain no more of it, so I must away, haste, tarry no longer, and tell of it, to the poplar, the pine, and they must know, and knowing no stillness, no ease, I must go and tell of it, that I know no ease, so intense is this joy, so unbounded it is, like a sea of no shore, and no thought, no word, can essay of it, and in this happiness, I can but still my heart, ease my heart, by listening to this sacred sacred sound, that I heard a while past, the blessed secret, that came to the earth, from far beyond the sea, from far beyond the sky, and that listening of it, too, fills me even more of joy, and I must away, so unbearing unbearing is this joy!

And I must away, go speak to the rose, to the lily, the pine, and the poplar, and all such, and do these deeds, for I know of such happiness, such joy, that I can brook no delay, and I must away, I must go, go speak to the trees, the leaves, and all such, and seek the lily, too, and wait, wait by, wait now, and hear the echoes again of the sacred sound, and remember the trail of light, the rose and lilac light, that passed me by, indeed, indeed, such remembrance brings peace, and stillness, and it brings such peace and such stillness, and the flame is calmed now, is steady now, and is by silence surrounded, surrounded, and it is peace, benediction, that is come, of silence, of sleep, the sleep by mercy of God, and I am still, at peace, and it is as if a raging sea were calmed, silenced by the hand of God, by the Will uncaused, and such is this soothing, healing peace, a precious treasure lovingly entrusted.

COLLECTED STORIES

–1–

The Valley of Lions

WHEREUPON, BY A COINCIDENCE, I ABIDED IN ITALY, IN A PLACE CALLED (IN ITALIAN) THE VALLEY OF LIONS, IN GOODLY COMPANY OF AN ELEGANT PET, A CAT, FOR WHOM I BUILT A SPLENDID CAT'S HOUSE WITH A FOUR-FOOT-WIDE BALCONY.

Preamble

ASKED I, *"Wherefore, am I here?*
Lodged in Valley of Lions
(With no lions in sight and none heard
But for the presence of their cousin, the feline?)
Speak! Materialize! Ancestor! Archetype! First Adam!"
WHEREUPON, THE SPIRIT MATERIALIZED AND CONFESSED:
"By the Maker that made me
I was given an eye and an ear
And he promptly forgot to make the sights and sounds
So naught saw I; and heard I nothing.
Unfulfilled and hungered were my eye and ear
The eye saw not itself; nor could the ear hear itself
Yet matured they as years went by
Untended, uncared; made, yet unmade.
Then one day the default roused the Maker
And thought he, 'How can my created that never saw, never heard

Be in the need *of such seeing and hearing!' (as indeed I was):*
PUZZLED, PERPLEXED, MUTELY SPOKE HE THEN . . . IN THIS MIEN
 AND IN THIS WISE . . .*"*
THE SPIRIT THEREUPON STOOD STILL LIKE THE YONDER MARBLE
STATUE, UNSPEAKING; AND THEN CONTINUED . . .
" 'I know not, maker,' replied I as mutely and unmoved,
'But something in me occurs me this lack of seeing and hearing
Such occurring urges me to lament
And I lament my lack of seeing and hearing.'
Said the Maker thereupon: still voiceless and by my ear unheard,
'It must be my own will in thy will.'
'Even so,' replied I, 'it is not yet I, that sees and hears!'
'See me and hear me with two eyes and two ears!'
 said the Maker thereupon
And I forthwith saw and heard him: then, now, and for ever!
'Moreover,' said he, in a voice beyond compare, 'for the satiation
 of thy kind I will gift thee an olive
And let it be multiplied in arid Italy; destined yet to be
 Italy evergreen!'
It is from such commerce and compliance, G.V. Desani!
Progeny of me! that all offspring of creation too saw and heard
From the will of the Maker: and so do you see the emerald groves
And the olives twilighted, and vibrant orange, and glistening gold
And hear too the gentle wind betwixt the tender leaves
And you hear, too, Maria mew.
So illumed, son, I bid thee adieu!*"*

THEREUPON, THE SPIRIT VANISHED.

AND I WALKED UP TO CASA MADRE, THE MATERNITY HOME, TO
FELICITATE MARIA AND GREET HER SLEEPING KITTENS. I THEN PRO-
CEEDED TOWARDS THE FLOWERING TREES BY THE LAKE, TO BLESS
THEM, AND I SAVORED ME AN OLIVE, FOR THE GLORY OF GOD AND
THE ONCE UNSEEING AND UNHEARING ANCESTOR.

 THANK YOU, READING CLASSES, IN ITALY AND OVERSEAS.

–2–

This Shrub,
This Child of God

Once, the light of all the world wished to have a face. The ageless one had a wish for age, so that he might live and die, as creatures created by him live and die. As he so wished, there appeared a face of great splendor, and it had a destiny in time, an age, and it was surrounded by a sphere of lightning. And it rose in the sky, in a cloud of flashing silver, which was as a mirror, in which the divinely willed face and the sphere were reflected. And the face found joy in seeing itself so reflected. When its age came to an end, there were flames, and the cinders and the ashes of it became a precious shrub, a sacred flowering shrub, sheltered in the hills, and with a living soul divinely willed. And when I saw this daughter of God, touched this child of God, I heard her say to me, "I would be kin and not be alone. I would be of thee. Bear me in thy heart."

And I said to her, "All that you and I have seen is in our hearts, even as we once were, in the heart of God. I have you now in my heart and whichever days and nights I would witness, we would witness together, and we would be as one, and your haunting dream of the body of human bone, the shape of man, in death, and washed away to the sea, with blinded eyes, buried in the salt of the sea, and the mourning woman of strange over-powering beauty, who weeps awhile by the sea, and about whom is the fire, the flames of red and black, with tongues far apart,

33

will not now be: it will be as a phantasy of days gone by, as a story carved upon stone, and you shall be at peace, because you said to me, '. . .I would be of thee. Bear me in thy heart.'

"Aye, beloved, I would bear thee in my heart. I would away to wonders, and even in the midst of wonders, I would bear thee in my heart, and say to the Lord, 'She and I are one, and all that she and I have seen is seen together, and this thy child has become dear to me, as beloved as thou art to me.'

"And when our ages end, as did the age of the face of splendor, we shall be cinders and ashes together, and if it is willed that I be a shape, a form, and if thou art not beside me, I would cry out to God, and say, 'I weep for my love! I weep for my child!' And the Lord would say to me, 'Behold, she is beside thee!' and so it shall be, thou beside me, as art thou now, beside me! beside me!"

–3–

Mephisto's Daughter

Being an old sinner, one of the worst living in this part of
western India, I have access to a member of Mephisto's
family. My first meeting with the Old Ugly's daughter happened
when I was seventeen. She tempted me with the latest super-
duper watch, model Swiss, thousand-jewel, all automatic and all
proof. It was made from the metal cooked in the Furnaces, and
hammering it for two hours didn't hurt it. It didn't even scratch
the crystal. That was years ago, and I was told never to speak to
girls.

Her father, Master Mephisto, lives in a sticky honeycomb,
the size of the Taj Mahal, with his arms and legs permanently
stretched to the four corners of the honeycomb. His daughter—
that is, my friend—lives not far from him, also inside the honeycomb, and she addresses him as *"Abbā huzoor."* There are burning hills and valleys fuming about—no stokers are needed to stir
up these flames, *ha! ha!*—and there Mephisto suffers mightily.
He has smothering in him the flames of overwhelming desire, the
urge for domination—undreamt of by any politician or man of
commerce. He wants to conquer *all* mankind and, of course, he
has no patience. She lives in terror of her father and suffers
likewise. She observes no proprieties, lives in the honeycomb
quite nude, and Mephisto sends her out on seducing errands, and
she obeys him instantly. *"I go, Abbā huzoor!"*

Not long ago, I had reason to make the secret *zero-minus-
zero* sign—it was given to me by my friend—and I called forth

Mephisto himself. I addressed him, appropriately, "Your dirty, filthy, censored, your mother's, your father's, *asterisking*, unprintability!" (the correct form, Mephisto loves it) and, although I was not permitted a full materialization, an indescribably fetid odor arose from an unused flowerpot, and it revealed that—being a friend of the girl—I would be allowed, as a special favor, to attend a *Tablet*. (This is an esoteric term for the graduating ceremony of the Devil's disciples, and it often concludes with a convocation address.) I could, alternatively, the fetid odor revealed, have the girl—such are the privileges enjoyed by those who know the secret sign!—but I preferred the first offer, the reading room of the town library, ahem, being no place for entertaining *her!*

II

So, I attended a *Tablet*. Hereabouts, in the Western Ghāts, I was waylaid by the omens to a banyan tree, and found a party of peasants sitting under it, all wearing turbans, and in the center was the largest figure of them all, about twice the size of an average peasant, and wearing a red turban—but for the size, exactly the kind worn by railway porters hereabouts—and facing him was a singer. His voice was like the cracking of drying ceramics, in a very high key, of course, and he had a single-cord instrument from which he produced a screaming sound, not unlike a combination of chronic catarrh and a dog whistle. He was improvising the phrase *Apavitro, o! o! o!* the basic *bol*, in all keys, up, down, high and low, in the manner of Hindu hymnists hereabouts. And, as he concluded with the . . . *o! o! o!*, an unseen drummer aided him. (The phrase means, more or less, *Un'clean, o! o! o!* or a better translation might be *Im'purity, ee! ee! ee!*) He seemed to have enchanted the company with his song, and they applauded him solemnly with *Vah! Vah! Vah!*

I appeared to have got to the meeting rather late. The proceedings were almost over when I got there, the *Im'purity, ee!*

ee! ee! was obviously the conclusion. Still, I was lucky enough to hear the big fellow speak. Here is what he said. *"Im'purity, ee! ee! ee!* Brethren, all is *One*. All is *Self*. Contentment is the greatest *good*. I *know*. I can *judge*. That is the *Truth*. All propositions are *right*. All answers *correct*. What thy right hand finds, that *do*. Self is *real*. All else is *unreal*." They applauded him again with *Vah! Vah! Vah!* Then they all got up, loosened their *dhotīs*—the fiendish ritual— and there it was, for anyone to see, the little stump of a tail at the backside of each, the sort of podgy things some bulldogs sport—the mark of Mephisto's offense, and it goes without saying that only his favorite disciples may have this tail, after they have duly become *un'clean, o!* with the necessary *Im'purity, ee!*

I got rather bored with all that *Tablet* and the speech. I recognized what the fellow said was mystic talk, and since I knew it almost by heart—it is common property—I returned home and cooked myself a curry.

III

The same evening, as I happened to be having tea in the kitchen, something reminded me of Mephisto—actually, it was a photograph of my father. I made the *zero-minus-zero* sign, sang out *Apavitro, o! o! o!* and followed it up with *Vah! Vah! Vah!* And very soon there was a materialization. Next to the kitchen table, where the bread board is kept, stood my friend, Mephisto's daughter—she never wears any clothes, in or out, at any time of the day or night—and after taking in the entire detail of her at a glance, I put it all to her. Now, what did the Devil's disciple mean by all that mystic talk!

She spoke fast, and was out of breath. She said, "Man dear, *Abbā huzoor* is sly. He has told us to make people happy . . ."

"Half a minute," I interrupted her, buttering a slice of bread. "Did you say *happy?*"

She nodded, and declined the kitchen cloth I offered her as

part covering. "Man dear," she said, *"Abbā* wants folk to be happy."

Then it all flashed on me in an instant, as it flashes on the mystics and the like. "Daddy, His honor," I said to her, "wants folk to be happy, yes? So that they would be content, no? So that they would do nothing to attain the Enemy, eh? They would be *immobilized,* yes? The Sly One wants folk to be *happy, content* and *immobilized,* yes? They would be *paralyzed,* no?"

She nodded yes.

Greatly encouraged, I went on enlightening her about her *Abbā.* "His honor has a passion, yes? He is troubled by doubt, no? He wants to conquer all mankind, but the doubt, that *one* of them might go over to the Enemy, agonizes him, no? The impossibility of complete, absolute conquest becomes very vivid day by day, eh? And another thing . . ."

I was interrupted. My friend was down on her knees, prostrate, shaking from terror. Convulsively, she was sobbing, *"Abbā huzoor! Abbā huzoor!"*

"What have I been saying!" I said, frantically moving about my arms and legs to extricate myself—right, I was caught in the honeycomb, the size of the Taj Mahal—as I realized that it was the Sly One speaking through me.

A full materialization indeed.

My father was right. It is wrong to speak to girls. No good can come of it.

–4–

The Lama Arupa

In the neighborhood of Vārānasī, Uttar Pradesh, India, once upon a time, there lived a lama, who was an incarnation of one greater than his present self, now fallen in station—he admitted this to himself, though rarely, and only when he failed in some undertaking or lost in a doctrinal disputation. All was well with him till a junior lama, a novice, also from Ladakh, sometimes called Little Tibet, and a small man, put a question to him which—although it had absolutely nothing to do with the Buddha's *dhamma*—yet had an indirect and subtle implication to it. It was a puzzle, really. Asked the novice of the incarnation lama, *"A chicken raced the fastest horse in the land. How was it that the chicken won?"*

The answer the novice gave—the incarnation lama having given up—was that the race had never been run, or won, and that the chicken was *already there*. (That *already there* was the indirect and subtle implication, involving, as it did, an assessment of space as a non-existent real, or an actual unreal, or a formal real, a concept actually, or a mere idea.) The novice added, with a flashing and malicious smile, something about its (the chicken's) being 'ended' (eaten) at the winning post. This frivolity added fuel to the fire, and the incarnation lama—whose name, by the by, was Lama Arupa—went pale, and the encounter plunged him into gloom and a grave dissatisfaction with things, and it remained with him for weeks. He was sure that people did not take him seriously, an incarnation though he was.

II

A month or so after the "disputation," he fell ill, and, in high fever, he kept seeing fireflies and human beings in a jungle of Burmese teak. The jungle was in flames, over which—as a crown of gleaming gold, flashing intermittently—hung the cloud of fireflies, and he saw agonized Burmese folk fleeing away from the fire, seeking safety, but without success, and the incarnation lama's pain became an anguish, because there was his opportunity to sacrifice his life, to save one or more creatures, and so earn merit and a better birth for himself, but—somehow—he felt incapable, and in despair, he kept groaning, and restlessly tossing in bed. Incidentally, while dreaming of the fire, he noticed a curious fact. He saw only the backs of the creatures, as if they were running away from him, declining succor. It was to him a fact of much import, and he was greatly saddened by it.

He got better, and, but for a lessening of appetite and a slight bitter taste in the mouth, he soon became quite well. And in thanksgiving he decided to offer worship to the Buddha.

Next day, he cooked rice with milk, and poured thick honey over it—the meal Sujātā had offered to the Blessed One—and he carried the bowl on a silver *thālī,* covered with silk. On his way to the *vihāra,* he was stopped by a small boy, age about three, and his sister, a year older, both wearing shirts, and the girl a silver waistband as well, and they smiled at him and asked him a question. What was it, they asked, the venerable one was taking to the *Baba?*

The lama answered them in a troubled voice—they shouldn't have asked a question about an offering made to the Blessed One—and he walked past them hurriedly, and when he reached the *vihāra,* he looked back, and the two children were not there. After his illness, that was the only miracle vouchsafed to him—that vanishing of the children.

The lama remained in Uttar Pradesh till a ripe old age, and one day—his hour having come—he felt unwell, and, presently, he felt a hurt in his heart, and so occupied was his attention with the hurt, that he forgot about the salutation to the Blessed One, and he was dead a moment after. Thereupon, as befitting a holy man, he was cremated sitting in the lotus posture.

III

After his physical death, the lama went through several states of consciousness—he knew this would happen to him—and those states, curiously, seemed to his dying intellect a kind of rosary, of an unaccountable number of beads, and he went not up, or down, or sideways. There was no movement, nothing of the property of extension as known to him could compare with what he was going through, but so progressing—a kind of progression was what he was conscious of—he found himself surrounded by mirrors, millions of mirrors, and in each he found himself reflected, to be replaced instantly by another image, also of himself, and after that had happened, he entered the caves of silence, each deeper than the foregone, and he felt himself—from habit, though he was separated from his body—shaking from terror, as those caves of silence were like nothing he had ever known. Shortly after that he felt a great tightness, a total constriction, a state of being bound, and he wanted to cry out, and was conscious of the inability to do so. This state remained with him for a very long time—so it seemed to him—and following that he went through a scattering process. Everything whatever he had known, believed, experienced, thought, read, heard, became scattered, and then all memories abandoned him, leaving him almost void.

He wanted to scream, from a sense of loss of identity and person, but he could not, and when that had come to pass too— all those curious, puzzling and tormenting states having vanished—his entire consciousness formed itself into a soft lump, or a fluffy ball, and that ball became an enormous worry, a puzzle, a question, a state not of strict awareness but of vacuity, more or less, leading to a true vacuum, waiting to be filled—a psychic affair altogether too difficult to ween or believe—and it got linked, somehow, in a manner most mysterious, with the novices' puzzle, of which the last state of the incarnation lama's consciousness grasped but one word, "chicken," and what was connoted by it, that is to say, its significance.

IV

So vivid became this entire summary of his experience on the earth—indeed he remembered nothing but the word *chicken,* and its simple meaning, and that was the whole residue of his experience, all else having been scattered—that, in accordance with the laws, like a flash of lightning, his consciousness passed out of the bubble of space surrounding his corpse, and forced itself into the interior of a hatching egg, splitting it into two, a true double-yolker, and it saw light as a twin of a real chicken, but a moment old, and it was the immediate cause of pleasure and surprise to the delivered hen, whose expectation was exceeded a hundredfold.

Thus, in spite of the appearances, as chicken, the laws caused the noble lama to become a creature of a truly lofty destiny: a little fellow fated to delight the human young as a pet, and foreordained, furthermore, as repast, to sacrifice his life—as indeed was his will—to save at least one hubristic sinner from hunger and distress, and so earn added merit for himself, forsooth.

May all beings be happy!

–5–

A New Bridge of Plenty

Hereabouts, in western India, once upon a time, a strangely understanding boy was born, and at the age of seventeen or thereabouts, he felt disgusted with life, with the never-ending curses—the want and the poverty. So disgusted, that he went to the bazaar, bought a rope, and on his eighteenth birthday, after making a declaration and an offering of curds to Wagle, the patron saint of these parts, quietly hanged himself.

(The good folk in these parts pronounce the name Wagle correctly as *Waag'lay*. Thank you.)

This matter was duly reported to the Guardians. They regarded it as a sacrificial death, and no suicide, since the deceased had given up his life after making a declaration of reverence and an offering of curds to Wagle. He was ordered up, to explain his conduct, which he did, and they referred him to the Examiners for final judgment. (The Examiners are the people nearest to our auditors and overseers. They see that God's laws are obeyed.)

Now the Examiners, by ably cross-examining him, condoned the eighteen-year-old ex-man's reasons for preferring death, and they granted him a *chit*, bestowing on him unlimited food, drink and sexual potency. (Those were the things that the ex-man still wanted and relished.)

II

He was duly born a very strange creature, a new and unknown species—an insect-worm combination—and made his home in

43

one of the wooden bridges in the Western Ghāts, eating wood in plenty, drinking water at will, and, having made from his body a female of his kind, had children by the hundreds, then thousands, all doing what their all-father and founder did, till—a few centuries after the Examiners' decree—it became an instinct with his kind, to eat and gnaw wood, of the bridge of plenty, and drink at will, and breed. So content were the creatures, that it was suggested to God that such human beings as are always complaining of want and poverty—of food, drink and free love—might be born as the insect-worm's progeny. They were.

The family now numbered billions, and the human souls that became members of it were happy: the whispered deathbed offer to them of unlimited food, drink and free love, having once been made, was never refused. It was a good life, and there was no struggle of any kind, no contests, no violence, and the simple proportions to which existence was reduced—the immediate satisfaction of one three-fold instinct of eating wood, drinking water and mating—made everybody content. Boredom, the curse of humanity, did not trouble the creatures. If they felt it at all, they ate, or drank, or mated some more, without suffering the consequences of excess.

III

Now in all divine plans and designs there is always—as has been said by St. Wagle—an unforeseen *something*. And there was an unforeseen *something* in the matter of these creatures too. For years the people living in these parts were planning to build new bridges, bridges of iron and steel, to replace the old wooden bridges, and there were, awaiting official consideration, schemes for building dams and canals too—all strictly in accordance with the evolutionary laws of God—and the planners, inspired by the Guardians (though they did not know it) were acting under compulsion and were impatient. The attention of the Examiners was drawn to their impatience and they reluctantly withdrew their protection from the wood-eating and free-drinking and mating worm-insect community and gave their blessings to the new plans and schemes instead. But, in their divine wisdom, they overcame the unforeseen *something* of the matter by decreeing that the entire community of the ex-man should die and be reborn, and— as a reward for suffering the pangs of death and birth—should become human beings, living exactly as they did in the past, under their own all-father and Adam, the late strangely understanding boy, and enjoying absolutely the same blessings.

IV

Meanwhile, the planners got busy, and the first move towards building the new iron bridge, where the old wooden bridge of plenty stood, was made, and, one day, wearing a red-and-gold turban, the chief justice of these parts arrived to lay the foundation stone, and he was greeted by the local dignitaries with applause.

While the second stage of the plan was shaping—the first being the laying of the foundation stone—a most important personage, an enormously wealthy and stout dame, was crossing the wooden bridge on her way to the shrine of Wagle, the saint aforementioned. She was in a *pālki,* carried on the shoulders of four men. And—this is an extremely difficult matter to account for, involving many and various exacting calculations of time, space, and such—she and her party set their weight against the exact spot, gone rotten to the core from centuries of gnawing by the insect-worm community, and in the exact split second when the resistance of the wood was the feeblest, there was an awful snapping and rending, indeed an explosive end of things, following which the bridge broke, and the apparent cause of it all, the stout dame, while proceeding towards the bottom of the river, was hurled upon the rocks and promptly hurled back by the stunning and blinding kick of a ruthless ass, the vexed devil who, so disguised, was waiting to collect sinners, and she was sent flying to heaven, boosted up by the petrified bearers of her *pālki,* as her last wish had been a virtuous one—to pay, be it noted, a visit to the shrine of Wagle, bless his heart.

There followed a terrible turmoil among the worms, at the breaking of the bridge, the most frightful calamity being the outrage—so it was dimly understood by the eldest and the ablest among them—of having to face a new situation, and there was, too, to be endured, however briefly, the struggle, the exposure, hunger and thirst, the denial of mating opportunities, and yielding, pellmell, they began to die by the million—one is speaking of a very large community indeed, grown fat and comfortable from centuries of the right kind of nourishment and pleasure— and soon it was all over with them, and they were dead and gone, having had their first and only taste of death and disaster. However, as decreed by the Examiners, they were immediately reborn as humans, suffering the least hurt, unaided by bib, towel, or midwife, a brand new community, on good virgin land, as pioneer creatures of exceptional fortune, to continue to benefit from the prime sacrifice made to Wagle, by their all-father, the aforesaid eighteen-year-old ex-man.

V

As one of them lay under a palm, watching the scene, and faintly recalling the thrill of his new existence, and not knowing anything of the unlimited food, drink and partners provided, his woman, wearing a divinely-provided grass skirt, joined him, and they looked upon each other with favor and desire. But their ardor was doused by fear, the fear of the morrow—the bane and curse of all mankind. Fathoming this, the Examiners took pity on them, and they heard the wind whistle, and the voice of the Examiners themselves. "Ye shall be glad of the morrow!" the voice said. "Ye shall bring the tidings of plenty to the many! Ye shall be honored of the many! There shall be a new bridge of plenty for the many!"

They ran away from the palms shouting, *"Plenty! Plenty!"* and were duly honored by their kind—the many—for the great and comforting tidings they had brought them. Indeed, as witnessed in the annals of their kind, they were known as the Prophets of a new bridge of plenty.

May God bless us all.

–6–

Sutta Abandoned

In the eastern end of the ridgy ground by the indigo plantation close to a certain village in northern India, there is a square piece of land, and nearby, next to the tranquil pond, an old temple—a tiny construction in yellow stone—and from the outside one can only see the brass bell, and nothing else, as there is darkness inside the recess, and in the chapel proper only a dim oil lamp burns, and no one seems to know the identity of the idol—they just call it *Baba*—and this is what happened in the chapel on a certain dark and windy night.

It was late—the hour of midnight—and nobody was about, and the *Baba*, the spirit of the idol, wished to incarnate, be embodied, and it assumed the form of an intensely luminous spiral, of the fineness of a hair-spring, and it issued from the mottled marble image, its former home, screwed out of it, and it faced the image, and looked at it in wrath, and to test its power, it willed the dead to moan and the dead did indeed moan. After that, with fearful speed, it flew out of the temple, and set upon a white mare, and she ran past the houses, not knowing that she was ridden upon by a supernatural thing, and she ran through the night, was abandoned, and came home in the early hours of the morning to die. And the angry spiral did not return to the temple, but hovered over the pond, by the indigo plantation, and past midnight, with the same fearful speed, it submerged, went to the bottom of the pond, and stayed there. The only living creature in the pond—apart from the green *singhārā* nut and the lotus which grow there—was a crane and it died instantly.

From that day, the pond became hungry, and whoever set foot in it—any living creature—was taken. One day, a young woman, till then a stranger to the village, hot and dusty, and not knowing anything of the spiral, or of the danger to young women exposed to a male spirit, wished to bathe in the pond. It was midday. As soon as she entered the pond, she had an experience akin to her bridal-night experience, when she was a little girl of thirteen—they marry young in this part of the world—and of such violence that for days she was as one dead. From that day onwards, she was possessed by the spirit—the spiral lived inside her as her lover—and the pond was at peace once more.

Had anyone seen the girl with the trained eye of an *ojhā*—only the *ojhās* know the ways of the spirits—he would have seen a luminous crescent on her brow, a thing of the other world, vivifying her looks so strangely, and at the hour of midnight, he would have seen her in the throes of an awful embrace, a ravishment, and seen her writhe in pain, for such are the embraces of spirits in carnal love with human beings.

Her husband, who had married her so young and was but a year older, had seen her in such a state, glowing and smouldering, and, terrified, had left her alone. Day after day, he saw her grow lovely—every bit of her person, the very down on her arms, acquired a strange, an ethereal kind of beauty—and very often the vision filled the peasant with desire, intense enough to be a torment, but whenever he approached her, a glance from her terrified him and he left her alone, feeling as if he were overcome, defeated, so exhausting were the two feelings warring inside him—the desire and the fear of the unknown.

II

As years passed, the carnal will of the spirit was calmed, and the flesh of Sutta—that was the girl's name, it is a tender word meaning *daughter*—was violated no more. And there grew in the spirit a true dependence towards her, as of a child on its mother, and it sought no fiendish satisfactions of the flesh, and knowing this change, Sutta was no longer in fear of her unearthly lover, living inside her, and she would often dream of it as a babe in arms, and imagine it lying on her breasts, often asleep, its crying quieted by a lullaby. And suckling it—so dreaming—she would feel an intense tenderness for her child that was once her fiendish lover—and in the years that followed, a calm content with her situation came to her, and it made her bloom as a woman of beauty, and everything about her began to shimmer with an unseen light, the light that was once the spiral spirit's, and now was hers, a thing not of the earth, and even the blind could feel her radiance and grace.

So nursed and tended by a human heart, the spiral lost all its awful power, and became a child, and so real that Sutta could feel it stir, often resting against her breasts, and so filled with tenderness and motherly love was she that it was the true fulfillment of her destiny—the happiness of being the mother of a dearly beloved child—and she was then thirty.

III

In that very year, a great and good *yogi,* who was a leper and who knew occult arts, arrived in the village. He went into the temple and spent three days and nights entreating the *Baba* to heal him. Failing to speak to the *Baba,* he breathed his *prānā*— his own vitality—into the empty image. That is the occult way, to infuse life into an image by an act of will, and so seek power and aid. Thereupon, a voice issued from the image of the *Baba.* It was the voice of the leper, though outside of him, made of his *prānā,* and from his own will. And assenting, the voice declared him healed on the eve of the next new moon, and gave him leave to go and wed, take to himself a wife, as indeed was his ardent unspoken wish, though he was a leper, despised and undesired, and forbidden the touch of those who were clean.

So heartened, and glad, he went into the village, and saw Sutta, the sight of whose beauty overwhelmed him, made him blind from passion, and he ravished her, as might a maddened fiend, and the child-spirit inside her remained powerless, innocent of the iniquity, and while the leper was savaging Sutta, he was set upon by the peasant—Sutta's husband—who, knowing no ease, from fury, beheaded both with his axe—his wife and, so he surmised, her man, the *yogi*—and denied them the rites of the dead. No voice was raised against him in the village because he had done what seemed right and just.

Thus, from causes unknown—just as a beautiful and endowed child ages, dies, and the days of perfect peace and happiness end, and often end in sadness—a revered spirit of a temple lost its awful power and was made motherless and would cry and endlessly seek its human mother and ache and endure: thus, too, was a great and good *yogi* degraded, by beauty and splendor, to the fate of a tyrant and a ravisher, and sorrowing for his sin, made to suffer for an eternity, from irredeemable guilt, remorse, a fate so forced upon one who was unhappy, needy, a leper, despised and undesired: and thus, poor Sutta, too, would abide in anguish, till the end of time, denied her child, denied love, denied home, denied the rites of the dead, beheaded, abandoned, and be as one unclean, wanting, thirsting, craving, craving for content.

The Fiend Screams
"Kyā Chāhate Ho?"

By the grace of God—not forgetting the blessings of my elders—I was appointed Overseer in the Survey Department of the Government of India the day I left college. That was when the British were here. *Mahakammā Sarwāī,* as the department was called, was a good department. My superior, a Scot, was a conscientious officer. The pay was not bad and they were liberal with promotions.

I was posted in a hilly northern district. A wave of fragrance from the Department's crimson and yellow rose garden welcomed me on arrival. A miniature stone house was allotted to me for quarters. A merry stream ran not far from the house. At night the gentle rustling of the water used to make me feel restless and lonely. I was young. I expect I was longing for a girl to share my life and my quarters with me.

I soon settled down to official routine. The Survey Department disillusions you, gentlemen. Within a month, I managed to survey every inch of the district and every resident. I did not find romance but I became friendly with the *jadūgar.*

A *jadūgar* is a sorcerer, a wizard, and wizardry was—it still is—a hereditary profession in these parts. People have problems: matters of love, employment, litigation, enemies. And they need a *jadūgar*'s help. He is expected to work wonders for them.

My *jadūgar* friend was known as Aamil Mia. I used to call

on him for a chat whenever I could. His wife did not mix with male callers. She kept *purdah*—wore the veil—and lived behind the gunny bag curtain. It divided their one-roomed cottage. She cooked behind the curtain, too, and made passable tea.

They had an unpredictable sort of a boy called Muglai. Aamil Mia introduced him to me as a *gustākh*—an impudent fellow. He was about thirteen. And judged by *any* standard, he was an entirely attractive person. I liked him very much. But he was the silent type and hardly spoke to anyone. I think young Muglai knew about his attractions. That is why he kept himself aloof. He seemed to know that he was a gift of God. And gifts of God should not be squandered. When I first saw him, I caught myself wondering about the heartaches so much charm could cause a young possessive girl, in the days to come. The girl angle was a part of my thinking in those days. If I may say so, it still is, gentlemen.

One day, Aamil Mia dropped in at the office to say that he and the family were off for a few days' *chhutee*—rest, relief, recreation. This surprised me. People in our parts—having so much leisure and not knowing what to do with it—do not understand the meaning of the word *holiday*. It so happened, Aamil Mia explained, that his brother-in-law, the widower—who was an army pensioner—had gone away to Delhi to join in a ceremonial parade. He had sent the key of the homestead with a neighbor that very morning and—Aamil Mia thought—the family could do with a train ride. In my district, next to a clandestine love affair, a *rupee* worth ticket for a train journey was the most sensational thing going for both young and old, men and women.

I returned his *salaam bandagī*, wished him well, and said that I looked forward to seeing him and friend Muglai after their return. To my surprise, however, I heard the family was back home the same evening. I called on Aamil Mia for news.

He gave me the news. Arrived at their destination, he and his wife—each carrying a bundle on the head—walked about three miles from the station. Carrying his canvas rucksack, Muglai followed them. Hot and bothered, the first thing he and his wife did on entering the brother-in-law's cottage was to stretch themselves out on the cots. The two green army collapsible cots, and a few baked clay pots, was all the household equipment in the cottage. The widower was a bit of a ... *er* ... miser.

After resting a while, Aamil Mia said to the wife, "Ah, *Begam*, this is comfort!" And the *Begam*—he always addressed her as a lady of rank—further refreshed by the cool breeze that blew over her, replied, *"Ji, Khāvind*. It is indeed comfort!" She always addressed him as *Khāvind*—master, and never missed an opportunity to bless him with a long life by the benign *"ji."*

A bare moment after that courteous exchange of words, I tell you, a *nāgin*—a racer snake—fell on her *pet* from the ceiling. Aamil Mia pointed out the spot to me—her *pet* would be just where Aamil Mia's stomach was. It flattened on impact, I imagine, recovered, and retreated fast, zigzagging towards an old hen house in the shade.

Although stunned, in a matter of seconds, the *Begam* had her bundle on the head, and, in tears, she started walking towards the station. Aamil Mia quickly locked up the cottage—and reluctantly—followed her. Nothing would make her stay in such a place. While his mother and father were walking fast towards the railway station, Muglai lagged behind, in the vicinity of the hen house.

Aamil Mia added that he was sure that Muglai had known of the *nāgin* trying to slither over the bamboo sticks supporting the ceiling of the cottage, probably to sun itself, before it lost balance, and dropped on his wife's *pet*. He was certain that Muglai—deliberately—hadn't warned his mother of the snake's presence. "I am shocked to hear it!" I said. *"Gustākhī!"* Aamil Mia maintained. "Impudence!"

The three got into a crowded third class carriage. The boy's calmness—and because he had agreed to go back without making any sort of a fuss—made Aamil Mia suspicious. As the train raced twenty miles an hour on the narrow gauge, he asked Muglai about the *haal*—the situation, the state of things, the news! Getting no reply, he threatened to search Muglai's rucksack. *Where-*

upon the boy opened it and—as Aamil Mia put it—"emptied it outside the window." Thereupon a middle-aged woman of girth, sitting a few seats down the carriage—and leaning out of the window, enjoying the prospect—screamed, and *swore* that she had been struck by a snake. It had slapped her face and flew past her, she complained loudly. Nobody would believe her. Snakes do not fly. But a red cheek and a developing bruise across her chin made matters quite obvious to Aamil Mia.

II

Not many months after the incident, Aamil Mia reached the conclusion that there was more than mere *gustākhī*—impudence—in the boy. He had real *shaitāni*—devilish stuff—in him. For instance, to handle a *nāgin*—to catch it with bare hands to take it home in a rucksack, this sort of thing—just isn't *done* . . . not by *boys!* As the result of reaching that conclusion, in spite of his tender years, he initiated Muglai into a secret *shaitāni amal*, a *jinnī* rite—to conjure a she-devil: a practice Aamil Mia had inherited from his *jadūgar* ancestors as an heirloom but, I may add, he himself did not practice, for want of *dilerī*—heart, courage. Such practices are forbidden to decent God-fearing folk, anyway. But the results—if you could tame a fiend—are worth the trouble to those who dare.

On the thirteenth night of the practice, about midnight, while his mother and father slept soundly behind the gunny curtain, Muglai saw a vaporous, sooty sort of a figure, sitting on the floor next to him, where the dim oil lamp was burning. It was a nude figure and, judged by the human female standards, huge. It quivered as if it were having hiccups, Muglai thought, and it sat there listening to the praises of the *jinn*—the fiends, demons and the like—that Muglai was reciting. . . . That was the concluding part of the blasphemous daily ritual, the *shaitāni amal.* Decent God-fearing folk pray to Allāh, and daily recite the *namaaz.*

On the thirtieth night, she spoke. In a voice that did not seem to issue from the figure—but rather from inside Muglai's own ears—she demanded that the praises be recited again. Muglai did not take notice. Aamil Mia, who had carefully cross-examined the boy the following morning, told me that this was an *unforgivable* thing to do! If there is a serious business in this serious business, it is this *jinnī jadūgarī* business. Absolutely no *gustākhī* or affront is permitted!

Convulsing violently, and raging, she showed Muglai the sights—such sights as make lesser men of magic go dumb for life or to pieces altogether. He saw corpses floating down murky rivers as logs, and graves being dug by corpses, corpses burying corpses, and along with certain profane and impious details, he saw a stampede of animals, the animals rushing at himself, their heads severed, bleeding fountains from the neck down, yet shrieking outrageously . . . and more. Not impressed, and reluctantly—he said he was tired and wanted to sleep—Muglai recited the praises again and the visions ceased.

III

On the fortieth night of the *amal,* she spoke again. Muglai had his ears bursting from inside, and he rubbed them from the outside—to ease the ache, he said—she thundered why had he summoned her? In plain, but a horrifyingly rasping Urdu, she demanded of Muglai, *"Kyā chāhate ho?"* (*"What do you want?"*)

Aamil Mia had prepared the boy for the moment. When asked what he wanted, he was to say humbly, but firmly, *"Kabza, huzoor!"* ("Control, your honor!") Reduced to obedience by the spell, she would agree to be controlled. Next, the boy was to request that her honor come to their *garībkhānā,* their mean and unworthy home, only when summoned. She would promise it. Her honor was not to cause any *pareshānī*—any sort of harassment—to the family. She would promise it. Lastly, she would promise to cause *hub*—attachment, love—in the family's favor: she would fascinate anyone at all with whom the family felt like dealing, in matters of the heart, money, employment, whatever.

"Kyā chāhate ho?" she demanded the second time and the third time and the fourth time. And Muglai—from sheer villainy, I should think—did not trouble to reply. Quite a rumpus followed that *gustākhī*. What little property the family had—a few pots and pans and two old trunks and what was inside them—were hurled about and the pots smashed against the wall. Their room divider was torn to shreds. What with her nerves, Muglai's mother, reposing on the floor, was rocked in her sleep, as if she were caught in an earthquake, and made to stand up. Aamil Mia was pulled off his cot, and by the beard. He too was made to stand up and witness. . . . And both had a feel of what passes for psychic terror.

Meanwhile, the sooty figure—now grown monstrous, every single limb and part of her nude person grown monstrous, her elongated neck stretching towards the ceiling and her waist whereabout Aamil Mia was—kept screaming, *"Kyā chāhate ho? Kyā chāhate ho? Kyā chāhate ho? Kyā chāhate ho?"* (*"What do you want? What do you want? What do you want? What do you want?"*)

While his mother and father stood petrified in their baggy *salvaar* pyjamas, transfixed in the humble stance of addressing a *salaam* to the enraged demon—and Aamil Mia recanting, imploring God for aid, silently citing, *"Allāhwand karīm! Khudāwand karīm!"*—Muglai answered her question. He said to her, "Ask *abbā!*"

It seems that of all the calamities with which a *gustākh* son can besiege his *abbā*—his papa—the worst is to invoke a creature from the depths of darkness, get her raving mad, and then tell her, "Ask *abbā!*" Having been won by the boy, she promised it. She immediately *asked abbā*, and has been *asking him ever since!*

IV

Without a moment's respite—from that very instant—the old sorcerer heard the terrorizing voice of futility, day and night screaming, *"Kyā chāhate ho? Kyā chāhate ho?"*

In the years that followed, he tried to fight the *shaitāni āwāz*—the devilish voice—and gave up fighting. If he replied to her, and made a request, "I want . . ." she screamed once more, *"What do you want?"* And if he were angry, and swore at her—familiarity with the *āwāz* through the years had lessened his fear of the fiend—she repeated *"What do you want?"* "Ask *abbā!"* was Muglai's demand—no more no less—and she had promised it . . . She was *asking*—and *granting nothing!*

Now a dashing and very handsome thirty—mustachioed and turbaned, too—Muglai is not on speaking terms with his father. At my suggestion though, Aamil Mia did unburden himself and speak to Muglai about it. And Muglai—impudently aspiring for the favors of the same fancy girl whom Aamil Mia happened to be . . . *er* . . . courting—put in a condition before he would intercede with the fiend and call off the *āwaz* . . . a condition, I may add, gentlemen, no man in his senses could accept. "What are you going to do?" I asked Aamil Mia, rather alarmed.

Stroking his henna-dyed beard—and steering clear of the words "castration" and "eunuch," these words . . . *er* . . . are a part of the social history of man, gentlemen, and Muglai had certainly addressed them to his father—the old man told me what he was going to do. He said, as far as he was concerned— and as far as I can quote him—the *asterisk*ing thing could do what she *asterisk*s well liked. . . . She could do her *asterisk*ing worst, in fact, for as long as she *asterisk*s well pleased. And as for Muglai Mia, he voiced some pretty unquotable Urdu, too.

Quite understandable though, gentlemen. If you had to choose between enduring a she-devil's nagging day and night, or a conditional peace with a rival in love, your own son, I bet you would decide to do with the *she-devil than to do without your mardī* . . . to do without his actual bull feature—that is what Muglai had demanded of his father, author, sponsor—his *abbā* . . . I have *never* heard of such a thing!—the ultimate *gustākhī,* gentlemen! *the* conclusive liberty, I beg of you.

–8–

With Malice Aforethought

There are a lot of people—G. Gurdjieff, Ramakrishna mission Swamis, J. Krishnamurti, Ptr Dem'yanovich Uspensky, Ramana Maharishi, the Zen masters, Meher Baba, Shri Aurobindo, Aldous Huxley, the holy Mother of Pondicherry, to name a few—who want you to go in for self-realization.

Self-realization is the absolute condition for happiness. To know this truth is growth, maturity, enrichment.

A fortunate self-realized victim might find comfort and fulfillment in martyrdom, in torture, and (at the receiving end of) flogging, assault, crucifixion. A self-realized adept doubtlessly finds fulfillment in martyring, torturing, flogging, assaulting, crucifying.

For the multitude, this esoteric knowledge is not easily come, not easily grasped when come, and—as *all* achievement—its arrival is conditioned by time, destiny, luck, God, *anti*-God.

II

I discovered my true nature and became a self-realized being very early in life. When I was a boy, I used to pinch little girls (how many of you, my esteemed friends, have not done that or dropped wriggling worms down their little backs, what do you think?) and *enjoy* watching them squirm.

Not yet twenty, I became a business man. I was a travel

agent. I had a one-room office and an elderly widow's savings. Travel agency was her idea. She wouldn't part with her savings for any other idea. She thought it was a "nice business" for a coming young man.

I drew full pay but no client for the first eight months. I might have been wool-farming in a sheepless country.

At the beginning of the ninth, I got a customer—an old classmate of the widow—and the classmate's thirty-five-year-old nephew, the name of Mr. . . I booked them a run of the East African coast on a tramp of tramps—a converted Arab dhow. The old woman was gone on such words as Mombasa, Kilindini, Cape Delgado, and the scum of the earth—the captain of the dhow—had a fifty-fifty split arrangement with me.

The woman—past her sixties, when I booked her—was never the same after her return from "the holiday". The scum of the earth, the dhow, the seas, the sun, the manners of the crew, and dysentery, all helped. And "the boy"—the nephew, the name of Mr. . .—was wearing around both his eyes monocles of raw and bruised beef—so the bags about his eyes from little hernias seemed to me—as he took refuge in a nursing home.

His aunt was courted by death exactly a month after. The dysentery bug was Arab and strong. My sleeping partner, the widow, followed her. I quit business and saved her savings.

By all reckoning, the two old women, and the nephew (the name of Mr. . .), cut a caper, or what do you think? I enjoyed doing business with them.

III

Man, by nature, is happy. Search for happiness is folly. Happiness must be realized within. This is an esoteric secret. The Hindu Vedāntin knows this secret. *Sat-Chit-Ānanda,* he says. *Ānanda* is bliss, joy, happiness. (See *Upanishad* books, chapter so and so, page so and so, verse so and so.)

One reason why we do not realize our true nature is our preoccupation with others: because we do things for others instead of doing them for ourselves, help others instead of helping ourselves. This perversity—trying to run a stream against its course and current—results in effort, exertion, struggle. All so-called religious and moral discipline is effort, exertion, struggle. It is anything but spontaneity. It is suffering. It is not happiness, my esteemed friends. As soon as all that folly is abandoned, realization of Truth results. The means of attaining this insight into Truth might be ever so trivial: squirming little girls, a duped widow, the departed dysenteric, or the nephew (the name of Mr. . .).

Post-realization, all service must be for self. All execution of such service is bound to be disadvantageous to others—who must be reduced, worsened, and, eventually, sacrificed. And this course must lead to true spirituality (since it is the Truth, and it must lead to a further conquest, a greater freedom, mastery, to self-possession entire, and, only then, not before, my esteemed friends, *all* would be won!).

To win *all*, the adept must not be satisfied with meeting the needs of his nature (self-realization, *etc.*). That is not *all*. He must forge ahead, be truly sovereign; and be a man of metal (not flesh). Not satisfied with mere happiness (*ānanda*), he must be a Force unto himself, an adept in tempting, tiring, and confusing creatures: a hunter of men, a whipper, a scourge, a punisher of those who desire and accept punishment: those who seek escape from fire to a greater fire, in fast, pledge, Lent, discipline, cruci-fixion, death.

Thus, my esteemed friends, the adept—by laws of Magic Eternal—gains *all*. He is never without his due: his *prey, feed, fodder*.

(These truths are not known to G. Gurdjieff, Ramakrishna Mission Swamis, J. Krishnamurti, Ptr Dem'yanovich Uspensky, Ramana Maharishi, the Zen masters, Meher Baba, Sri Auro-bindo, Aldous Huxley, the holy Mother of Pondicherry, to name a few.)

IV

My own night of achievement was rayless. There was an ebon gloss upon the darkness too, I thought. And, with my heightened susceptibility, I could discern a premonitory amalgam of scents: the seasoned teak of the coffin, the woolen suit and the silk tie (shrouding the corpse), the odor of palsied flesh (present premonitorily, no other than the nephew, the name of Mr. . . HIC JACET, Auntie's pet and kin!). Following these omens—having chosen to be a sovereign man of metal—not yet thirty, I was ready to forge ahead. Dispensing with all ritual, all ceremony, chant, spell, forsaking all vestment, naked, legs astride, head lowered, towards and below the navel—the-face-to-the-pelvis posture, as prescribed—I invoked Him.

My aim was to be a peer of the All High Himself, be second only to the premier plenipotentiary: the tusky grandee, who wears the morning coat made of male hide and hair, the top hat of tarred female hide and hair, and sweats tongues of flame and smoke from his honeycombed hide and hair: the solemn *sultan* who, forever, reviews the All High's state of the Estate report: so many dead, devoured, sacrificed—by war, pestilence, disease, ignorance, confusion—and so many on the way, fasting, laboring, struggling, courting the grave!

V

So resolved, on that night of achievement, I soon passed beyond the reaches of aspiring minds, and beyond the range of the man-devil, warlock, werewolf, vampire, the comforter of witches, the leader of carnage, the master of whoredom.

I asked for a sign from Him.

In my library, in the farthest corner—where the reading lamp stands—I was enveloped in a virgin radiance: an aquamarine light, cooling, comforting, consoling. Then the rays were gathered off me, became a girdle of a still purer splendor, throbbing with life, laughter, joy: all the smiles of babes that kick and gurgle when lying on their backs, when suckled, when kissed, when lying face down—all that *and* the jasmine, the rose, *and* the soul of sandal, the memory of myrrh!

In the girdle of supernatural light, my esteemed friends, then emerged dancers, dancers of fantasy, nymphs, creatures of such entrancing beauty that I cried curses upon the poets, painters, sculptors, for never having known such *richness!* Then the girdle was gathered, and became a swan: a swan of ultimate, immaculate, intrinsic beauty, symmetry, majesty: a swan so conjured, and breathing, its wings opalesque, and glittering silver, sapphire, gold and rose!

Then the swan was gathered and became a hand of absolute perfection: a masked woman's hand, and, on her wrist, I saw a bangle, gently shedding the light of the rarest rarest beryl, the greenest greenest green!

The hand *blessed me!*

Appalled, betrayed, cheated, I stood upright, my posture broken, and stamping, cursing, I cried, "Deceit!" "False!"

VI

Wherefore, my esteemed friends, the *true* symbols—the soothfast signs? Wherefore, the oozing, suppurating corpse—the fouled grave? Wherefore, the Master's cloven hooves—His sulphurous smell? Wherefore, His witch-kissed fundament—and wherefore, wherefore, the immense phallus of our Father?

Spitting on the Glory—the hand of beauty that was blessing me—I invoked Him again, crying aloud my aforesaid thoughts: "Wherefore . . . ?" "Wherefore . . . ?" "Wherefore . . . ?"

Instantly, the hand became viscous—a splash of bloody red—and it coagulated a brownish muddy red, and in the middle whereof was an emptiness, and the emptiness was aflame with a malignant glare, an infra-red, uneven glare, and it jumped off the emptiness and touched my bare flesh!

By that burning, searing touch, I knew it was He. Trembling from rage, and mocking Him, I said, "Have you come to me for *pity,* Beelzebub?" Standing straight, naked, and facing Him, I defied Him. "Do I expect *justice* from you, now, Beelzebub? Are you cultivating the *virtues,* now, Beelzebub?"

Meekest of the meek, Father replied ever so humbly. "Did you say, 'deceit!' and 'false!' your reverence?" "I said, 'deceit!' Beelzebub! I said 'false!' Beelzebub!" "What is false, your reverence?" "Beauty is false, Beelzebub!" "What is deceit, your reverence?" "Joy, benediction, perfection, is deceit, Beelzebub!" "You asked for a sign, your reverence?" "I asked for a sign, Beelzebub!" Gently, and pleading, our Father said, "The Glory was the sign, your reverence!" "Deceit!" "False!" I cried again, blind to Truth.

The glare jumped towards me again and penetrated me viciously. Scorched, scalded, seething, that very instant, my esteemed friends, I attained *all!*

I *was* His peer, His son, His chosen, the chosen of the Great Magician, the perfidious Pretender!

"Hail, Most High!" I cried, assuming the pelvisacral posture, as prescribed, legs astride, face lowered, towards and below the navel. And I hastily read the oath and litany of the chosen: *"I promise to protect, to serve, love, shield, shelter, the multitude. Thy food, Father! Thy weal, Beelzebub! Woe be to the multitude! The plagues of Egypt upon the multitude! Amen!"*

VII

Today, my esteemed friends, I am a man of religion, a convert, *Deo gratias,* a penitent among penitents, a reformed whore, a Mary Magdalen manifold. I endorse and support all self-accusation, and doctrine, idealism, mysticism, symbolism, all Hindu

Sat-Chit-Ānanda, and profess love, chastity, propriety, decency, justice, charity, beauty, and I urge faith upon all, and I believe in Santa Claus: and I plead compassion for the creatures, the multitude.

Sheltered, protected and *loved,* the creatures are His *meat,* His *feed,* His *sacrifice!*

Deprived of safety, protection, caress, love—their *needs!*— the creatures seek other pastures, seek the anti-Most High, the First and the Last Enemy, the Adversary called God. They stray away from the world—which is the domain of *our* Father—and so many of His sheep—His *feed,* His *fodder*—are lost!

It is upon creatures, my esteemed friends, that our Father's *existence* depends. That is the cross He bears. Enthroned in their hearts, He lives, He reigns, He laughs. In barren, broken hearts—what do you think?—He is as dead. Ailing, eclipsed, lonely, and molested, aye: lost of His domain, forsaken by His subjects, deprived of His church, His sacrifice, is our Father!

So much is revealed and affirmed by the sign, the Glory, the hand that blesses!

This Truth, my esteemed friends, is revealed *only* to the chosen of Beelzebub. This Truth would be realized *only* by the gifted of Beelzebub. This Truth would be understood *only* by the elect of Beelzebub. And the purport of this unpardonable *treason* by G.V. Desani—the publishing of this most secret commerce with the Master, our *āgha,* this *sinister* betrayal by an arrogant renegado channel, which, by the laws of Magic Eternal, the multitude *must* believe to be fiction, a random philosophic fabrication by a crackpot gownsman, a parable, peddled to earn himself tainted *cowries* for pin-money *and* at the expense of his Sovereign Owner and Prompter—would be known *only* to the very own *sons* and *daughters* of Beelzebub!

Devil take! Confusion seize! Woe betide!

The Last Long Letter

Dearest Father,
Remember me? It was you who sent me away to visit his people and to see him again and if I fancied him get engaged to him.

Everything here is as you had said it would be. The mist over the hills is always blue and everything as peaceful as you said it would be. The sea is a few hours' drive.

I have fallen in love with this house and with everything— even with the stationery. The weather is ideal. It will be ideal all through the years, so everybody says.

They are all such wonderful people. The dog is so dignified and the baby of the family is the prettiest-ever kitten. It is a pedigree Persian and temperamental. It purrs, too, of course. It is at my feet, pawing the loose ends of my shoelaces and purring itself silly.

He is as you had described him. He wears the breeches in the morning and is such an accomplished rider. I cannot connect him with the little boy I once knew and played with. He has grown up and is beautiful. Being a man, you wouldn't understand this. He has traveled, has culture, several European languages, to say nothing of his magic with the piano. He has all the classics at his fingertips. As you see, I am terribly impressed.

He received me as an old friend and with the courtesy due to the daughter of his father's best friend. He calls me by my school name. I am accepted.

Love,

I——

Dearest Father,
Everybody calls him Nanhe sāhib. Rhymes with *none* and
hay. Young sāhib. It sounds nice. In spite of his twenty-six years,
he seems so young to me, too, a child really. Sometimes, I feel
a bit afraid of him.

Thank you, thank you, for introducing me. In this house,
surrounded by the orchard, and the hills, it does not seem that I
am in India at all. It is a different world. It is still the old world
too. Nanhe's people were India's princes and princesses not long
ago, perhaps that is why it is still the old world too.

I must find out what is troubling your prospective son-in-
law. Something is.

I am not posting these letters or dating them. I want to give
them all to you as my last long letter before I wed.

Love,

I——

Dear Father,
You taught me to be truthful and always accurate. Nanhe
spoke to me last night. I have written it all down and as accurately
as I could.

That is what he said, but it *does not read as it sounded*. I
am quite sure. He spoke so earnestly and sincerely. From him it
sounded all so natural and spontaneous. My *notes,* joined together, do not read like that at all.

We were sitting in the library and talking of symbolism in
art. Nanhe said, "Whether you call Pope Agapete, Agapeto or
Agapetus—I am not sure of my names—or il Benedetto Agapito,
does it make a difference? His identity is established if you call
him a man—or an Italian man, if you must—a man and therefore
different from God.

"Either your God, who has become your man-god in art, is
to be identified with the high symbol, the very Highest, or with

the mere man. Either your man-god's beard and locks carry the
dirt of the streets, and the smell of the streets, the smell of earthy
things, or he is of the stuff of the stars. Then his hair carries the
luster of which the stars are made.

"Your man-god would cry at his birth and suffer in death.
Wouldn't he? Would you drown his cries of fear and pain with
your devout chants, prayers, and pious moans? Dare you do that
to God made of the stuff of the stars?

"And if your man-god is in the image of a woman, an
exquisite woman, she would be an obsession, wouldn't she, Millie? She would be of the *soul,* and of the *subtlety* of the soul,
though clinging to her is the scent and the savor of the lily, the
jasmine and the rose—bright, bright as a beatific pearl, set in the
blue of the sea! Dare you compare her to a woman prostrate
before an image, an icon, or a symbol of God—an earthy
woman, aging, sweating, and periodically bleeding? Dare you
compare this woman to the Deity—though celebrated as an image of the Deity, her icon bathed in the incenses of Lebanon?
The symbols of the Goddess—the Goddess that is fragrant, fragrant as a celestial lily, the very *soul* of the sacred things, a thing
superior even to the morning star—are of the earth, Millie, made
by man, therefore *different* from God.

"To deify a man or a woman in art! Kings born in bed and
murdered in bed! Some stifled, some strangled, some blinded,
left to weep from hollow sockets, tears mixed with blood!

"I think of the dirt of the bazaars of Khurāsān and of the
beauty of the emeralds of Peru, of God made of stardust and of
man tormented. What is the substance of man, Millie? What is
the will of God for his created? What has God, the Inspiration,
to do with that which is made from Inspiration? What has the
substance so subtle, the starlike substance, the Spirit, immortal,
self-existent, to do with the blood and the bone, with life and
death?

"I think it would be an embrace, though. The starlike thing
can do no other than love. The substance so subtle, the Spirit,
will embrace the flesh. It could be no other than love. It would

crush the bone, and stifle the breath, so intense an embrace it
would be!"
Yours,

I——

Dear Father,
We agreed that while I am here I need not write, though I
have written and not posted my letters. Just shows you that you
are never out of my thoughts.

Today, Chhote, my youngster, our Nanhe sāhib, said such
wonderful things. He sees visions, Father, and they are so real
to him, and he makes them so real to me. I tell you these things
in the strictest confidence.

He said, "I saw a lake. In it reflected I saw the temple of
God. Then I saw flames and sparks upon the temple of God.
'This is the wrath of God,' I thought.

"Then I saw a tree. On it growing I saw leaves of gold.
Then I saw a fountain of fire. And I saw a fountain of gold. I saw
a crown of gold. It hung over the temple of God.

"In the lake I saw reflected the temple of God. Again I saw
the leaves of gold.

"Then the temple burned, its walls burned, the trees burned,
the fountain burned, and the lake burned, the crown burned, and
again I saw fire, and flames and sparks.

"Then I saw the Spirit walk towards me. Untouched by the
fire, I saw the Spirit walk towards me. In its hand I saw a star.
In my hand, too, I saw a star."

I——

Dearest Father,
I have never had any secrets from you. After Mother left us,
and I was three, I have looked upon you as everything and you
have been both mother and father to me.

I feel terribly guilty to keep these secrets from you. Do not, *please*, ever judge my Chhote—my Nanhe sāhib—from my notes. These are his words and translated by me. But he does not speak like that. He is different. And do not, *please*, forget that these things are confidences to me. These things are a secret between us. And if, speaking of his visions and hurts helps him, I am glad that I know, although I now like to be alone and often want to cry. It is not difficult to be alone. The people in this home are gentle and understanding and nobody would presume to ask why one wanted to be alone in one's own room. These are the most wonderful people and this is the most wonderful house I ever visited at home or abroad.

I have written the way I have to protect him. Is this mental illness, Father? If you only knew him as I do, and if he spoke to you as he does to me, you would never believe that of him. He lives through a whole story and it is all so terribly real to him.

He told me this last night. "Millie, I have seen a creature die. Before she died, she spoke to her killer. I heard and understood. He heard and did not understand.

"She was a snake. But she was not a snake. It was under that tree, in the dark, in torchlight, that she spoke to her killer. To him, she said, 'You enticed me because I was hungry. Release me, let me go!

"'Before I became a snake, I was human, a girl, and I was nineteen, a servant of God, and I lived in a temple, by the *sangam*, where the rivers meet, and where the waves play, and there, before the dawn, I had gone to bathe, and none saw me, and none heard me. Release me, let me go!

"'Before I went to the *sangam*, where the rivers meet, I went into the temple, the temple of the Devī, the beloved of God, whose bounden slave I was, and when none saw me, and none heard me, I stole the garments worn by the Devī, the garments worn by the image of the beloved of God, and all her ornaments, and then I went to the river, and none saw me, and none heard me. Captor, let me go!

"'I had bathed, and none seeing me, none hearing me, I dressed as the beloved of God, the green satin, the sandals of silk, her crown of gold, with the pearls strung, silver upon my ears, the ruby and the emerald necklace as red and green stars strung, and I wore her yellow robe, and the veil of the Devī, the beloved of God, whose slave I was, the veil of woven gold, and I saw my face in the mirror of the beloved of God, and I loved her slave more than I ever loved the beloved of God. Let me go, let me go! Release me, let me go!

" 'Then I saw upon me the shadow of an eagle, and I heard the cry of the early kite. Fearing, I hurried to the temple, and then upon me fell the shadow of a man, the shadow of the priest of the Devī, the beloved of God, and lured by the sight of the living image of the beloved of God—whose chosen slave, servant, and priest he was—he took me, and I was trembling—not seeking him, not seeking his limbs, but desiring him, yet desiring him—and thus was I taken. Then he cried, cried for his sin, the priest that was like my father, the holy priest of the beloved of God, whose bounden slave he was, and I fell at his feet, unrepentant, and I vowed to die, to die with him, and I vowed *sahamarana,* upon the polluted garments of the beloved of God, upon the woven gold, the garments which the priest of the Devī in frenzy had torn, and I vowed upon my blood that was upon the garments of the beloved of God, to die with my lord and love. Release me, let me go! Let me go!

" 'I returned to the temple and I bathed and worshiped the image of the beloved of God, whose slave I was, and I dressed the image of the Devī in the polluted garments, the garments that I, her sinning slave had worn, and the Sister of the temple saw me, and blessed me, for my head was upon the marble feet of the beloved of God, and I was adoring, and I was content, for I was willed to die with my lord and love, and so atone for my sin, as if it were so willed by our mother, the Devī, the beloved of God. Let me go! Let me go!

" 'While I worshiped, I looked in the temple mirror, and I saw as if the mirror could no longer see, but the shell eyes of the Devī all-seeing, and then I saw my lord and love, that was blinded, come into the temple, and dying, his blood washing the marble feet of the beloved of God, as his penance for his sin. Then I was blinded, as was the great temple mirror, it did not see true, not see true, for my vow was unfulfilled, and my lord and love was gone, and I was truly blinded, as was my lord and love. Let me go! Let me go!

"'I died of my hand, as did my lord and love, torn in the breast with the sword of the Devī, and I was captured by a blue mist, rising from the sea, as a blue monster of the sea, and I heard nothing, nothing, but the cries of pain of my dear one, my father, my lord, my dear love, calling *Devī! O Devī!* and not calling for me! not calling for me! and in torment, I called the beloved of God for mercy, mercy, mercy upon my beloved! my dear one! till I was in a *koopa,* a pit of gurgling waters, and I heard the waters speak, and say to me, woman, thy lord and love shall be healed if thou wilt be forgotten of him, be forgotten of him, not be remembered of him, and be limbless, and near-blind, as thou wert in his embrace, desiring him, thy garments and the veil of woven gold torn, thou near-blind and trembling! and so living, woman, seek, seek a coral leaf, the shape of a cotton seed, and marked in vermilion, stained as if in thy own blood, the carnal blood that was upon the garments of the beloved of God, and place it, woman! upon the foot of the image of the Devī, the beloved of God, whose handmaiden thou wert, and whom thou hast wronged, and so do penance to the beloved of God, thy mother, and the mother of thy man! Oh, release me! Let me go! Release me, let me go!

"'To be forgotten of my father! my love! my dear love! In anguish, to heal him, to heal him, I willed to be forgotten of him, and I prayed that it were so! And I was limbless, earless, trembling from fear, and near-blind, a creature snake, and I was hungry, and you enticed me, and I was captive. I cried till the sunset, weeping, still hearing, still hearing the cries of my beloved, my lord, my love, he who had forgotten me, till the Devī, the beloved of God, forgave me! She forgave me! And she gave me back the gift of joy! My mother gave me back the gift of joy! There fell upon me, from that tree, a leaf, a coral leaf, the shape

of a cotton seed, with the mark in vermillion! There fell upon
me from that tree a coral leaf with the mark in vermilion! And I
heard it said, child, take thou this leaf and place it upon the foot
of the Devī, the beloved of God, in the temple by the *sangam,*
where the rivers meet, and waves play, and so heal thy lord and
love! Let me go! Let me go!

"'Here is my coral leaf, and my lord and love cries in pain,
and my lord and love waits in pain! Let me go! Let me go!'

"When she had so spoken, her captor said, 'It is a dream!
This cursed creature gives me dreams!' And I saw him pick up
the lighted torch, and strike her till she was dead.

"Millie, I must find the temple of the Devī, by the *sangam,*
and place a blood-stained leaf at the foot of the image. I must
find the temple of the Devi! Help me, Millie, find the temple of
the Devī!"

I spent last night crying. I am so afraid.

I——

Dearest Father,

Today my boy spoke of *us* at last and this is what he said
and I want you to know that *nothing* would make a difference.
No wall ever could. It is impossible not to love him. It is not from
pity that I love him but for himself, for everything, and for his
dreams, and his visions, and his hurts, too.

He is so troubled. And I want to know everything. That is
what I am here for, aren't I? You said, get engaged, if you
approve of him. I approve of him. Nothing would make a difference.

"This is not my home," he said. "And there is a wall between you and me, Millie.

"In the evening, the darkness is awake. The light is lost in
shadow. Yesterday, I saw death. Death looked at me as you look
at me. How can I be happy, be glad, when there is this wall
between you and me, Millie!

"The king of the gods forbade a woman a male child. In rage, she stabbed herself, and her still-born daughter. She fell, her still-born dropped, and she was burnt on a hill of thorns. That, too, was yesterday. Tomorrow, I will wear a wrap, the wrap wet with the blood of her kind, and their still-born, and I will go to the charnel-ground, and sit by a pyre of thorns, and there await death.

"When I am dead, then, Millie, there will be no wall between you and me."

I am so terribly afraid for him.

I——

Dear Father,

I have not posted any of my letters and have sent you a wish-you-were-here card today. It was the only thing on the table.

You taught me to be virtuous. To love my little boy, and to be consumed by his love, seems all of virtue and religion to me.

Somewhere, some place, the terrible turmoil in his heart must find a resting place. I think so. When that happens, I want to be there, and with him. If it is death, to the death with him.

We drove past the hills to the sea.

It was noon, and warm, and beautiful.

We were sitting on a high rock.

In his hand, Chhote had his *neelam* ring, and with the sun shining upon its bluish convex dome, the sapphire made a lovely six-rayed star. "I had lost it," he said, "and found it by the sands. It was given to me as a token, not far from the sea.

"Watch now the image of the star! In it is mystery! In it is the image of all things! Watch now the star!

"Once the universe had no color. She was a colorless conal mass, opaque, cold, and in her happened nothing, nothing in her was born. Yet, bound in the darkness, as is the sea by the darkness, in her was the essence of all things, all time, all wisdom, all art, waiting, waiting to be born, and be true, be realized true.

"Then the Spirit, mystic, lone, unique, shone upon the conal mass, was reflected in the dark of the conal mass, even as this! this star!

"Nothing that ever moved now moved. Nothing that ever happened now happened. The whole became parts. Parts moved towards parts. Shape moved to shape. And there was color, strange color, and lights, each reaching towards the other, and another, farther into the conal mass.

"After that magic, as the sudden setting of the risen sun, the Spirit was gone, to be lone again, be unique, and death happened to the beatified mass. Nothing moved, and all was darkness once more, nothing a shape, nothing a part, waiting, waiting again to be born.

"Watch now this thing enkindled, and watch again the star! In the star is mystery! In the star have I seen the Spirit! In it I have seen the universe! the mystery of all, of birth and death! It *is* the Spirit! It is the universe! In my hand, Millie, I do now hold the universe! *all! all!*

"It was given to me as a token, this *neelam*, with its Spirit, this star. It was given to me as a token, by the one I loved, and the one to the sea I lost!

"Watch now the waves. Deep, beneath the waves is the silence, and the dark. Water lies upon water, heavy, so heavy upon a silenced heart. But watch again the star!

"To the sea I return the token. To the sea I return the star. "You will see the blue of the sea, and never again the blue of my *neelam*, or the star.

"To the sea I have returned the token, to the sea is gone the star! "Thou, token, wert given me by my phantom love, and thou, the star, wert in the image of my phantom love, the one I loved, the one to the sea I lost! Tears are of love, and I shall mourn, mourn even in joy!

"Ever, in remembrance, I will seek sorrow, hear me, my love! for sorrow is of love, and is to me of the nature of joy!

"She shall be resplendent! be precious! as the beatific Spirit shining upon the dark conal mass! She shall wear a crown! a crown of stars! Yet, I shall weep, for thou, lost star! fallen in the dark of the sea! token! image! sign! near-beloved! art *all!* art the universe! art the creature! art the phantom! art the Spirit! art light! love! God! *all!*

"Mourn ye, for my beloved is dead! Mourn ye, for my beloved is dead! Drowned in the sea, drowned in the sea, my darling is dead! My darling is dead!"

I——

My dear Father,

As I get to know Nanhe, I have a feeling that all this has happened before. That we have gone out for walks or that I have driven him to the sea and that he has spoken to me exactly as he does and that I have written it all down and that I have known and loved him before.

Hearing him talk, I forget everything, even you, and my schooling in Europe, the years at the university, all the things I learnt, and I remember. I remember as if everything he says he has said before and I have heard it before. I cannot explain it.

I seem to remember too that he had died and that I had died after him and was happy because I had to go and look after him.

He dreamed up this yesterday.

"I saw a stream running into a pool. I was happy, Millie, looking into the pool. And I prayed to God. So it was yesterday.

"Then came the wind wailing from the sea and I heard stones falling. So too it was yesterday.

"Then I saw animals, like hounds, fly close to the earth, till the sky was dark with the creatures. From the trunk of an olean-der tree, from the knot, blew air, tinted air, the color of the clouds, and in the whirlpools of air, I saw the face of my love, fair as the young of the oleander, and I saw the face in a frame of wrought iron, and so it was yesterday.

"Then the sea became the color of burnt saffron, and, upon a rock of copper, I saw my shape, and I saw chains of kindled iron surround the rock, and upon it I saw logs of rotted wood, and then the wind wailed again, and the sound of the falling stone was as one with the wailing. 'Thy hour is come! Thy hour is come!' And I saw the sky become red, and the kindled chains burn and the rotted wood burn, and I saw the sea burn, the rock burn, my shape burn, the hair and the face alight, and it was so willed by my God, thus yesterday, thus yesterday!

"From the fire, I heard a voice, 'Thus it would be! Thus it would be!' If I am in pain, need I weep, need I wail? Thus it would be, Millie, thus it be!

"So the voice spoke to me and it was the voice of my God! It was the voice of my God that spoke to me! And burning, burning, I was weeping of joy, aflame, I was weeping of joy, for he spoke to none other! none other! none other! none other!"

I——

Dear Father,

It was only after I had begged him, over and over again, that Chhote told me the things he did. Please, please, *never* judge him from my words. I have tried to be truthful. I may have been unjust—is that the word?—in rendering his words and perhaps making up the idiom. I do not know why I write this except to beg you not to judge my boy by my words.

That vision about the burning rock was the last thing he told me and he has killed himself. When I saw him early this morning, it was as if something from another world tore me to pieces. I never thought a gun could do so much evil. This house is now dead and my thoughts are with everybody close to me and especially with you.

As long as I can remember, I have loved you and honored you. It is a terrible thing I am going to do. Nothing would change. As your only child, there can be no death to the love that I bear you.

I wrote these letters about the things my boy told me, things I tried to remember when I was alone, not knowing what else to do. And now I leave these to you to explain it all and to beg you to forgive me.

I do *want* to die, and to go and look after him. If there is a life after death, I want to be with him. He was ill, beautifully ill, and now that he has gone home, I must go to him. It seems so right for him to go and wrong for him to be of the world and right for me to go after him. I think of him now as someone sacred. It is not possible for me now to see him as a man or husband or a human being. He seems to me now of God and I want to be of him. Do you understand this?

Thank you for all the good and beautiful things you taught me and thank you for teaching me to love good and beautiful things. It is ironic, isn't it, that I should want to die for them instead of living for them? Chhote became all the good and beautiful things to me these last few days. He was good and beautiful and I would want no other man or child here or here-after.

It is terrible without him. The years I was away from you to another continent, schooling and learning, I had always known, that whenever needed, you were there at home, to protect me and to comfort me. Now, without Chhote, in my hour of need, all of a sudden, everything seems empty, without any hope of protection or comfort. I have no home.

I thought it wonderful of you to give me this boy and to send me to his house to meet his people and see their orchard and the garden. There is a beautiful mountain stream running day and night next to their lovely garden. I cannot bear to look at it today.

I am not crying. I am too stunned for tears. I have been overwhelmed these few days by Chhote. I want to go to him and I am ashamed that I do not know how to die. Is it too terrible to burn oneself? I only know the rock upon which we sat once and it was from there that he threw away his ring. If one jumped from it, avoiding the sands, one could die on the rocks. Something I read once in a sea story. I can't remember it.

I am sad to think that I could not make a return for all that you gave me. I never called you by any name other than "Father." I *feel* all the endearing names now. I want to pray that God guide me as you guided me. It is now that tears are coming to me. I see myself being led by the hand in a street. You are taking me home and although you are with me I feel alone and afraid. Although you hold my hand, I am crying, because I am afraid.

I want to say that in all my twenty-two years that you brought me up in the world, fed me, clothed me, educated me, sent me travelling, made me, I never once found a fault in you. When once you told me to go to my room, and I cried myself to sleep, it was I and not you who were found wanting. I have forgotten why that happened.

You gave me the choice to wear my hair long or short and wear a frock if I wanted to, and not the sari, if I didn't want to, and to keep the name they gave me at school. I remember these things.

I remember all the lovely things you gave me, the Rājasthāni costume, too, and Mother's jewelry, which I could have for keeps only after I married. That is what you said and I can see you now, as if you are with me, saying that to me, and I want to cry to you, and I want to say that I can't marry him because he has gone away. Now I can't have those beautiful things Mother left me, and that seems yet another reason for tears.

Please think kindly of me. I like to be a traditional Indian daughter to you, however independent I have been, and place my head on your feet and humbly beg your forgiveness, dearest Father.

Yours, for ever,

I——

–10–

A Border Incident

At the Indian frontier, on the border of P—n, there is a narrow estuary, opening into a quarrelsome river. It is hilly country: cool, sunny, and a very pretty green. The earth is good and fragrant hereabout, and mothers apples, peaches, the lotus and the rose.

There are powerful currents in the river. Deaths from drowning are not uncommon. No enemies of man live in the river. Crocodiles are said to be settled in the shallows, many many miles downstream. All the treachery is in the currents.

The estuary, being on the border of two countries, is guarded by sentry posts on both sides. Sentry duty, in this part of the world, is hard work. A day-and-night vigil must be kept. The most trustworthy sentries are on guard.

Some time ago, on the Indian side of the river, the post syce's little boy—age eight—happened to be fishing in knee-deep water. Losing his foothold, he was caught by the ebbing water. And, in a matter of minutes, he was off, making for the currents.

His cries attracted the sentry on duty. His name, I.M. Sharma, an entirely fictitious name. Sharma trained his binoculars on the river to be sure.

After uttering an oath, naming the boy's mother, I.M. Sharma hastily renounced his binoculars, turban, boots, belt, rifle, uniform: and plunged in. Within a few minutes, he was beside the boy, half way to P—n, and, after a manly dispute with the river, he brought him back to safety.

The sentries on both sides applauded Sharma with *shābāsh!* and *āfreen!* The little boy's father, the post syce, fell at Sharma's feet. It was his way of showing gratitude. This concluded the all-too-brief adventure.

Finally, having dried himself with a pair of army trousers, Sharma put on the uniform, belt, boots, turban, and, the rifle and the binoculars at the ready, he resumed duty.

The incident was reported to the Captain in charge of the post. He queried it. Whereupon, full details—as ordered—were furnished to the Captain.

The next day, he summoned Sharma. Looking at the papers on the table, the Captain—translated fair—said, "What you have done is done. It is well done." After a pause, he tapped the papers on the table, pointed obliquely to a red slip of paper, and drew Sharma's attention to the charge. Sharma was charged with absence from duty without leave—while he went rescuing the boy. The Captain added, "Of that only, you are guilty."

He queried if Sharma accepted the charge. Further, did he plead for a summary *faislā*—an on-the-spot punishment?

Finding Sharma speechless, and stiffly standing at attention, the Captain assumed acquiescence, and sentenced Sharma to syce-duty, the duty being to curry and groom the post horse, once only, make ready his meal—chopped grass, gram, water, oil, molasses, *masālā*—one feed only, as from the next morning.

On being commanded to dismiss, Sharma saluted briskly, and backed.

II

Presently, he went into the dormitory. He lay down on the bed. Staring at the ceiling, he smoked some fifteen *bidis,* one after another. He uttered sundry oaths, in the interim, tarnishing the boy's mother and sister. And he struck his forehead with his palm twice, and offered up *laanats*—curses—to his *kismet* twice. To be degraded to syce-duty, even though for once only, he thought, was worse than garden fatigue—the business of manuring the cabbage-patch with night soil—the post scavenger's exclusive chore.

He had a very disturbed night, moreover. It was a hard drill he lived through, a condition near enough to bed-wetting, or almost, so sudden and violent was the urging, doubtless from acute anxiety, and which anxiety—as the night wore on—he tried vainly to fight with fervent and repeated prayer.

In the morning, red-eyed and still bothered with his bladder, he reported for syce-duty. Then an amazing thing happened. A miracle, no less, was worked in Sharma's favor. He found the horse at the ready, curried and groomed, his feed made, the *masālā* and all. And the Captain duly inspected and passed both, very pretty and very smart, and that was that: the end of that. Indeed, it could not have been nicer for Sharma: everything squared, off the record, and the Captain most pleased.

III

This thing was told to me by a border man. It was the will of God to reward the righteous, he said. It was God's will that saved Sharma from disgrace. Indeed, God Himself had taken upon Himself the good sentry's punishment. God exists. He had no doubt. This was the proof.

Now. In spite of this belief, says another border man to me (concluding a considerable converse), there is nothing miraculous, or even mysterious about the incident. The post syce, the little boy's father, had curried and groomed the horse, had the feed ready *et cetera*. Obviously. It was he who had aided Sharma. It was not God. It was the syce, you understand. The syce denies it, of course. He daren't cross the Captain, you see. But for that, he would own up. Of course.

Well. Whatever might be your view of this business, some people, I know, would insist upon a more viable proof than— they might argue—a cock-and-bull story about a duty-bound

Captain *versus* a vulnerable sentry, not forgetting the demurring syce. Surely, Bertrand Russell, who is a forthright man and a very clever man, would not accept a prettily groomed horse as valid proof of the existence of the Godhead—or would he? The last word on this matter has not been said, I don't think. We need to write to Lord Russell, *airmail*.

Lord Russell replies, *airmail*.

Plas Penrhyn,
Penrhyndeudraeth
Merioneth.

I shall certainly not regard any horse,
however well groomed,
as evidence of the existence of the Godhead.
(*Sd.*) Bertrand Russell

The Barber of Sāhibsarāi

Not too long ago, in this part of north India, lived a young man. His fellow-villagers had nicknamed him Bhola—Innocent—because he appeared innocent of guile.

One fateful Saturday, after talking it over with his widowed mother, Bhola left the village for a day to visit the nearest town on the railroad—Sāhibsarāi. He was looking for a dog. He had three *rupees* on him. Like most villagers, he traveled without a ticket.

Bhola reached Sāhibsarāi at four in the morning. He walked past the railway offices and, after a struggle with himself, bought himself a flashlight for a *rupee*—such things are still a great novelty to the village folk and the shopkeeper had to restrain him from playing with it. (The shops and stalls open very early and close very late to meet all incoming and outgoing trains to and from Sāhibsarāi. It is a railway junction.)

On his way to the bazaar—it was nearly daybreak and his plan was to look out for stray dogs and if one should catch his fancy, take it home—impulsively, without need or a reason, he decided to visit a barber shop and have a "town haircut," such as you never get in a village. He found a shop open at that hour, went in, and told the barber what he wanted: a "town haircut."

The barber was an old man with thick white hair, and growing very low down on his forehead. He had the manner of the never-grow-up kind. Everybody called him Sticky—the original Hindustani of the word was fancied by himself—and not being taken seriously, he had the ways of the very young—and like most clowns—he was not aware of his years or the dignity of age.

He looked at Bhola and affected great astonishment—apropos of nothing—that being his usual way with the village folk. This, as the barber had expected, embarrassed Bhola and put him on the defensive. The next thing Sticky did was to mimic the manner of receiving royalty in his humble parlor. That, too, made Bhola obviously uncomfortable. Then Sticky actually asked his name, and on being told—not without awkwardness, but by then Bhola could not resist the barber—Sticky asked, "And what do they call your *father?*" (That was an insult and Bhola mentally filled in the unspoken word—a very rude word— insinuating that the father of an innocent one must be—an euphemism—more blank *innocent!*)

II

Now, for the barber, this was getting to be quite a treat. "Town haircut," he said, emphasizing his words, ". . . right you *are,* your honor!" and he got on with the job, humming, and fussing all the time.

Bhola sat on the chair—to which he had been invited with a flourish—wrapped up in a dirty sheet, under the kerosene ceiling lamp, and the barber poured a lot of water on his head from an old aerated water bottle—and he went on massaging Bhola's head, softening the hair, and in a rough manner, to cause actual discomfort.

While this was going on, this softening of the hair—and the barber hadn't touched the clippers or the scissors yet—an old friend of his came in. From that moment, between the two of them—Sticky and his friend—it was a riot, and Bhola's ordeal really began.

Quite unable to resist his impulse, the jovial manner having got the better of him—Sticky might have restrained himself had his client been a townsman—he began soaping Bhola's head, and presently, without further ado, he picked up a razor, and went over the center of the head and *shaved off* a bit!

Sticky saw in the mirror the effect of that move on Bhola. There were no words spoken or any sort of a protest made but for a tightening of Bhola's facial muscles and a distortion of his mouth. Except for that, he sat in the chair, immobilized, and Sticky, with a quick glance at his friend, asked, "A *shave,* you said, your honor?" And with a feigned seriousness, he went over the rest of the head and shaved it clean and close. He left a bit of hair on the crown, where the *chotī,* the Hindu crown lock is worn, and tapping Bhola's head patronizingly, he asked, "Leave this much here, your honor?" And Bhola, now very tense—his eyes were quite red, but he was unable to resist the barber's questions—nodded. (That done, anyone would have taken Bhola for a bereaved person from a village, who had "given"—sacrificed—his hair to a recently deceased elder, possibly his father: a custom in this part of the world.)

He paid Sticky who smilingly accepted the change. And Bhola was out of the shop fast, having covered his head with his country scarf, to hide his shame, and he walked hastily. As soon as he was out of earshot, the two—Sticky and his friend, who had followed Bhola to the street—were quite unable to restrain themselves. Nearly splitting his sides, and wiping away tears, Sticky managed to mimic Bhola, "I like a town haircut, barber!" It is doubtful if the two had ever laughed as much as they did that day.

III

Bhola spent the rest of his day by an old creek, sitting under a tree, and looking at the water. He did not go to the bazaar to look for a dog and he did not eat or drink. He stayed by the creek to be alone. It might have done him some good—he was not yet twenty—had he cursed, or indulged in unrestrained weeping, young men in this part of the world are not ashamed to do either, but he did nothing, just kept looking at the water, and all the time, he was seized by an oppressive feeling, something quite unknown to him in all his born days.

He got up when the sun had set, and he walked past the shops, not daring to look at himself in the shop mirrors. He did that usually—he was not at all bad-looking—and impulsively— as indeed he had acted earlier in the day and sought a barber for a haircut which he did not need—he stopped at a smith's and asked for a farmer's pointed-edge knife. The smiths in this part of the world do not use tempered steel for these knives: rather, bits of crude iron, fastened or hinged to wooden handles, as you wish, and they fashion a blade for you, while you wait, and give it a good edge, too. Bhola chose a fair-sized pointed blade and he kept watching the sparks intently, as the smith worked on the knife.

The rest of Bhola's doings that evening are briefly told. After paying a *rupee* for the knife, he went back to the barber shop, and found Sticky sitting on the barber chair, and alone. He seemed scared—something in Bhola's manner made him afraid—but he stood up, managed to smile, and raising the wick of the kerosene lamp a mite, he leaned against the wall and asked, "Another *shave,* friend?" The words were hardly out of his mouth, and he was struck a violent blow, and Bhola did not have to cut through him more than once. He left him, the pointed knife stuck into him, got out of the shop, and his last sight of Sticky was of an old man sagged against a grubby wall, drooping forward, and his hands, Bhola could not quite remember, if they were on his stomach, or holding the wooden handle of the knife, as if the barber were busy, very busy, in the process of stabbing himself!

While walking down the street—there was no blood or any sign of violence on him and no one had seen him go in or come out of the shop—Bhola did not feel any satisfaction, or anything like a conscience, or guilt, or even anxiety—and he continued to be oppressed with a sense of loss, of being overcome, ridden upon, and laughed at.

On his way to the railway station, however, the fear of God prevailed on him. He had no education of any kind, but there were, in his manner of thinking and speaking, as indeed of all village folk, scores of references to God. Every next word, and exclamation, recalled the might and omniscience of God. He did not try to resist the feeling and made straight for the police *chowkī*.

There, with hands folded in humility, he said to the *Dārogā*-in-charge, "My mother and father, I have killed a barber!" (An equally accurate translation of his, *"Ek hajaam ko mārke āyā huh, maī baap!"* would be, "Having killed one barber, I have come, my mother and father!") And he told the *Dārogā* all about ordering the "town haircut" from the barber and getting a shave instead.

The *Dārogā* heard his story in silence, all the time looking down at the papers on his table—and after Bhola had finished, almost in tears, as he recounted the loss of his flashlight somewhere in Sāhibsarāi—he shouted for two constables. Both of them, signaled by the *Dārogā*, attacked Bhola by showering blows on him, and not sparing their nailed boots, they kicked him too as he reeled on the floor. Stunned, bruised, bleeding, and groaning, they threw him out of the *chowkī*, ordering him to *"Jāo, randīpoot!"* ("Go, son of a whore!")

Bhola accepted the beating as a proof of the might of God and just punishment for killing a barber. He managed to return to the village by the late night express and earned a worse name for himself, for not only being a simpleton, but actually the idiot of the village, the sort that go to Sāhibsarāi hoping to steal a man's dog, and end up by being shaved, beaten and bruised for it. They laughed at him and that hurt him more than anything else yet in all his teens. (Meanwhile, at Sāhibsarāi . . . There was great excitement at the police *chowkī*. A list of some ten "suspects" was prepared, and each—Bhola did not know this—had to buy back his freedom, and the rewarding prospect of all that bustle and scramble, made the *Dārogā* and everybody else expectant and happy. For months, *bayāns* and *havālās* would be taken down, questions asked, statements demanded, folk detained—before the case could be written off as an unsolved crime, a murder without a known motive—and that was no small piece of luck for those responsible for conducting inquiries—once Bhola, who wasn't worth anything, had been driven off the scene.)

IV

A year or so after the incident, an itinerant *kathā*-reciter, a pandit, visited the village. He was reciting from the scriptures and Bhola, and his mother, heard his discourse. Horror gripped Bhola as he thought of being ripped open in hell, again and again, by his victim—the barber—and his parents, too, suffering the same fate. Such were the punishments decreed for *hatyā*—murder—the pandit said.

After the *kathā*-recitation, late at night, while his mother slept soundly, he slipped out of the hut, and called on the preacher. He spoke in a hushed voice, afraid he might be heard by someone outside the *kathā*-reciter's tent, and related in detail what had passed between him and the barber, followed by the beating by the police and the loss of his flashlight in Sāhibsarāi.

The pandit heard him, took four *rupees* off him—not without some resistance from Bhola who had two in hand and two concealed in a fold of his *dhotī*—and citing from the scriptures, the pandit advised *shāntī-karma:* an act of peace-making with the gods. He promised, for the offering made, to recite the requisite number of *mantras*—invocations addressed to the guardian gods—and counseled Bhola to go and have a bath in the sacred river—at a walking distance from Sāhibsarāi. These acts, he assured Bhola, in the idiom of the scriptures he quoted, were all the *prāyashchitta*—atonement—needed for *hatyā*—the killing of the barber of Sāhibsarāi by the suppliant sinner Bhola.

"Do recite the *mantras,* my mother and father, never forgetting," Bhola said to the pandit earnestly, and wholly relieved, "and I will go tomorrow to Sāhibsarāi, and have a bath, never forgetting."

-12-

The Pansārī's Account
of the Incident

With a show of calmness, and in a confiding tone of giving
away professional secrets, the pansārī—*druggist*—said,
"I had a preparation of tāmra—*copper*—and it could make a
dying man bātur—*loquacious*—and keep him in honsh—*awareness*—for an hour at least, so that he could make his will. Sudden
death is bad. A man has no time to speak his will. My remedies—
gifted by the guru—are a blessing. They never hurt . . ."

To which the policeman—to whom the pansārī was speaking in a confiding tone—replied, "But your patient was hurt!"

The pansārī said, "Our medicines never hurt . . ."

With obvious impatience, the policeman said, "But he bleated!"

(Which was a reference to a man whom the druggist was
supposed to have treated with arsenic and killed. An inspector
of Calcutta suburban police was inquiring into the incident.)

The pansārī explained, "The medicines are good. They are
dayāloo—*kind, merciful.* They are kalpa remedies. These reju-
venate. This even a mooka—*dumb*—person should know. Our
kalpa remedies are built around loah—*iron*—, mandoor—old
iron, *rust*—, mirch—*chillies*—, heeng— *asafoetida*—, tāzi
adrakh—*fresh ginger*—, aafeem—*opium*—, sankhiya—
arsenic—, and lahasun—*garlic.* Lahasun is like mother to us.
It is merciful. There are no poisons in our recipes. All poisons
are drivya—*material, stuff.* In the yogas—*prescriptions*—the

drivya—*material*—is always written as amrita—vivifying *ambrosia*. It is *never* written as poison. A poison is written as vish. Vish is tīkhyana—*sharp*—, vikāsi—*penetrating, fast permeating*—and its vikās—*penetration*—is towards the sookhyama—*subtle*—granthīs—*knots*—inside the body. It even reaches to the nails. Vish—*poison*—has prabhāv—self-manifest *extreme effect*. Its vikās—*radiation* is implied—is tīvra—*fast*. Vish is fast working. Take away the tīkhyanatā—*sharpness*—and let vikās (far-permeating characteristic) remain, and let prabhāv—*effectiveness*—be, and it is *no longer* vish—*poison*—but drivya—*remedial stuff*. Sublimated, the drivya is amrita—*ambrosia*. In the yogas—*prescriptions*—sublimated drivya—*remedy*—is always written as amrita, because it *is* amrita. Once there is viyoga—*separation,* as between lovers—of tīkhyanatā from poison, it is amrita—*ambrosia*. In amrita also is present vikās (penetrating potential) and prabhāv (extreme effectiveness) but it has no tīkhyanatā—*sharpness*. Vish is no longer vish. It becomes dayaloo—*kind, merciful*—like a mother to her only son . . ."

Although interested, the policeman reminded the druggist of his ex-patient who, keen on being rejuvenated, had died of poisoning.

The pansārī said, in a deferential tone, "Mahāshayajī—*noble sir*—in all my life, I have found *one* thing (*one* significant thing or wisdom). It is tears. Take them as the impure saltwater of this body or as *Gangā jal* (water of the sacred Ganges). As you wish, mahāshayajī. They are an offering to you . . ."

The inspector mentioned a possible charge of murder by poisoning, and he asked, "How do you go about making ambrosia out of arsenic?"

The druggist replied, "The yoga—*device*—is taught only by the gurus. It is secret. Lemon juice and goat's milk are used to sublimate sankhiyā—*arsenic*. It must be pure goat's milk. It is then siddha—a *success*. It is then amrita—*life-gifting ambrosia*. The power of vikās—*penetration*—and prabahāv—*effectiveness*—will remain. Only tīkhyanatā—*sharpness*—will be gone. My father took amrita (ambrosia). He used to wake up at three o'clock in the morning and croak (hem, a ritual, with an air of authority, to loudly hawk phlegm). People knew it was three o'clock in the morning when they heard him croak (hemming). After that, he wanted to smoke his hooka. Only the bahū—the *daughter-in-law* (the druggist's wife)—made his hooka right. He would not even look at the tobacco cake if anyone else touched his hooka," the druggist went on, with a tolerant smile. "Only the bahū made his hooka right. She got up at three in the morning to make his hooka. He called her bahū-rānī (queen-daughter-in-law). By temperament, my father was a rājadrohī (a revolutionary, a rebellious person). But he never objected to the pathya (medically prescribed *diet*). He drank seven glasses of milk every day and took butter in his tea. As long as he lived, he ate bājarī-kī-rotī (millet flour bread) with cheenee (sugar), and ghee (clarified butter), and he did not touch salt, rice, meat, fruit or a vegetable. He was ninety-six when he died. One day, he said to his servant, 'Gorkhā Girdhārīlāl, give us a slice of mango,' and in fifteen minutes he was gone. That was sudden death. He did not speak his will. He wanted to reward the bahū. She had made his hooka for ten years. He wanted to leave something to his servant. He was not in *honsh*—awareness. This did not happen because of the kalpa yoga (the rejuvenating remedy). It was from his own vish—*poison*. The vish was shed by the sookhyama—*subtle*—granthīs—*knots*—inside his body. Vish is tikhyana—*sharp*. The tīkhyanatā—*sharpness* . . ."

Weary, the policeman mentioned to the pansārī the seriousness of poisoning people, and he spoke of less serious matters such as possessing drugs without a license, administering proscribed drugs, and dismissing a man's bewildered widow with remarks such as, "Your man died of his own vish." He added, "You cannot give a death certificate to anyone, pansārī. You are no doctor."

"Mahāshayajī, in all my life, I have found *one* thing. It is tears. Take them as the impure saltwater of this body or as *Gangā jal* . . ."

"Sipāhī," the policeman addressed an expectant sepoy, "lock him up!"

13

In Memoriam

I n the united provinces of Āgra and Awadh—the present Uttar
Pradesh—not many years ago, lived an Englishman. His name
was E.C. Clay. He was a member of the Indian Civil Service.
This was in the days of the British *rāj*.

Akasmaat—as the rustics of Uttar Pradesh are wont to say
of any *sudden* occurrence whatsoever—Mr. Clay, being on a
tour of the district, was taken ill and although his bearer did all
he could with quinine and tonic—it was reported—he died that
very day, before a doctor could reach him.

Now, the news of *akasmaat* events travels very fast. Mr.
Clay was an important person. He was the district magistrate.
The news about his passing on reached his Indian deputy within
hours. (Before proceeding further, let it be made *quite* clear that
the report of Mr. Clay's death was false. It was a bazaar rumor.
He was alive and well.)

Now, the deputy: he was in his fifties, about five years
senior to Mr. Clay. It was Mr. Clay's habit to entrust to the
deputy minor administrative responsibilities. One of those responsibilities was the presidentship of the local branch of the
Temperance League, although—Mr. Clay knew this—the deputy drank heavily, or as much as any civilian in the district.
When the news concerning Mr. Clay reached the deputy, he was
presiding over a meeting of the Temperance League.

He dismissed the audience in a hurry and immediately attended to the formalities. He was a man of few chosen words—

he had risen through the ranks and hadn't been through the competitive examinations—and he equated himself well with Mrs. Clay. He spoke no more words than strictly necessary, although he expressed his grief to her by silent and copious weeping.

As a necessary part of his official duties, he called a public meeting to mourn the untimely death of Mr. Clay. He was anxious to make the gathering representative. He did not forget the pandits—those particularly versed in the Hindu scriptures—with whom, in the normal course of his work as an official, he had little to do.

II

It was the largest meeting the town could muster at so short a notice. There were about two hundred men and the only woman present was Mrs. Clay. She was absolutely prevailed upon to come. She had resisted the deputy, but the deputy had put it to her plainly. "Your presence, dear madam, is *imperatively necessary* to console the poor souls of this town," (or a few words to that effect). She sat next to the deputy on the improvised platform—wearing black. As she had declined to speak, or be chairman—this the deputy had suggested—it was the deputy who had—as he put it—"humbly and regretfully" occupied the chair. (The large Union Jack on the table was also the deputy's idea.)

Now, the town—apart from the deputy—could boast of no more than three speakers with any experience of public speaking or appearing. The three spoke up for Mr. Clay. They were followed by the president of the Pandit Sabha.

Now, the president of the Pandit Sabha: he certainly had a voice. But he had no experience of appearing before such high company—which included the local dignitaries, the deputy, the entire police force in charge of the town, and the widow of Clay sāhib herself. He too had been prevailed upon to come although he had no sort of acquaintance with Mr. Clay. He would not

have missed the honor for anything; yet—as he later on confided
in his brother—while waiting for his turn to speak, he suffered
gravely. The physical part of it all was the most distressing. His
mouth went completely dry and there was no strength left in his
knees. He had, moreover, a terror of being compelled to suffer
an *akasmaat* demand from his kidneys. And considering everything, and the fact that the dryness of the mouth was now extend-
ing to the throat—as he later on confided in his brother—there
was not the remotest chance of a man excusing himself, however
compelled, in the middle of a funeral oration. (That is what, he
thought, was expected of him.)

While so absorbed, and dreadfully anxious, he heard the
deputy announce his name. He had little recollection of what
followed that announcement although, had Mrs. Clay raised her
eyes from the table—which she never did throughout the proceedings, not so far—she would have seen, as everyone else
saw, a little man—wearing a cotton *dhotī*, a shirt, and a *tauliyā*
scarf on his shoulder—hardly five feet in height, entirely bald,
and all blood drained off his face, with the look of no martyr but
of a lamb led to slaughter, and supporting himself on his palms,
which were riveted to the table, standing there, blinking, and
alternatively staring into the space ahead of him. It was a most
awkward pause—a minute or so and it seemed incredibly long—
an acutely embarrassing matter for all, and certainly for the
chairman who was toying with the idea of concluding the meeting
without hearing the pandit by putting to vote the condolence
resolution, to move and support which the three seasoned speak-
ers had already risen.

It was then that the old man—as he later on confided in his
brother— received supernatural aid. He had, of course, forgotten
every syllable of his prepared speech and the words he had copied
from his grandson's *English to Hindi Dictionary.* Yet, he was
aided supernaturally and given guidance about what to do. Accordingly, in a ringing voice, he began reciting a highly erotic
sonnet in praise of one surpassing in beauty an *apsarā*, a courte-
san of the gods. He knew it by heart—it was a poetic composition

of his own—and the finesse and the energy of his utterance made even Mrs. Clay look up once. Although—his brother and a few pandits excepted—hardly two or three in the audience understood the pandit's Sanskrit, still, it was absolutely the most extraordinary thing to do.

The song took the best part of two minutes. By the time the old man was through, there was little initiative left in the chair to intervene. The deputy was gravely surprised and he was afraid that the meeting for his late lamented chief might end in a *fiasco,* after all, as most meetings in the town willy-nilly did, end in a *fiasco.* There was absolutely no warrant, none whatever, for doing what the pandit had done.

Meanwhile, the old man had recovered himself completely. As he opened his eyes—(while singing the *stotram,* the hymn of praises to the *strīratna,* his gem of a woman, his eyes had been closed and he was oblivious of any presence except of his supernatural counselor, the shade of the late chaste and unsullied lady to whom, as a young man, he had addressed the sonnet)—he surveyed the men, and Mrs. Clay, with absolute confidence and self-possession. After a moment's pause, and without further formalities, he spoke up and told his audience that he thought, nay, he was sure, that Clay sāhib had been justly *degraded,* and *stigmatized,* for his *sins!*

These words made the deputy sit up and *suffer:* altogether more than he had from the sonnet. With a guilty look, he glanced at Mrs. Clay more than once. She understood the pandit's Hindi as well as the rest of the audience. Meanwhile, proceeding, the old man insisted that to anyone versed in the scriptures and astrology, the *jyotish shāstra,* as he himself was, it was obvious that the late Clay sāhib's name was *bad, inauspicious,* a *disgrace,* and that it was a result of *bad karma*—sins and misdeeds of a previous birth—and it was *bad* for those whom he had left behind (obviously, the relict).

Those words, spoken with such energy and conviction, caused a sensation. Never in the history of the town was such a thing known to have happened. It was not only an abuse of privilege, a grave discourtesy to the dead, of which the old man was guilty, but it might have led to a well-merited report to the higher authorities against the deputy, with whom the responsibility for what the old man said and did must lie, and the deputy, let it be added, had a few unfriendly friends in the town.

"A *disgrace,* of an evil omen," the pandit went on, and he paused to beam at his brother who, perturbed, and convinced that the old man had had an overdose of *bhang*—hemp, the nearest thing in that part of the world to abusing the bottle—made frantic signs to him to stop and say no more. There were, too, several voices at the back—friends of the deputy, who took upon themselves to defend Mrs. Clay—demanding that the pandit should sit down. Had there been a person or two to shout *"Order!"* the local press, with perfect justification, would have described the meeting as a *fiasco.* That is what the deputy feared most, a *fiasco.*

III

Oblivious of the disturbance he had caused, but mindful of the voices at the back, the pandit allowed a few moments to pass, to drive home his point that the late Clay sāhib had been *stigmatized* for his sins—of a previous incarnation—he was *sure,* being versed in the scriptures and astrology. "Otherwise," he continued, putting to good use his grandson's *English to Hindi Dictionary,* "the sāhib would not have been named '*mitti,*' (clay)." "Fate," he added, "would not have caused that to happen!"

"But I say now," he went on, turning to Mrs. Clay with a sympathetic, paternal smile, "that by being a good servant of the King, the Englishman has expiated for his past *bad* karma, and he should not now be called 'Clay,' but Silver, or Gold, or even '*Heera*' Diamond!" Very pleased with the word, he raised his voice, and his right arm, and repeated, "Diamond! I say, *Diamond!*"

The applause which followed that pronouncement, the rushing to the platform by his brother to embrace him, the mobbing of the old man by his fellow pandits, and the congratulations showered on him—all that is a part of the wonder of mere *mitti—akasmaat*—turned *Diamond!*

POSTSCRIPT

Hereunder, with apologies, a few words related to Mr. E. C. Clay's rise from earth to the stature of Diamond. Credit for this happenstance must be shared between the pandit and deputy. It was the deputy's concern with the proprieties—with *rank, precedence,* and *class*—that made him yet once more urge Mrs. Clay, "The stricken citizens, Madam, are here. Join them." Pointing at the vacated chair, he said, "Clay *Sāhib* is in heaven. The chair is yours and yours alone."

When Mr. Clay (hereafter honored as *Heera Sāhib*) reached home, he was angry. Mrs. Clay (hereafter, *Heera Memsāhib*) complained to him. "Earnest, you were not at home. What was I supposed to do? I must admit I was intrigued when the deputy said one of his speakers was an astrologer." "I am not blaming you," *Heera Sāhib* said. "He had no business to drag you to the meeting. Dammit, Beth, a death certificate must be filed before ceremonies are authorized. Astrology has *nothing* to do with it!"

14

Correspondence with Sister Jay

Praiseworthy elder, *jīo!* (live!) From India Amritsar city receive our remembrance. You would be well there.

Remains (to be said) that I have received some photos of Canada, pictures of your dog, and warm clothes for Sisters. We praise you for helping us for so long.

Elder, the old teaching is good. We must not sin. Hazūr (Presence) Sardār (Chief) Sāhibjī, our Guru Mahārāj, *jai!* (Victory to him!) says we ourselves can be without sin right here. We have no need to go to the jungle to be *pavitar* (pure). When we received this teaching, we built this *āshram.* We do our own household work. We have renounced the world that way. We give the same teaching to the people who come to our *āshram.* Remains, I asked some questions from Hazūr Sāhibjī only. He told me to ask you the questions. So I need to ask you the same questions now. Sāhibjī has told me to ask you.

Elder, who are we? Where have we come from? Where is our *aslī* (real) home? This world is a *musāffirkhānā* (a travelers' inn). One more question is we *bandā*s (slaves, slaves of God) pray O *Prabhū!* (Lord!) Come! Make us *patita* (fallen) *pavitar* (pure). Mahatma Gandhi also prayed the same way. *O patita pāvana!* (redeemer of the fallen!) make me *pavitar* (pure). So I ask, why do we not see our *Prabhū?* Is he hidden somewhere? The one who gave us the *Gīta* (the scripture), where is he? What was his real name? I also ask you the date when Parmātmā (Supreme Soul) caused the war of Mahābhārata (the war described in the epic *Mahābhārata*).

Remains, was the *gyān* (gnosis, knowledge) of the *Gītā* given by Krishna (God of the *Gītā*) or was it *Prabhujī* Shivjī (Lord Shiva) really? Is *Prabhū* Shivjī not greater? Did Shivjī make (by his grace) Krishna *sampooran* (full, entire) *nirākarī* (formless)? With your true *meharbānī* (merciful friendliness) surely answer these questions. We will all wait here. Hazūr Sāhib *santjī* (saint) has told us to wait. We will tell others.

Remains, one of our older Sisters Gangoo has been to the villages to teach religion. She has now returned. In one village, she found a rainwater lake just like a very big boat. The boat was full of water. It is so funny to see. We have laughed at this too much. If you come here in the rainy months, Sister Gangoo will show it to you.

Remains, I and the Sisters want to see your face. Many new Sisters have not seen your *peshānī* (forehead of destiny). If we could, we would come to see you in Canada. Let us see your smile again. We think you are one among many many thousands. Sāhibjī, Guru Mahārāj, *jai!* (Victory to him!) says you are a *lāl* (a ruby, a precious gem).

Written by Sister Jay in Amritsar. Live! Shivjī *madadgār!* (Shivjī be your helper!)

Good Sister Jay, live!

I reply to your letter after one year. I reply because of Sāhibjī's order, Victory to him!

Your questions were so difficult! Remains, also, I have not read or written Multānī (dialect of Panjābi) for twenty years! Forgive many mistakes, Sister Jay.

A *bandā*, be he man, woman, animal, bird, angel, or other, has *'aql* (light, intelligence). *'Aql* tells him a thing is hot, cold, *dukhadāī* or *sukhadāī* (cause of pain or pleasure). Remains, all *bandās* do not have the same *'aql*. Among *bandās*, there is *farq* (difference). Why is that, Sister Jay? Because in everything and everyone there are *hadd*s and *kinārā*s (limits and boundaries). A *bandā* knows only from his own *roshinī* (light, in proportion to the limits and boundaries of his *'aql*).

If you ask me who you are, I will say, you are surely reverend Sister J., the first letter of the name in Panjābi of a singing bird, whom I call Jay. If you ask, where is your home? I will say surely Amritsar city. If you ask where is your *aslī* home? I will say wherever you make your home and that is surely your real (*aslī*) home. You say, this world is a travelers' inn. In my *'aql*, it seems so too. It seems so too because *bandā*s stay awhile here and go away (die). Is the *bundānawāz* (protector) hidden somewhere? Why don't we see him? Well, some good Chiefs (gurus) say, he is not hidden anywhere. Some good Chiefs say we see him. He is everywhere. He is in *bandā*s too. Who gave us the *Gīta?* A *mussāfir* (traveler) gave us the *Gīta*. They say, his name was Ved Vyās. Now, Sister Jay, if the Supreme Soul himself caused the war of *Mahābhārata,* then no *bandā* did cause it. So, we need not feel happy or unhappy because of it. If Parmātmā didn't cause it, and the travelers did, then some travelers among those who fought, were not *pavitar* (pure). I am happy that you and the Sisters are pure. Hazūr Sāhib himself has said so.

There is *farq* in us. Some Chiefs say there is no *farq* (difference) in God. There is no *hadd* and *kinārā* in *Prabhū*. When we say *this* is greater than *that*, it is because we *think* this. There is *farq* in our *thinking*. Some good Chiefs say *Prabhujī* is an *ākārī* (with form). He is, also, they say, *nirākārī* (without form). If he is everywhere, and inside *bandā*s too, is both seen and unseen, then we must love him as seen, as *ākārī* (with form). I have answered your very difficult questions, from the *hadd,* and *kinārā* of my *'aql*.

Suppose Sister Gangoo's *roshinī* were different and she were an engineer sāhib? I can see you and the Sisters laughing without restraint. I can hear you chiding the Sisters, "Sāhibjī has told us, not to laugh so much, even if the praiseworthy elder makes us laugh." Remains, this is said not to make the reverend Sisters laugh. So, if the engineer sāhib Sister Gangoo saw the lake, she would not be surprised. There is a very big boat, full of water, and it should sink, but it does not sink! That is very funny. But an engineer sāhib will not be surprised. An engineer sāhib would see the lake with a *farq* (difference), you see. It will not be the same boat-shape lake, Sister Gangoo might show to me. *Hadd*s and *kinārā*s change almost every day. The shapes of rainwater lakes change every day. There would be new white and blue lotuses too, almost every day. I have seen beautiful panther cubs drinking from the lakes at night, when it is so very quiet.

Live! Written to Sister Jay in Amritsar. Remains, my remembrance to Chief Sāhib. Victory!

15

Country Life, Country Folk, Cobras, *Thok!*

I had been under a severe strain and did not need a doctor to tell me so. Some doctors don't talk enough. Some talk too much. My condition had something to do with the family of an old Indian bachelor who used to live in the U.P. I am not sure if it is still the most populated state in India.

The bachelor's sole surviving family was an adopted daughter. She was twenty-five when we met at a culture revival meeting. Her name translated into English as Good Friend or Friendly. I often added to her name the honorific suffix, *jī*. The Hindi terminal *jī* descends from the Sanskrit anticipated wish for the person saluted. "Friendly, may you *live!*" (*"jio!"*) Did you know, that the term turf, too, descends from the Sanskrit? I think it is scandalous to refer to the potential human victims, living in the self-proclaimed U.S. gangster's territory, as his *turf—darbha,* Sanskrit for tufts of grass—intended for a gangster's or his rival's mowing!

Friendlyji was about to wind up her father's estate, she said. Her father was a professional hunter. The panther was his animal. She had a collection of panther skins. Panther skins were not an interest of mine. I do not think those were a collector's item either. She said she would throw in half a dozen if I accepted from her a freehold acre in a village nearby. It had been left to her by her father. He had wanted her to build a cottage on the land and to cultivate a fragrant jasmine garden around it. Moved by the refined characteristic of his wish, I confided in Friendly. I told her, in artless words of youth, of an esteemed childhood memory of my own: the sight of a green nursery of miniature lilies, sparkling in a still pool, and being bronzed by the setting sun, as if of an avowed design. Presently, I deferred to her view that you needed to own land to raise lilies of your own. I was deeply moved by her observation that I loved lilies, as poets did.

It so happened that I was reading an almost impassioned book by a French doctor who had left a successful practice in Paris for the bounteous fresh air of Sicily. When I discussed the extreme relevance of the book with Friendly, she said to me, "Would it not be better to live in one's own country than to go and live in Sicily? There is plenty of fresh air here!" Once again, the element of logic in her opinions appealed to me. At twenty, I respected her for her age too. She was five years older than I was. I had my hair cut short because, she said, my long hair made me look like a girl.

Friendly was giving away the land only to a *supātra*. She thought I was a *supātra*, a well-deserving person, who would benefit himself and honor the wishes of her late father. She told me about her father's views concerning the virtues of country living and the country folk. The severe strain I spoke of was the result of my accepting responsibility for the land. No bargain hunter, which I was not, can resist what is thrown in for love. I took her father's panther skins too. Had he left us tiger skins, we might have been better off. Tiger skins were a collector's item.

Sometimes, life lavishes on you years' education within hours. Men have been known to nurse a private image of a cherished woman, as a source of all physical, psychological, spiritual and *financial* comfort. If you would lay claim to velvet, wealth is a necessity. Well, after a fierce encounter, involving excessive familiarity, adherence (overt and clandestine), bruised, the same men are known to name such a treat of a woman *hog!* and address all womankind with a hidebound hate thereafter.

Contemporary love-inspired image and metaphor being mostly derivative, the worshiped *hogs* are known to reciprocally compliment their ex-angels, sweethearts and pets, as *pigs!* There is no substitute for *experience*.

The capacity to measure accurately, to assess and appraise, is a condition for success in any enterprise. If you wanted to set yourself up on the high pedestal with Shakespeare, and to compete keenly, with a line or two of your own addressed to Robin, alternatively spelled Robyn, your best girl—whom, for an equally abstruse poetic reason you named Myrtle, to remind you ever so tenderly of her pet turtle, and then named her Dove, for love—you are likely to fall off the pedestal, because, Robyn's no rival to his Julie, Juliana, Guilietta, Romeo's *cara spoza;* indeed Juliet by *any* name! Although I was convinced that I had discovered my direction, country life, a country cottage, lilies shortly to be my very own, upright country folk for neighbors, and fresh air, too, my measure of things was unsound. Life was about to lavish on me a lesson. *Experience!*

After we signed the papers, Friendly, very happy, left the scene. Before she sailed overseas, she threw in a whole yardful of lumber, household goods and garden tools. I might marry and have children, she wrote, and I would need these things. Splendidly endowed with stocks and supplies by Friendly, to say nothing of her faith, I boarded the crawling train to the countryside.

On arrival, late in the evening, and awed by the starlight, I met a bearded old man and his nephew, the sole work force of the village. It did not take me long to discover that the old man had been hired by a petty cottage builder a few years ago and never since. The nephew was green and underdeveloped and obsessively devoted to his uncle. Sensible men in the village had migrated long ago to the nearest town and found work. The old man and the nephew had lagged behind because they lacked stamina. Meanwhile, up to their necks in pauperism, they seemed to be subsisting on air. These two sons of the soil, the old man and his nephew, had no knowledge whatever of building, and yet, soon after we met, they unblushingly arrogated to themselves the combined functions of architects, carpenters, bricklayers, concrete masons and roofers too. Victims of widespread village illiteracy, these two did not know the *meaning* of the words *project* or *planning*. There was not much plumbing done in the U.P. villages, but they knew all about plumbing too. There were, in the village, matchwood outhouses attached to the few cottages occupied by government and railway officers. For reasons known to themselves, these cottages with the outhouses were called basket system cottages. The basket system is a rage in these parts. It is regarded as *class* by the village folk who, of necessity, are driven to transact their business *sub jove,* rain or shine, braving storm, hard rain, deluge, cloudburst, monsoons. Some nature-loving informed parties call it making the most of the freedom of the wide open spaces, the whole world their private prairie, savanna and outhouse; although, stalking them under cover are the peekers, to be sure, waiting to violate their privacy: the graffiti *virtuoso,* the *voyeur,* the hardened lout, the pervert: *and* the anti-pollution lobbyist, not to mention the environmental vigilante! "Who cried *'Woe!'?"* "*Je,* Jacques-Yves Cousteau!" And how do you respond, Yaqui sorcerer Don Juan, who frequents the bushes as frequently as el señor Castaneda narrates you frequent the bushes? (On the occasion of an unexpected meeting with the two of them, following their visits to the bushes, you squeeze your hat against your chest and say: "*Salud!* . . . *Buenos días, caballeros!*" If you happen to meet others, who are not taken so seriously, to them you say, "*Hola*" or "*Amigo!*" or simply "*Qué pasa?*")

My own knowledge of building and construction and design might not have been astronomical or infallible. After weeks of killing labor, goaded on by the old man and his nephew, all I remember is that I hauled. The aching muscles, the blisters, are forgotten, but I remember hauling; hauling lumber, bricks, cement, gravel, rocks, mud, and the malodorous water from the communal well. An ultimatum to the two being out of the question, periods of self-pity and depression followed. I was disposed to be very irritated with the two blockheads and there were disputes between us about everything. These two, the old man and his nephew, had assumed the status of experts and specialists and they were not experts or specialists. Finally, I felt I needed to defend my health over and above all else; to cope with their systematic scorning of all the known laws of hygiene, and a passionate courting of infection, septicity, contagion; in spite of the substantial benefits reaped from abundant fresh air, the lack of electricity, the lack of safe water, the lack of laundry and other only too plentiful rural amenities. I needed to get away for a few days. But there was the face-saving factor.

I was at war with the two of them, my hired employees, bosses and taskmasters. I did not know then that the village folk hereabouts loathe and detest manual labor, which is their luckless lot, something of which they are heartily ashamed, such activity being, in fact, a punishment for the sins committed in their past lives. Now, if a prosperous soul, and a favorite of the goddess of prosperity, an *actual* landlord, should volunteer to serve as workhand and galley slave—indeed I had offered myself to help build the cottage, the garden and the lily pond—then these two bigots and empty-headed snobs would make an issue of it, take hurt from working for such a subspecies, and nurse an arrogant and a lofty contempt for him, as the lowest of the low, almost an outcaste, a renegade from his own feather and kind, the high breed that has you flogged with rawhide, to inflict summary damage to your backsides, if you so much as paused to breathe before complying with the command *chul! chul! move! move!* Anyway, I knew that it is not manly to admit defeat. In these parts, it is called *naak-katāi,* cutting off (one's) nose. (Did you know that the word *nark* is Hindustani for nose—*naak*—and that it is grafted into the substandard English through the gipsies?)

I was searching for a credible excuse to get away. It so happened that we in the village were very close, a matter of a hundred miles if not fewer, to an acclaimed temple. The temple happened to hold up to view an image of Lord Shiva which was very *awake.* In our idiom, that means that the image was particularly attentive to the suppliant's petitions. An ancient Indian book on statecraft advises the king to give rise to rumors through paid agents, to advertise the miracle-working powers of a temple, so as to profit from the augmented income by taxing the temple. The value of donations made to a temple, in cash or kind, are a reliable guide to its influence. That the gifts made to the Lord by devotees are investments, returned a hundredfold, is an article of faith proclaimed by the priests.

I asked the old man and his nephew if they could do without me for a few days. They were eager for me to go. Actually, they were overjoyed. A visit to the temple was the greatest good fortune. My land was so close to the Lord's, they said, and my home and my children's future home well within his *rājya*, that I had better go soon. He was so powerful. He fulfilled all desires.

I did not know then that thieving in that part of the world is entirely justified, if, for any reason whatever, including a visit to a celebrated temple, the owner of a property is half-witted enough to absent himself from his property. A basket system cottage, which you put together by the sweat of your brow, like a bonded slave, under the heel of two humorless and capricious louts, can be dismantled by every household in the village, and your yard emptied, your trees uprooted for firewood, all within an hour or so. If you were foolish enough to make inquiries, at your next home-coming, your neighbors tell you, "Thieves! Robbers! Thugs! *Who knows!*" "*Kyā mālum*, sāhib!"

I want to tell you about what happened to me on the way to the temple. The only means of transport available to pilgrims in that part of the world are the free-plying buses. These are driven by anyone at all, with an old motor and a mother-and-father, the money-lender. They build a very low-ceiling body around the engine somehow and anyhow and with anything at all. It is unpardonable. It is inhuman. There is a total indifference to the safety of life and limb. I feel very strongly about it still, as you see.

The temple was situated in a raja's territory. I did not know this when I boarded the bus. I would have avoided the trip. The petty rajas, with a few exceptions, were the worst of autocrats.

As we entered the raja's territory, we had to acknowledge the fact by stopping at his *chowkī*—the toll post. Our bus was due to reach the temple—and the adjoining dormitories provided gratis by well-meaning almsgivers, as pilgrims' roosts—at two in the afternoon. As we did not have the full quota of pilgrims, we started late, and reached the *chowkī* at eight in the night, six hours off the arrival schedule by my entirely reliable watch. They do not invest in watches or clocks in these parts. It is real country.

It was very dark when the pilgrim bus approached the post, lowered its lights and stopped. The *chowkī* was a wooden shack about eight feet by eight, which is to say, approximately three feet larger than a basket system outhouse. There was dense smoke around it. It gets very wet and cold in these parts. To keep his scullions warm, the raja dispenses wet logs. Dry wood costs more. So, the government property is veiled in smoke during the rains and in the winter months. They do not provide chimneys in *chowkī*s. We were waiting for the *chowkīdār*, the keeper of the post, to inspect us and wave us on.

Presently, I saw a hurricane lantern moving towards us. I could barely see the shrouded figure as it emerged from the curling smoke. The shape, wrapped up in a pressed felt sheet, the legacy from the ancestors, inherited by the poorest of the poor hereabouts, looked like a monster germ, making for caverns measureless to man down to a sunless sea, to borrow an image from Samuel Taylor Coleridge. As it came closer, the fantasy began to melt, and the man, having acquired a false magnitude from the felt, a sculptured sideways stretch added to his puny figure, looked to me like a shivering reef fish of great girth, piloted by a hurricane lantern, and groping for the bus. It was obvious, as he came closer, the *chowkīdār* was annoyed with us for turning up at that late hour. It was getting cold but the inspection was supposed to be cursory. The keepers of the toll posts briefly speak with drivers, glance into a bus and contemptuously order you to move on *jaldī! promptly, fast!*

I must detain you: this is relevant. I have before me the facts sheet. The door of our bus was either the top half of a double-door affording egress from an old duck barn, or—possibly—it was half of a hatch on the deck of a tugboat. Quality timber, massive, superbly preserved, obviously stolen property. It was about four feet by four feet, and fitted vertically, not horizontally, as in the barn or the tug boat setting. This door, at the rear of the bus, was the only opening provided, the chasm you had to cross to enter or to escape. It was supported by two hinges screwed into the left of the bus. Opposite, on your right, as you entered, was a wooden post, about four inches by four inches square, and I recognized it at once as a historic old *kos* distance road marker, a genuine antique, also obviously stolen property. The post, nailed to the corpus of the bus, was about five inches taller than the door top on the left—but for a village smithy's home-forged spike, about half of its point-end hammered into the door top. Now, the post's five inches or so extra height, level with the shaft of the spike, was an ornamental carving, actually the bald head of a goblin, a figure with antecedents in Hindu mythology. With no regard for the utilitarian intent behind the design of the vehicle, and passenger safety factor, or the beauty of the carved artifact, the door was kept shut by dropping a discarded dog collar over the upright spike on the left, and the goblin's neck on the right. When the door was open, the leather quoit hung loose, ringing either the spike, or the goblin's neck, at your pleasure. I noticed several dovetail grooves in the goblin's neck, whittled, I suspect, by the driver, thereby, making the scarred road marker worthless as a valued antique. Although rattling at the least provocation, the door, when shut, remained anchored; the leather collar looping the spike on the left and equally at home roosting into the grooves on the right. In either position, the spike jutted out ominously, silently voicing warning of personal injury and harm to all comers. An appendage to the door was about nine inches below. It was an iron folding step, a sagging relic of salvaged miscellany of an old luxury bullock cart owned by a landlord, I imagine. As you stepped on it, to draw closer to the door, it squealed like several cornered rats, and while the bus was in motion, it dispensed notions of panic and perturbation; sincerely, matter-of-factly, unmistakably. As if that was not all, you had to double up, as you entered the bus, to avoid your head running afoul of the low ceiling. This sort of thing is *dabbling* at its worst. I will not endorse amateurism. The bus driver politely lifted up the dog collar from the antique's head and held the door open for the *chowkīdār*. With the bus at the mercy of the raja's man, the *chowkīdār* faced the driver and wielded his prerogative. He hurriedly mumbled a list of goods. Drivers of vehicles are not allowed to bring for sale and resale tobacco, cloth, hay, cooking oil, rice, kerosene, salt, sugar, potatoes, flour, onions, spices, hair oil... If they did bring any, for sale and resale, they must produce a receipt showing that they had paid raja sāhib's toll. The bus driver nodded with folded hands. All bus drivers understand such proceedings. Distribution of the basics in the list is in the hands of the wholesalers and the money-lenders who know all tax and toll procedures and so do their expert transport personnel. The recitation of the list to pilgrim bus drivers is a stupid formality to assert the raja's *hukoomat*—authority, sovereignty.

Apart from this body, and one other, whom I rightly guessed to be a hay farmer, we were some twenty passengers in the bus—men, women, children and infants. We had, too, four goats with us. I had seen them for the first time—as I had paused abruptly on the folding step, unnerved by the fearful squealing under my feet—and as I stooped to enter the bus, my face level with their beards, I had counted them, one by one, as a silent protest against the outrageous freight hauling operation I was being asked to defer to. I had decided to swear out a complaint before the District Health Officer against the owners of the bus for transporting goats in a pilgrim bus.

The driver hastily pulled out a piece of paper, tucked in a fold of his turban, and showed it to the *chowkīdār*. The man shined the shaking lantern on it. Other than fogging the glass with his steaming breath, nothing happened. No problems here. The goats belonged to the raja sāhib. The *chowkīdār*, holding fast to his felt wrap to resist the biting cold, now recited the list again, this time for the benefit of the passengers: ". . . for sale and resale, any tobacco, cloth, hay, cooking oil, rice, kerosene, salt, sugar, potatoes, flour, onions, spices, hair oil, *thok . . . ?*"

It was at that stage, a passenger at the rear, sitting nearest to the entrance to the bus, where the driver and the *chowkīdār* were, interrupted the reading and answered, "Yes," contending, thereby, as far as I could make out, that he carried the last item in the list, *"thok."* I assumed this, since none among us was visibly carrying any goods for sale and resale, certainly no article on the *chowkīdār's* list except this *thok.* Following that disclosure, a veritable confession, incited and stirred, the *chowkīdār* sucked in a quantity of air, loud enough to be heard by one and all as a whistle in reverse. Soon after registering his reaction, he shouted, "You are all under arrest!" and still shaking, he and his hurricane lamp disappeared into the smoking *chowkī.*

Peering through the grimy window, I asked the entranced driver, "Why?" He pleaded with me. *"Please,* sāhib!" I did not question him further. Presently, not daring to approach the *chowkī,* he noiselessly entered the cage separating him from the passengers, where the convict-type front and side view photograph of his face was hanging; got into his seat, turned off the lights, and he said he was in trouble. It was a raja's territory— and I gathered from his monologue with unmistakable clarity— you don't talk that way to a raja's man. No passenger talks to a raja's man. Only the driver talks to a raja's man. He then struck his brow with the palm of his hand—I heard this happen since I could not see him in the dark—and he swore on his mother's life that in all his years he had never offended a raja's man. Always, he had said *"Ha!" "Yes!"* to a raja's man. And now he and his passengers had been arrested! I could not intrude upon his thought further. He was choking from spasmodic sobbing.

Well, I do not wish to recall the details of what happened that night. All the devils who unfailingly escort and loyally attend upon Lord Shiva, because he loves them as much as he loves the good folk, were loose in the night. This is a blessed land. You always hear the gentle murmur of the river. The Ganga flows by, never too far, on her way to the Sāgara, her very own sea, to become the Sāgara, her very own sea. The echoes of that gentle dance of waters, towards immersion into the sea, the river soon to become the sea, her very own sea, is the music of these hills. In their kind of sky, the stars are a lovely sight, as is their gracious and yet gracious, and yet gracious moon. In settings like these, beauty melts and softens your heart, and the soul has remembrance of God. I have so thought. Yet, as it was, to hear an owl hoot filled you with fear and foreboding. We endured the night freezing in cold. There was unbearable crying by the infants, as if the end of the world had come. I complained about the noise and demanded of the hay farmer, sitting next to me, that he answer one simple question. His teeth chattering, he complied in a whisper, ". . . milk." At twenty, I did not know that the human infant feels hungry and would raise the squall, day or night, to sue for milk. You heard groans, sobbing by young women, laments addressed to Lord Shiva by everyone, including the man who had caused it all. It was he who had confronted a raja's man with a *"Ha!"* when the *chowkīdār* was doing his bounden duty, and had alluded to *thok*—and to whom he had said, unmistakably, by implication, "I have *thok*. And let's see what you do about it!"

It is in situations like these that you rate a woolen blanket several rungs above your very life. Having abandoned all hope, I nevertheless saw the day break, the first light upon the frost, and heard the man sitting next to me on the rough hewn wood, implore Shiva; voicing in his usual Gorakhpurī my own unspoken thought: Innocent Lord! O Innocent Lord! for a sight of the sun before we all die! That prayer was immediately fulfilled. Though the skyline had no contours yet, I had a fleeting glimpse of a celestial thing: a sheer shawl, woven of the young sun's gold, hanging as a canopy over the blue and amber haze, veiling everything far and near! Meanwhile, down in the pilgrim bus, we looked like bundles you see in the railway yards, huddled together, and wrapped up in whatever *dhotī*, sari, turban, towel, scarf, handkerchief we could find. The wind, blowing free from all the windows and through the bars in the driver's cage, felt like needles and it hurt the face. My ears had lost all sensibility. Weary beyond endurance, I dozed off for a few moments. Soon after, I had a confrontation with a king cobra.

This is relevant. I have the facts sheet. The great cobra, the king, is not *Naja naja*, Sanskrit *nāga*, the cobra. It is *Naja hannah*, the hamadryad. To see one is *experience!* Reliable hunters have seen fearless king cobras stare at them standing erect well above fully grown stalks of corn. Witnesses have watched elephants fall and die following an argument with a king cobra.

Shiva, Shiva, it is an auspicious thing, a merciful thing that others do not partake of one's nightmares! Well, as soon as I dozed off, I saw this magnificent king cobra, in a witness box, standing erect like a rod and testifying against us—the humanity. He was wearing a tiny turban on his head, and an elastic cord chinstrap, to keep it secure. He was raging, all fifteen feet and better of him, and speaking for all snakes, he said, "You despise us! You despise us! You step on us! You step on us! Is this justice? Is this justice?" His hood spread like a mottled dish of aged iron, and, hissing from passion, he said, "You cannot count two and two! You cannot count two and two! We will wipe you out! We will wipe you out! You dust-eaters! You scum! You bastards!" I woke up, still hearing his testimony, and I cannot own up to a cold sweat. It was so cold. The sun was up, but it was as cold as it had been all night long.

Everyone, without regard to age, had difficulty in moving the limbs and getting out of the bus as ordered. The *chowkīdār* had sent for the law to back him up. A sub-inspector of police, wearing a brown waistcoat, khaki breeches, boots, and a red turban with a brass badge on it, dismounted from a bicycle, searched the bus, the peasants' meager belongings, and our benumbed persons. I was the only one with luggage. An exhibition of your personal effects in such a setting causes resentment and active anger among the deprived classes. The *chowkīdār* and the lawman belonged to the deprived classes. The sub-inspector held up my magnifying glass and asked me what does it do? I could not explain why was I carrying it to the Lord's holy abode, to the temple, myself being on a pilgrimage, bearing gifts for the Lord, except that I had always carried a magnifying glass along with these—and I pointed out the items to him—a compass and a set of four screwdrivers. These were my possessions, I explained. They were displeased with me, too, because I did not have an overcoat. Sub-inspectors of police, hereabouts, take a coat off your back for your own good. "Your family is rich, yes? You have two coats, no?" Actually, I had more than two. The old man and his nephew had advised me that the overcoats would be safer in the village.

Presently, the sub-inspector spat on the rear tire of the bus and said to the *chowkīdār*, *"Jānedo!"* "Let go!" He signaled us with his thumb to get into the bus immediately. The bus driver, red-eyed and humbled, stiffly saluted the two, gently folded and boosted up the step, dropped the dog collar in place, the spike on the left and the goblin's neck on the right, and tried to start the engine as noiselessly as he could.

Within half an hour we sighted the temple and everyone sang loudly of the glories of Shiva. We were constrained because of our own deeds, our *karma,* and we magnified the Innocent Lord many times over because we were free and forgiven and with our Baba, our Father, after a night long separation.

As we sluggishly stepped out of the bus, one by one, every passenger, man, woman and child, avoided the man who had owned up to carrying *thok.* We feared him. Unable to resist it, I approached him guardedly and questioned him. "You had *thok?*" He said no. "What is it?" He said he didn't know. I asked him patiently, "You don't know what is *thok?*" He said he didn't know what is *thok.* I raised my voice. "Why did you say 'yes' to the *chowkīdār* when he asked if anyone had *thok?*" His mother, he said, had told him always to say *"ha!"* "yes" when spoken to by a government man.

To this day, after all the inquiries I made, I do not know what is *thok.* Speaking as a student of Hindi, however, and outside of our context, *thok* means *wholesale,* and *phutkar* is

Hindi and Hindustani for *retail*. The relationship in Hindi and Hindustani between *thok* and *phutkar* is not quite syzygial; the terms, as you see, are not yoked together, in a condition of *yoga*, as it were, and yet, being correlative, and, in spite of the discernible quantitative difference between the two, and the corresponding volume/profit dependence factor—you sell to *one (thok)* and you sell to *many (phutkar)*—they are syzygial, inasmuch as you cannot have *thok*—wholesale—without there being *phutkar*—retail, or, retail without there being wholesale.

Well, whatever it was, the keeper of the *chowkī* must have understood that one of the pilgrims was smuggling it and smuggling it *thok* (wholesale) for sale and resale (*phutkar*), in defiance of the authority, and our detention and subsequent search was a search for contraband—and therefore—legal and justified. I had been thinking of filing a First Information Report against the *chowkīdār* and the sub-inspector, to protest in the strongest possible language I could command, quoting chapter and verse, and let the raja's own procedures take their course.

As I got out of the bus, I noticed the goats in the temple compound, basking in the sunshine, waiting to be collected by the raja's men. They were young goats, hardly three years old, intended for the raja's prized flock, as traditional symbols of his dynasty; in fact, one of his titles was goatherd. There are rajas whose titles honor the cow; for instance, His Highness the Maharaja of Baroda, the Gaekwād, the cowherd. As I approached the goats, I noticed they were Indian specimens, pure uncrossed breed, from the Jamna riverside, and *such* lop ears, *such* convex faces, *such* prominent foreheads and *such* Roman noses, as to shame all other such ears, faces, foreheads and noses! Superior to the Nubians I had known and befriended in the outskirts of Cairo, and again in Jerusalem, their ancestry goes back a few thousand years in Indian history. *Ajā* (goat) is mentioned in the *Vedas*. You should have seen their great soulful eyes, as they looked straight into yours, three doting does, and one solemn stalwart buck, who moved up a few feet, with his head raised, with an unmistakable demand for "me, too!" He wanted his chin tickled—and they ever so irresistibly drew you to themselves, by their excelling child-like faces, their beauty, and it all certainly merited your love, and a hug for each besides, and many passes with your fingers, from the noble forehead to the noble nose, ever so gently and ever so friendly. I muttered guilty apologies too for overlooking in the pilgrim bus such solid charm. And we had endured so much together! This conference with them was the only happy thing that happened to me since I arrived and left the village. I have never subscribed to the old English/Scottish superstition that once in every twenty-four hours a goat needs to go to the devil to have its beard combed. Fiddlesticks!

Soon after, having bathed in the sacred pond, I stood in the line, along with other pilgrims, to offer the customary worship to the sculptured snakes on the temple wall, and I was not at all lighthearted about the king cobra's testimony. We do *not* despise snakes. We do *not* step on snakes. We *honor* snakes. But the king cobra might not have been denouncing the Hindus, and addressing his slurs and insults to others.

I have not been in those parts for many years. Before I left the village for good, I wrote to my gentle sister Friendly to forgive me. I paid a Brahmin to pray for her father whom too I had failed. I expect the old man and his *supātra* nephew informed everyone that I had been overcome by the sight—*darshan*—of the Lord and was *stilled*. A rustic paraphrase of this sudden mystic *stilling* means that, being blessed in the shrine of the Lord, one renounced all earthly possessions. And it was the Lord's will that all the lumber, bricks, bags of cement, the leftover gravel, rocks, nails, tools and my precious books—the construction having been appropriated by thieves, robbers, thugs—and the panther skins, the overcoats, too, were the old man's and his nephew's by rights, won through their meritorious *karma*, their deeds in the past and the present incarnations. "Who knows!" "*Kyā mālum,* sāhib?" This *kyā mālum* is very idiomatic; literally, "What's known?" Translation: "*Nothing*'s known!" "Why do you ask?"

If they, the old man and his nephew, had been able to sign

their names on a piece of paper, the freehold land would have been theirs too. The illiterates in these parts, and their fathers and forefathers, have been in trouble so often by signing their names by seal and such other devices, and stamping their thumbs on paper, too, pledging themselves, ignorantly, inadvertently, to everything, from lifelong serfdom to contracted slavery overseas, that they will *not* do it even if they were made landlords in perpetuity. I have fewer illusions about country living, country folk, fresh air and so forth now, than I had in those days.

William Cowper was pleased to reveal, "God made the country and man made the town." Nathaniel Hawthorne was born four years after Cowper crossed the Stygian ferry, as they say, and lived to be sixty-four. Having partaken of some accommodating wisdom, meanwhile, Hawthorne has written, "There is nothing good to be had in the country, or, if there is, they will not let you have it."

16

The Merchant of Kisingarh

The following is the translation of the Hindi, spoken by
Lachhīsing, the merchant of Kisingarh, deceased, speaking
through his son Rāmsing, self-confessed spirit medium and
suspected arsonist. He is speaking to his father-in-law Kanāising and addresses him as *burrādar* (equal to brother):

In the Kristi years of World War Two, we were prosperous in
the city of Bombay. Kristaan was killing Kristaan. There was
a rain of *rupee*s in Bombay. Everybody was buying. One day the
razor blade was one *rupee* for four. The next day, it was two
*rupee*s for four. The third day four *rupee*s for four. Merchants
got what they asked for steel. Our village men always had beards.
They too shaved. They looked like women. They could not show
their faces for shame. Everybody had to shave to get a government job. The army said no beards, go away! Only the Sikh army
and the public had beards. There was big demand for razor
blades. The god of wealth Raja Kubera said to Bombay, *"Lo!
Lo!"* "Take! Take!" Take the *rupee*s! I broke a ten *rupee* note
without a care in an eating house. I ordered potato fritters and
sweets after eating a full meal. I said, "Let go!" We had never
known such prosperity, O God!

Now and then there was a lack of care with money. I have
already said that. Otherwise, we were humble brokers only. We
could have had a motor of our own. But we did not want to tell
the government of our good fortune. If we had shown our prosperity, the government would have robbed us. We did not tell the

public. The public would have robbed us. We did not tell our relations. The relations would have robbed us. We let our losses only be known. We ate good bread and lentils. My mother had served my father the same simple food. We could have bought milk, butter, even honey.

I had always been a broker. Now I had capital. I could invest. But we did not want to show our capital. I have already said that. For services without wages, a railway clerk taught me accounts. As a poor boy, another man taught me A-B-C-D English free.

The same year, I got married to an orphanage girl. Orphanage girls are taught good obedience, we knew. We also wanted it made very well known that we were only poor brokers. Why would we otherwise marry an orphan? We spent almost no money on the marriage. The girl brought with her what she wore. We gave her a spare sari, one petticoat for underneath and one blouse. Also, one *rupee* present.

At that time, an important thing happened. My father worshiped Shivji. He always carried *bilva* leaves and some milk to the temple on Mondays. I always followed him with the same offerings. One day, a naked man saw us in the street. He said to us, "*Sālo!* you are going to the temple to worship God? Have you *seen* God?" My father could not reply. He whispered to me not to get hot. The man had called my father and me his *sālā*. He had said we were his brothers-in-law. So, as their husband, he mounted on our sisters. My father said to him, "Mahātmāji, if not God, whom should we worship?" The man said, "*Sālā,* worship God you *see!*" My father was silent. He was afraid the man might curse us. He then said to my father, "Dog! does your woman cook for you? Do you eat, *sālā!*" My father said, "She cooks, rājā. I eat, rājā. We are poor folk. We only beg for your blessings." Then the naked man said to us, "If your women cook, don't you see Agnī, *sālo?*" Then I understood. I fell at the mahātmā's feet. The holy man then touched our heads with his foot and said to us, "Go, worship Agnī, *sālo!*" So he became our guru and we became fire-worshipers. We always folded hands whenever we saw fire. We offered to Agnī food also. A pandit told us Lord Agnī is the eldest son of Brahmā. There is no creation without heat. Our faith was firm even before I heard that.

The same year both my father and mother made their home in heaven. I got into brokerage same as my father. I rented a room in a humble building. It was a *chāwl*. Many poor people lived in it. We lived in one room. My wife and I lived on the same simple diet. It made good bones, my grandfather had said. There was one more thing. Now that my mother no longer ran the family stove, my wife's craving for *mirch* became known to me. The green small *mirch* is very hot. She also put in so much red pepper in the lentils. When I bit the first morsel, I ran for a drink of water. Even then I was burning. For years, I ate with my right hand, and drank from a *lotā* of water with my left hand. I said to her, "Why do you make me eat and drink like this? I am not a cotton fluffer working with both hands!" She would not stop when I told her to stop. I did not want to shout. Our walls were very thin. The people in the rooms could hear everything. That is why everybody in that building always whispered. We never raised our voice. Neighbors were always listening.

I gathered *rupee*s in the Kristaan war. I have already said that. We had no friends. Friends would have robbed us. We had one son, Rāmsing. The midwife came and delivered him. Rāmsing was given to us by Lord Agnī to do our last rites. For his sake, too, money had to be saved and kept hidden. We hid it in jute sacks under wheat in our room. Our soul was in our son and in those sacks. When we were so happy, we had a robbery. The wife went down to see a procession, and all our money was gone. It was taken from the sacks by unknown persons. A neighbor said they were communists. I said they were thieves. He said communists say all money belongs to everybody. Neighbors from other floors came upstairs to ask how much was taken. We said, who would steal from the poor? Some little grain was taken, yes. The thieves were sorry for their trouble, I joked with the neighbors. They went away satisfied. Inside, we drank up our grief.

We could not open our hearts to the police, my *burrādar*. They would have asked where all that money came from. I had done things which would have been bad if opened. I had bought and sold English gold coins too. The English put anybody in jail for buying and selling gold. If anybody had their guinea coin, the police called his father a dog and took him to the station. They asked him questions. Which son of a dog sold you this gold guinea? Was he not a German spy? Where does he live? The English said buying and selling gold was very bad for their war. They did not say why. Hanging was not good enough for such dogs, they said.

Our gold was gone too. I had paid high for my gold. I used to weep very often. I wanted to kill myself or kill somebody, even little Ramsing, because he kept crying. Twice I laid hands on the wife. I slapped her hard. It was always the same reason. There was too much green and red pepper in the lentils. The third time I raised my hand, she answered back. She whispered, "If it burns you, isn't that your Agnī?" The name of God! My woman! The mother of my son! I said, not loudly, "You, whore!" and I got the hammer in hand. Seeing death, she screamed. The neighbors came running. I became sober. "She thought she saw communists. I say it was only mice," I said to the neighbors. After that, I wanted to renounce the world. I wanted to become *sanyāsī*. I went to join the Ramakrishna Mission. The swamis said they wanted educated *sanyāsīs*. I never again complained of her *mirch*.

Those were lean days, *burrādar*. Money was hard to see. Burma had fallen. There were victory parades by the English. The public was joining too. I was in brokerage for anything, even country whiskey. The government stopped country whiskey supply. This brokerage was paying more than marriage brokerage. One time, for full two weeks, we lived on bread and plantains. We could not pay for lentils and *mirch* was high again. The farmer was supplying to the government. It was helping the war effort, they said.

At that time of need, we had a new neighbor. He took a

room on the fourth floor too. The fourth floor was cheapest. We died every day climbing the stairs. We shared a small balcony with this new neighbor. He was a retired school master. He got *rupees* thirty a month pension. He worshiped Lord Krishna. We let him play with our son. The wife often left the little one with him. We let him be foolish over our two-year-old. He said our son was the image of the child Lord Krishna when he was on this earth. We called our new neighbor grandfather.

One day, I saw grandfather sitting in his easy chair. His eyes were closed. I asked him why did he close his eyes. He said a man was fighting cancer. Grandfather was cursing his cancer. I told my wife about this. We were afraid. We were afraid he might curse us too. We stopped speaking to him. After a long time we met and spoke. He said he had a hobby. He told fortunes by cards. I asked him, "What is in the cards for me, grandfather?" I was happy that day. Brokerage from one consignment of top leaf tea brought me good money. I said, "Do I become rich, grandfather?"

He made four stacks on the balcony floor. One for me, one for the wife, one for Ramsing, and one for himself. From those stacks, he picked up four cards and looked at them. He took the name of Lord Krishna and said we all four are one family, Lord, guide! Then he was silent for a long time. I wanted to go away. I became afraid. But I wanted to know my fortune. Will our robbed gold and money come back? So I sat quietly saying nothing. Little Rāmsing crawled up to the balcony. Grandfather looked worried. He said he saw misfortune. Then he closed his eyes again. I quickly picked up Rāmsing and went in and shut the door of our room. I vowed never to speak to such a man. He was cursing. Why say misfortune? If it is misfortune, do we become beggars? Do I die? Who would look after the little one? Someone might touch the wife. They pull up the petticoat of a woman and take her if her man is gone. I lost my appetite that day thinking like that. I could not enjoy the wife that night. I could not give her happiness for many days afterwards.

I stopped going out to the balcony. Grandfather tried to

speak with us. One day he left a letter asking to speak to little Rāmsing. My wife had learnt to read and write in the orphanage. She read his letter. But we did not reply. He then wrote that our plantain peelings on the balcony floor were collecting flies. I was very hot with him. We eat plantains and bread because the lentils are high. Why mention our shame? I wanted to kill him. I had killed one man before, a brother broker. He had spoken bad words about my mother.

The same day I received the letter, I saw grandfather on the balcony. His eyes were closed again. I wanted to go out and say to him, "Grandfather, you rogue-man, who are you cursing now?" He opened his eyes and saw me from his easy chair. He got up and came to me to embrace me. He had, now and then, embraced me in the olden days. Seeing him coming towards me like that, I got very hot. I said, "You, *sālā!* I lie with your mother!" I then quickly pushed him down from the balcony.

Everybody understood it was an accident. His eldest son came for his things. He sent us *rupees* three thousand after one week of the funeral. Grandfather had given this in his will to little Rāmsing. One day after we received this money, a man came. He asked for grandfather. I told him he was old and had fallen down from the fourth floor. I had been to his funeral. He wanted grandfather to curse his cancer, he said. I asked him what is that? He said it is English language for *naasoor.* I said to him, "Why do you speak English language with us and not say *naasoor?*" He said doctors call it cancer. Grandfather used to curse people's cancer, "Go away, go away!" Some got well. He used to lay hands on people too. He took the name of Lord Krishna, then laid the hands, the man told us.

With three thousand *rupees, burrādar,* we left Bombay. We moved to the lucky town of Kisingarh. I rented a small house. I invested the *rupees* in poor women's saris. The wife dyed them green, yellow, red, also blue. She dried them herself. Our stock was cotton. Silk is for rich women. We worked in the yard. With all stock ready, ironed, also starched and folded, I swore before fire a partnership. O Lord Agnī, little Rāmsing is ten *anna*s in the *rupee,* me and my woman, remaining six *anna*s in the *rupee,* total sixteen in the *rupee.* For three years, there was turnover of the same cotton goods. I made more than I had lost to the communists or the thieves. It was more than my seven ancestors had made in their lifetime. I was a merchant. The poor were buying from me day and night.

That same year, Hindus and Muslims were going to fight. Government was buying. Jute, khaki cloth, and cotton goods for women police. Mill owner was selling to government. I went back to brokerage. Thanks to the luck of my partners, I flourished. Now Rāmsing was grown up. He learnt fourth standard English in school. I paid fees. For some time, he joined one Annie Besant Theosophy psychic development course. I pulled him out and said we are rich, son. Poor men learn to earn and read and write. He obeyed. Then, on his own, he became a very good medium, and often spoke with the dead souls. I made him a very good marriage too. So he became the sole son-in-law-heir. It was a rich man's only daughter, but the rich man said he was poor! We were happy. Then more good fortune came. We became grandparents three times. Rāmsing was father of three sons. I paid back the principal *Rs.* 3,000 with interest to a widows' welfare home. All three partners were now free of debt. Rāmsing then decided on partnership with his own father-in-law rich man Kanāising. I said, it is your own capital, why not? If your father-in-law cheats you, Agnī will eat him. You will see his ashes, Rāmsing, my son. I have already said that to you, Rāmsing, my son.

At the age of 61, my *burrādar* Kanāising, one night, I thought somebody was pressing my throat. I could not breathe. The doctor came. He wanted to chat and joke with a rich man. He was a social man. But I screamed. They put me in the doctor's motor and we ran to the government hospital. They made x-ray photos. They said, in their English, it was embolism. It was in the lung maybe. They said to Rāmsing there is a bad clot. Both my partners were weeping. I wanted to shout, be happy, partners! We can pay the dogs! We are rich! Then one dog spoke to a nurse. He said, arrange oxygen, nurse. I wanted to say, dogs, I *guarantee* payment even for a more expensive thing. Get the thing! But in a few minutes I was gone, even with oxygen.

Now that I was dead, same as he, I saw him waiting for me. I asked him if it hurt when I pushed him down. He said when he touched the cement, his head hurt very bad. Then it didn't. He said his death was in the cards. He had to go that way. I said, "I was hot, grandfather." "It was nobody's fault, Lord Krishna's will. The cards said, 'the family will separate.'"

I died a man of property and a happy man, *burrādar*. Some days after my rites were done, I went to see my senior partner Rāmsing. I visited his bedroom. He had a real man's beard, *burrādar*, and his side whiskers were like wings. There were curling hairs on his chest and below. Like a jungle! My own son! I waited for him to be done with his woman. It was too hot for the innocent to put on her blouse and petticoat. She was sitting on the bed fanning him with a hand fan. That is how my woman used to do after I was done. Dear Rāmsing's eyes were closed. He was happy. I was happy. I sang to him the *Song of Six Million*. I made it up in my head.

One million, there's a lucky town the name of Kisingarh, *ohoho!*

Two million, there live merchants and their servants, *ohoho!*

Three million, there are Hindus and Muslims, some young and some old, *ohoho!*

Four, there was a rich man, now dead and done, *ohoho!*

Five, there lives in Kisingarh, a son-heir, earning and earning, *ohoho! ohoho!*

Six, there's a lucky town the name of Kisingarh, *ohoho!*

Again, six million, there lives Kanāising, the richest man, *ohoho! ohoho!*

He will have six million, Kanāising! . . . Why are you afraid of Rāmsing, *burrādar?* I have given him all my *rupees!* Now you give him all your *rupees!* Order of Lord Agnī, *burrādar!* Make a fire, say, Lord Agnī my witness, I give now everything to my heir-son Rāmsing!—otherwise, Lord Agnī eat me! eat me! ...

"Why are you crying, Kanāising? Rāmsing will be happy with you! He will not hurt you! Why would a merchant hurt his own father-in-law, Kanāising? Why would Rāmsing break his woman's father—make unhappy his own wife, who makes him happy and gives him sons? Tell me, tell me, Kanāising!"

I am Lachhīsing, dead. I have spoken the command of Lord Agnī to father-in-law Kanāising—through the mouth of my own blood, my own Annie Besant medium-son, good Rāmsing!

Lord Agnī witness, who witnessed the stocks and the sari goods of the rivals burn, witnessed the senior partner Rāmsing, fearless, lion-hearted, spit on the face of the policeman who caught me and my woman with a torch and a barrel of government kerosene!

Hear me good! Take care! O Kanāi! Kanāi! Kanāi!

17

The Second Mrs. Was Wed in a Nightmare

In clouds so dense that I could see no more of myself than the shoulders, I saw an oval opening, and I walked out of it, and found myself on a nearly flat ground, and in the dead center of it—towards which I walked—I found an enormous dome, with no under-structure, nothing to support it.

Under the dome, I saw a huge ape, about the size of eight or nine average-size apes, sitting on a revolving stool, and most intently playing an organ. And—as the music issued from the organ—I felt the vibrations through my very bones, and I asked a passing shape—forms were passing all the time and there was great traffic about me—who the ape playing the organ might be. He replied that the great ape's name was Eric, and that he had been a-playing that very organ—J.S. Bach's music exclusively—for centuries before J.S. Bach was born, and that he would continue playing it for all he (the passing ape) knew, for centuries to come. Appalled, I asked him, "Is this a nightmare?" "No. You are in the fifth dimension," he replied, lying to me.

I left the traffic and got myself under the dome, and I was trying hard to attract Eric's attention, and failing to do that, I picked up a wooden plank, and landed it on his exposed backside—as much was outside the seat of the revolving stool—and there was an awfully loud report, but the ape did not stir, remained seated, and, although one of his paws went to his back-

side automatically, to soothe the hurt, he continued to play J.S.
Bach on the organ.

In desperation—I was feeling desperate by then—I began
to shout "Eric! Eric!" as loudly as I could, causing a frightening
echo under the dome, and although there was the magnified
returning "Eric! Eric!" he remained seated, his back towards me,
still a-playing J.S. Bach on the organ.

Thereupon, I walked behind him and—having had an intuition about it—*I blew on his neck*. Immediately, Eric turned towards me, and he spoke to me fast, in high Gothic and Sanskrit—
which I began to understand instantly—and he said to me, first
in Gothic, next in Sanskrit, (that bit I remember perfectly) that
his name was not Eric, not exactly, but Sandoes, and that it was
an occult secret, and he pronounced the S in his name with a
sibilant hiss, and if I could—he challenged me—pronounce his
name, he would be my Guru, my spiritual guide, and tell me
more secrets.

Now, I did just that for him, and perfectly: "Sandoes! Sandoes!" I said, and I pronounced the S with a sibilant hiss. Eric
was astounded. He said, he thought, it was *impossible* for a
human being even to attempt to pronounce his name: still, according to his promise, he became my Guru, and the first secret
he told me was that an initiate-to-be (which I now was, by Eric's
grace) should always maintain silence, a brief silence—the secret
mute—after he had pronounced the full name. I did that, too, for
him. I said, "Eric, Guru Sandoes," and was silent for a moment.
He blessed me and said that I had done something that was
impossible for a human being to do. Accordingly, he declared
me no longer a human being, but an initiate—like himself.

The news about my having been gifted with a spiritual
guide, and no other than the great Eric himself, created a sensation among the traffic passing outside the dome. Everybody
stopped reverentially, as I approached, and if anyone didn't, he
or she turned into a crow—there were thousands of them now—
and a word came from Eric, which was passed on among the
traffic, that such sinning crows could revert to their original

blessed shape—become apes, and no longer be crows—if they would repent, and go to the Wishing Well and wish, with the reservation that *they would never know the Wishing Well when they see it, verb. sap.*

Getting quite cross about this reservation of his—a puzzle, really—I started a frightful disputation with Eric, and shouted my arguments, (*"I demur!" "I grant!" "I assent!" "I deny!"*) all of which echoed under the dome, and it was a very fast debate between us indeed, involving metaphysical, theological, cosmological and phrenological (I couldn't understand why phrenological) matters, and it went on for a day and a night, carried on entirely in a nasal sort of German, with umpteen *Ja*s and *Nein*s, and Eric said to me, by way of conclusion, *Ja*, there was no more to be said, and that such sinning crows could become apes, if they repent, and go to the Wishing Well and wish, but that *they would never know the Wishing Well when they see it, Nein.*

The *finality* of it, and his cocksure attitude, got me so worked up that I started looking for another plank, bigger than the one I had used before, and while I was searching, a passing shape told me—to my utter amazement—that the *whole* thing, the *entire* argument with Eric, the metaphysical, cosmological and phrenological disputation *had been broadcast* by *Radio Baghdad* and overheard by humanity, lord and lay alike, and that, (continued the ape), it had already become a human tradition, the latest French thing, and that its adherents included prime ministers, publishers, actors, medical men, statesmen, all sorts, and women, the clergy, and that it had attached to it a secret school as well, with its own theosophy, and signs and symbols, which the initiates alone understood, and that the occult side of the doctrine had already become a most elaborate cabala. In awful alarm, I asked him, "How long has this been going on?" and he replied, "Why, back into centuries!" I shrieked, "We *are* in the fifth dimension!" "I agree," he said, lying to me.

Getting no farther with Eric—he continued to play J.S. Bach—I composed a hymn of praises in my honor, and I was looking for a platform on which to stand and sing it to the multitude. It was then that I was suddenly swept off my feet by about a million apes—so many they seemed—all members of a grand chorus, who rushed in from all sides, to the center of the dome, to sing something entirely mighty, and epoch-making, all to the glory of Eric, Guru Sandoes—embellished with the secret mute—my spiritual master, that I began to feel less than dirt under his paws, and I threw away my hymn of praises in disgust, and myself melted into the mighty chorus, which was half male and half female, mile upon mile of apes, standing in strict order, all adoring Eric—who continued to play the organ, and now led the chorus with music—and I knew then that this adoration of Eric would become a mighty tradition in the three-dimensional world, and that it would survive a million years, while my disputation with him would have been forgotten, and my praises unsung, and this realization made me feel sorely unhappy.

I was weeping silently, and Eric, seeing this, took pity on me, and said to me, that the chorus incident would be wiped off the slate of time—it would be sacrificed—and he prophesied that my disputation with him would survive instead, and my unsung hymn would survive, too, remain for ever, till the end of time, to my everlasting glory, with the reservation that *I should perish first, be wiped off the slate of time myself, and become the world's sacrifice, Ja.*

Lured by the promise of immortality, I agreed to his reservation, and walked outside the dome, and met a passing shape, who told me that Eric and I were being worshiped on the earth, by all manner of human beings, that very day, as symbols of a most sacred craft, and that a certain musician of far-East and near-East was, in fact, at that very moment, being inspired to compose a symphony in our praise, with words taken from my piece, and hearing this, I felt reassured of my immortality, and I heard myself proclaim to the winds, "Hark ye, apes have become gods! apes have become gods!" It was a moment of great triumph for me.

Yet, as soon as I had said that, I realized with utmost rigor that I myself must have become an ape! *"Like Guru, like Chelā!"*

In utter melancholy, and fearing more than I had feared anything on earth—including the ex-wife, the former Mrs D. (at present enjoying the enviable status of the Most Loyal Reader and voluntary Mender of Socks)—I dared not look behind me, or feel, because I might find something showing and hanging, to my everlasting shame!

At that stage, a female ape stood by my side—Eric's eldest—and she addressed endearing ape-terms to me (which I began to understand instantly) and she said to me, concluding her address, that from now on, it was to be home cooking for me again, and let's make music together (she said). I thought quickly, and realizing that I did still need the kind of love and support which a woman alone can give, I accepted her suit, and approached her father—who continued to play J.S. Bach on the organ—to marry us, be the priest, father-in-law, best man and witness, and grant us his blessings.

As minutes passed, however, and the moment for marriage vows approached, my human nature got the better of me, and I lamented loudly, in words which seemed to come from the very depths of my soul, "Woe is me! Fates, here I am, a creature man, turned an ape!"

Eric's eldest tried to console me and she smoothed the hair on my head, with gentle strokes of her paw, and my hair stood on edge at her touch, and I went on lamenting, spoiling it all, and addressing the multitude, I wept, "Oh, woe is me! I am turned an ape! Ah, regard ye well!"

Finding my grief overwhelming his eldest—at that crucial stage—Eric imparted to me two terrible secrets. "Because my wife is crazy, *I cannot make you an immortal,*" he said (imparting to me the first). Hardly had the words "You swine!" escaped my lips, he imparted to me the second. "Because my wife can bake cakes, *my wife can give you immortality.*" Sobbing piteously, I begged him, "Introduce me, Eric! *Please, Eric!*"

She materialized out of the multitude riding a tricycle, and wearing a Taj Mahal-shape straw hat. She was about the size of five or six of our kind, bar Eric, and she went round and round, as they do in the circus, and ringing the tricycle bell, she said not a word to me, but stared at me steadily, now and then, as she stopped cycling, silently willing power and wisdom on me.

After a few moments of this, she stopped once more, and fed me a piece of her Cake of Immortality. A bite of it, and I was as one awake, as one transformed, and with her grace, there came to me then the greatest illumination of my life, a real Cloud of Unknowing, a super-*satori* barred to Suzuki, to Roshi Ruth Sasaki, the supreme *Sat-Chit-Ānanda,* and I attained to an exalted intuition denied to any other aspirant to immortality, literary or other, Shakespearean or Alexandrian, genius or non, and all my doubts vanished, and I was *sure.* I *knew* that the cause of my grief was a fatuous illusion, a falsehood, a mirage, māyā, and that, in truth—although on my way to be sacrificed and wiped off the slate of time—I was on the threshold of the greatest voyage and gain of my life. Yes. A new formula! Immortality through *convention, kids, marriage—an unspeakably unhappy, unhealthy marriage!*

Beholden beyond words, in abject gratitude, I went lower still, down on my nature-bent knee, and with folded hands, I told the Super-Intelligence, cutting circles on her tricycle and ringing the bell, that as an ex-man and an ex-married man, mine is already a genuine tragedy, O Holy Mother! and my life with the ape—my new woman and your daughter—had yet to be lived. Those were no small assets, no: the tragedy enacted, and the martyrdom to come. And we could together—the creature and I, although ape and female, she was innocent of the vast issues at stake—for pity's sake, for a reverend saintly sorrow's sake, by *rights,* claim the tears of the unborn millions, ape and man, the posterity, everlastingly, and so attain, by thy blessings, O Mother-in-law! a marveled memorial: achieve a perennial fame, yea, *immortality:* A true *le Mort d'* (present) *Author,* a living *Tibetan Book of the Dead:*—the epic-Supreme of an initiate turned ape, and mark you, *voluntarily* agreeing to marry an ape, and *voluntarily* agreeing to live on a mockery of home cooking—twigs, leaves and such—and having apes for issue, his little boys and girls, and suffering at all hours of his day and night,—a tragedy and plot unheard of, unknown, uninvented, *unimagined!* Truly a tale of travail and woe, a story to sadden, appall and agonize, and haunt, the hearts of the *ages* to come, the *yugānī,*— and so become an imperishable evergreen!

And she understood me perfectly, and said not a word, and as she continued to go round in circles and ringing her tricycle bell, Eric, certain, too, of my illumination, and eventual immortality, through suffering and sacrifice, shook me warmly by the paw, as an *equal,* and placing on it a penny, my dowry, with becoming courtesy and growing respect, asked, "Shall we proceed with the ceremony now, friend?" and I replied, not a moment too late, "Amen, Ericus. Let's! Naked we come, naked we go! Ashes to ashes, earth to earth! Lucky man! Lucky ape! Lucky me! Lucky her!"

Since a Nation Must Export, Smithers!

I was crossing one street after another, thousands of them, and did not know that I was asleep and dreaming, and I stopped in a large white square—it was in Delhi, India—and all around me were stacks of cardboard boxes, millions of them, piled one upon another, and I asked a lady official, who was stamping them, what might be inside them, and she replied, "Mahātmās." The boxes were intended for export, she said, to help overseas trade. "Some of us must die," she added, "so that others might live." Moving on, I stopped again, and saw thousands of airmail parcels, neat little things, each the size of a medium cigar box, awaiting dispatch, and, on being asked about those, a lady official opened one, and showed me that they were coffins, in each of them was a tiny body, a miniature man, lying straight, swaddled like a mummy, wearing only a *kopeen*—less material than a doll's diaper—neatly powdered with ash, and wrapped up in tissue-paper, and she told me that those dead men were indeed mahatmas, clean, guiltless souls, meant for export, to further our overseas trade. "A nation must export, or die, you understand," she said. "This is our best product. There is a demand for it."

I kept wondering about it all, but nobody seemed to know anything more about it, so I decided to quit the square, and again found myself in streets, till I was worn out crossing them, and just when it seemed that there was no way out of them, I saw a man—he was an Englishman, wearing a *sola* hat, shorts, and a thermos flask—and he approached me and said his name was Smithers and that he would swap me a map of the place for a lock of my hair. I felt frightfully distressed—he might be a magician disguised as an Englishman—still, feeling helpless, I cut a lock of my hair with the penknife he offered me, and took his map, and found my way out of the streets, straight into a suburb called the Busti. It was as if I walked out of the day into the night. I saw street lamps burning, drops of perfectly still molten gold, framed in yellow, *astir!* and surrounded by round discs of crushed yellow gold, some still and some *astir!* a pattern of strange unearthly beauty, and repeated in rhythm—I had never seen such lamps, *ever!*—and I kept walking under them, helped by the map, till I came to a place, where the map indicated the Opera.

II

I showed my complimentary pass to the manager and got into the vestibule. A most enticing scent came from the auditorium, in ripples, now some, then some, and, entirely enchanted, I lingered in the passage, to savor it. Shortly after that, I walked in, and found myself to be the only person in the auditorium, but for the people on the stage—they were *Kathākalī* dancers from South India—and the orchestra (seven drums and seven pipes) went through the entire program for me alone, and it was only at the end, when the velvet curtain with silver flashes playing on it was lowered, and I was applauding lustily, that I noticed a young lady sitting next to me. She bowed to me and we got to talking in the Punjabi tongue, and I felt an overwhelming desire to ask her why was she so overdressed—charming though it all was—but the array was more for a court occasion than an informal evening at the opera. She—somehow—understood my question, and smiling, made a sign to me to look at myself, which I did, in one of the enormous mirrors on the wall, and when I saw

that—but for the map and the complimentary pass—I was carrying and wearing *nothing,* I fled, protesting loudly that there ought
to be a law against indecency in theaters. I walked straight into
the open mouth of one of the decorative animals—the figures on
the wall—and by the time I reached its stomach, I began to feel
waves of awful heat, and knew that I must be inside a living
animal, a whale, and I remembered reading that people get
bleached inside these things, from their juices, and I requested
aid. "Get me out! Get me out of Moby Dick!" . . . And inside the
whale, by the left lung, under the magnificent arches, her ribs,
or whatever. . . I met Smithers again, and for another lock of
my hair, he offered to save my life. I immediately accepted his
offer, and was out of the mammal, and was running through the
streets of the Busti, to daylight, and I was back in the white
square, where the boxes were, and the little mahatmas, clean,
guiltless souls, all dead and stacked up, since a nation must
export, and I wished that the Englishman were near by—and he
was, instantly—and I offered him the last remaining lock of my
hair—the one mother used to *love*—for the satisfaction of having
an answer to all these riddles.

While I was gratefully accepting the *kopeen* he kindly offered me, yet another lady official approached me, and adjusting
her sari over her head, she said to me, indifferent though I might
be to my mother's feelings, but it was her *duty* to warn me against
Mr. Smithers, who was a magician (as if I didn't suspect it!) and
that, with his magic, worked on my hair, he could export me to
doom, to eternal slavery, and—she continued—torment would
be my lot, she swore on her sari and upon her Guide's honor, and
that the remaining lock of my hair, still on my head, prevented
him from working his magic, here and now, there and then, *dear
brother!* I lost my temper with her—going about calling strangers
dear brother!—and told her straight, my mother's feelings were
none of her business, and it is my *duty,* scout and sportsman, and
no *brother* of hers, having made an offer, to stick to it, surely, a
deal being a deal, here and now, there and then, *dear sister!*

Smithers applauded me, and asked for the remaining lock

of hair, and a mustard seed. Given those, he said, he would explain it all to me—the boxes, the mahatmas, the Opera, the scent, the young woman, being without my clothes, everything. "My readers would be most obliged to you," I said to him. And I asked him, in despair, "Where am I going to get the mustard seed?" "One of these export inspectors told me to wish for it. Go on, wish for it!" he replied.

I did that, and there it was, the mustard seed, on my palm, and it seemed quite an appalling thing, this incident, and I asked him, if he needed the mustard seed that badly, why didn't he wish for it himself! He replied that he *couldn't*. I insisted, and asked why *couldn't* he, and he replied, impatiently, because he *couldn't*. "Why, huh?" I shouted. Losing his temper, he said, because he *couldn't*. "But why *couldn't* you?" I asked him, meaning to have the last word. And he said, with some heat, because he *couldn't*, that's all. "Is it *illegal*, man?" I demanded. "Maybe," he said, evasively.

I gave him the mustard seed, and the lock of my hair, and he said that he had been waiting for these two things for a bloody eternity. For centuries men like myself had walked the streets of the city, got into the white square, into the Busti, the living animal—and had had all the other things happen to them—and again and again, for centuries, the Englishman had rescued them, causing himself much suffering, and all because he needed the bloody mustard seed, and the locks of human hair. "And now," he said, triumphantly, "I bloody well have 'em!"

I felt alarmed, and asked him what was it that he was going to do with them, for pity's sake! He made no reply, and started walking away from me. I followed him, first walking, then running, and we kept running for miles, neither giving in—it seemed a matter of life and death to both—and I realized, while chasing the man, how *wrong* I had been not to have listened to the lady official's advice, and she had spoken from a sense of duty, as well as for my poor mother, and, I conceded, as a sister might to a brother, and on her Guide's honor, too.

III

Suddenly, something made the Englishman stop, and soon I was on him, and we both encountered the same obstacle, our heads struck a wall of rubber, or something like a wall of rubber, and we both fell into a deep well—I heard the muffled sound *plop!* following *plop!*—and there the chase continued, and we kept swimming, going round and round, and it seemed ages before someone lowered a paraffin lamp down to us, and a rope, demanding what were we doing inside the well, at that hour of the night! And while I kept going after the Englishman, gasping for breath, I shouted back to the man above us, that I had been cheated of my last remaining lock of hair and the mustard seed, and if the man was a policeman, he should arrest the Englishman, and the reply was shouted down to us that the man, in fact, was a policeman, and he ordered us up, in the name of the law, and we obeyed, climbing up by the rope, panting and dripping, and he arrested us, in spite of my protest that I was the complainant. We were produced before the Magistrate of the Busti, a Shri Karsanji Dauji, at that very hour, and he was shocked beyond words when he heard our story, and it was then that I knew that the mustard seed was absolutely a forbidden commodity, and *wishing* for it, or *possessing* it, in law, amounted to the *same* thing, and carried the death penalty; and, accordingly, we were both sentenced to death, to be shot, electrocuted, or hanged, the choice being ours, according to our wish, which, the Magistrate explained, being our last, would be honored.

Fate having brought the Englishman and me together, in dire misfortune, we discussed our next move together as a thing of joint concern, and we both agreed to ask for death by drugs—sleeping tablets, fanny barbitones—as our last wish, but it was refused to us, as, to provide the requested tablets, Shri Dauji sent word to us, would mean a delay of at least an hour—the pharmacists were asleep and had to be summoned—and it was insisted upon by the law that men sentenced for the meanest crime in the realm should die immediately, so that others might live. We thanked the Magistrate, and—reluctantly—withdrew our request.

Immediately afterwards, we were hanged—it didn't seem to hurt a bit, no swollen veins, no scarcity of air, no blueing of the face, nothing like that happened to me, and I realized once more the value of direct experience versus secondhand reports or theories. We were simply stood up on a plank, hands and eyes tied up with black cloth, the plank was withdrawn from under our feet, and we were hanged, and that was all there was to it. We were dead, executed, and although our eyes were closed for ever, we could still see what was going on, and hear everything that was being said.

IV

They took our bodies to a mortuary-like building—it seemed more like a laboratory to me, I recognized the bottles of formaldehyde—under the charge of Shri Karsanji Dauji, the Magistrate. He took delivery of our bodies, signed a receipt, and pressed a button, and we were pushed, mechanically, into an enormous tank, a very deep receptacle indeed, and liquid was rushed upon us from all sides, and our bodies were reacted upon, and we began to shrink, and, in a matter of minutes, we were perfect miniatures of our former selves, and were washed mechanically, dressed in *kopeens,* and Shri Dauji pressed another button, and we were taken delivery of, in an office tray—each body the size of a small cigar and no more—and the office boy signed a receipt, and the packing department powdered us with ash, wrapped us up in tissue-paper, placed us in the little boxes— there was certainly no Oriental contempt for the hour and the minute here and all this was so methodical that I could not help admiring it all—and the boxes were heaped up on other boxes, thousands of them, waiting to be taken to the square, to be airmailed overseas. It was then that I saw a man making inquiries about the boxes, exactly as I had, and the same lady official

opened one of them, and said to him exactly the words she had
said to me. ". . . This is our best product. There is a demand for
it."

V

"So that's how it's done!" the Englishman's ghost told me, red-
dening. "Bureaucracy forbids you mustard seed in the first place.
You begin to want the bloody stuff for dear life. You can get it
by wishing for it. They find it on you and sentence you to death,
because you challenged their protocol! They make a corpse of
you, shrink you, put you in diapers, turn you into a ma-
hatmawalla, all for beastly trade! You see it, my friend, don't
you? Don't you?" "I see it," I replied, thoroughly scared. "We
are done for, Smithers," I said, melting in tears. "You got a
handkerchief, brother?" "You don't need a handkerchief, you
dam' fool!" he yelled at me. "You are *dead!*"

"So this is *death!*" I said, presently, recovering and looking
Oblivion straight in the eye. "Having lived dangerously, and
receded dangerously, I feel staunchly and unaccountably *optimis-
tic!*" Addressing the fuming ghost standing next to me, I cried,
"Io triumphe, Smithers! One life, one *death!* So these are the
agonies of death! *Rigor mortis,* eh? We have joined the choir
invisible, Smithers! And England expects every man will do his
duty! Excuse me laughing, but . . . *ha! ha!*"

–19–

'Abdullāh Haii

The candidate for sainthood—who possessed the honored name 'Abdullāh and an unusual or even an absurd surname, Haii—it rhymes with *huh* and an *ee*—suffered from a distemper of imagination. He was an habitual liar. (The things narrated below, therefore, are lies.)

II

As a young man, he told me, he had received an occult instruction from an *ustād*—a master of the craft. (The *ustād* hailed from Mohallā Fojmal, Ittāwā Bhopajī, Thikānā Chamoo, Rājasthān, in the heart of India.) It was meant to compel spirits to his will. However, whenever he recited the incantation the *ustād* had confided in him, Haii saw a glass coffin, nailed fast to the earth, and himself in it, set upon by crawling things, his hair and beard turned white from terror—breathing but helpless. He asked the *ustād* for the import of the vision, seen once every afternoon, but the *ustād* would say nothing.

One night, Haii saw four huge and turbaned figures descend on him from their strangely oversize camels, truss him up, cut open his chest with the points of four daggers, one to each, get at his heart, slice it up in four equal parts, one to each, spit upon it, replace it, sew up the chest as surgeons do, and vanish. The *ustād,* on being told about that vision, too, remained silent. Further pressed, he lost his temper, called Haii a liar, and showered blows on him.

Within a week, Haii found several grey hairs in his beard. He considered both the beating, and the grey hairs, as punishment inspired by God's mighty ones because he pursued false *ilm*—gnosis—and on that very day, he decided to renounce the *ustād*, and the occult crafts, and he became a *namāzī*, one addicted to prayer.

III

On the evening following, as he was bowed in prayer, Prophet Solomon appeared and offered to kill him. Complying, as a true *namāzī* should, Haii said to the Prophet, "By all means, Hazrat Suleimān. Kill me!" On being so informed, the apparition cried out horribly and was mortified. Following that, an angel appeared, having assumed the shape of a silver star. In an absurd, childish voice, it said, "All your prayers are accepted, *barrādar* Haii. Pray no more!" As soon as Haii blessed it with a benediction—as a true muslim and *namāzī* should a *brother*, the angel *had* addressed him as his *barrādar*—the light was torn asunder, as if struck from all sides. (Obviously, a false one, no angel that, who dared to say, ". . . Pray no more!" The tradition refers to a similar exhortation addressed to an elder, a famed saint.)

Then Satan himself came. Before tempting Haii, he revealed his own history—flashed it on the wall, like a projection on a cinema screen. Satan wouldn't bow down to Adam. Said he to the unseen God, "I am of the fire. Adam is of the earth. How may those of the *superior* clay bow down to those of the *inferior*?" Following those words, a frightening thunder issued from the wall, and declared Satan a Denier and a non-Believer. But— this was the point—Satan was *not* punished by Allāh for *takbar*—pride—and his disobedience and argument: instead, in the scene that followed, he was seen in a breathtaking regalia of flames of fulgent gold, enthroned as the high lord of his own dazzling domain, with a beard of fire. "Name anything, dear 'Abdul, kin of Adam," the Tempter said, concluding the show on the wall, "and it shall be thine."

Haii was shaken for a moment. All his appetites and desires—for flesh, treasure and conquest—were sharpened from the long period of continence. But mindful of his vows—he told me—he reiterated his resolve to be a *namāzī*—a praying one. Thereupon, with an eerie scream (and a *Hā!*), the Devil dissipated in sparks.

Angry at his dismissal, Satan sent affliction to Haii. He caught a skin disease and itched all the time. A Christian doctor—although not of his faith—took pity on him and made him a present of some sulphur ointment. Not being able to read, Haii ate it, instead of applying it to the skin, as the label on the green jar plainly urged, and he complained of a severe stomachache for several days.

Meanwhile, a harder ordeal awaited Haii. He was no longer to be tempted by visions, but by the solid, matter-of-fact creatures. (This part of his story might not be all lies.)

IV

In the village where Haii lived, a party of minstrels arrived one morning. They were six elderly and heavily-built men with white beards, and wearing Lucknavī mull caps, and a girl—she was about nineteen—and she had on her an ankle-length petticoat, and nothing underneath: and she wore a *cholī*, showing her fair and flat belly to great advantage, and half of her young breasts were exposed by her economical use of the *cholī* cloth. Her cheeks dimpled deeply, moreover, whenever she smiled, which was often, and, all in all, she was a *prodigiously* charming some one.

The minstrels pitched their tent in the village, and announced their presence by singing songs, strange songs, of *ashiks* and *māshooks*, the wooers and the wooed, and of passion, and wanting, and of far off places, too, deserts, seas, and such, and the girl danced, to the accompaniment of the *sārangī* and the *dholak* and her own ankle-bells, holding up with the tips of her forefinger and the thumb the loose end of her veil, and she would go all a-quiver, this way and that, left and right, her face, half-hidden behind the veil, and this business went on at all hours of the day, till the men in the village began to rave about *the one*, none but *the one*, and there were strong words spoken by young men and some old, about sacrificing themselves, having their throats cut, hearts and livers hung up as butcher's meat—their manner of speaking was vehement—all for the love of *the one*. Indeed, they were all vanquished by the creature of near-nineteen, scantily concealed in her veil, her *cholī* and petticoat (with nothing underneath).

The song and dance went on for days till Haii himself could think of nothing but *the one* so filled was his heart with the gay echoes. Her voice, moreover, whenever she cared to join in— and render a *thappā*, a *thumrī* or a *ghazal*, to a lover in Kābul, Kandhār or Bandar Ibbas—he found altogether captivating, but in particular—he was partial to childlike women and the young *houri* was mightily endowed—it was the business with the veil that won him over and over again. He lingered on the roadside, oftener and longer, and enjoyed watching the girl sing and dance as one might a child at play, and, now and then, the flashing silver on her feet made him smile absent-mindedly. He had been afraid of evil visitations. He did not deem it necessary to fear a child of Adam (he told me).

V

One morning, while the six elderly men were away to the bazaar buying provisions, *the one* walked up to Haii, as he stopped by the roadside, and said to him, quite simply, "You are *the one*. To you, I have given my *all!*" And she gathered up the tips of her delicate fingers in a graceful shape—the pericarp of a flower—to indicate her *all*, and she placed the pericarp on her forehead, to signify her *kismet*, her destiny, her inescapable lot—the self-same Haii.

Face to face with these possibilities, Haii felt as if he had taken a sudden jump—off the rump of an unruly horse. He was surprised, too, to find the child of Adam look and speak like a woman—offering her *all*. Following the surprise, he was angry with her—at her *gustākhī*, her impudence—her brazen lack of shame, and in a street, in broad daylight, he a dedicated *namāzī*, a middle-aged man with greying beard—and there was, in general, an upheaval inside him, a surging forth, near enough to riding the rear end of a mutinous bull, and—as a consequence—he indulged in violent thought and phrase—he cursed in the vehement manner of his kind—not for the love of *the one*, as most men of the village had done earlier, but from anger, because he wanted to set her right from her wanton ways, even if he had to kick her and whip her to do it, and it all amounted to his being guilty of the three sovereign sins, an abomination to a true *namāzī:* egoism, anger, and pride.

Being designated *the one*, by *the one*, he was not unmindful of his arbitrary eminence as an assessor of conduct—that is egoism, surely—and the submissive girl heartened him further with guilty looks, downcast eyes, and blushing smiles, causing the winning dimples in her flushed cheeks, and—giving vent to irritation and indignation against *luchīs* and Jezebels in general, and *the one* in particular—Haii spoke in anger, indubitably, although he spoke as a guardian of morals, and as a keeper of the peace, but he spoke, too, unmistakably, as an executor of God's will to punish (and make an example of) the lewd and shameless creatures like *the one*. That, unmistakably, is *takbar*—pride.

All these dealings led Haii off the street, into the roadside tent, and astray. The six elderly and heavily-built men with white beards being away to the bazaar buying provisions, he was, indeed, *aabaad* with *the one*.

VI

No visions, or phenomena, were ever vouchsafed to Haii after his fall: fall it was, although, to reflect a mild reproach upon him, it has been said that he was *aabaad* with *the one* (that is, to relish an irony, albeit versionized, he *prospered* with *the one!*). It seems Haii no longer enjoyed the privilege of being tempted by Satan—and he was spurned, too, by the Tempter's wild and vicious clerks: the familiar ones with horn and hide, and those appearing as angels, stars, bearded minstrels and as Prophet Solomon, as well as those wearing veils, *cholī*s and petticoats (with *nothing underneath*). Praises be to Allāh, most merciful!

Gipsy Jim Brazil
to Kumari Kishino

J. Brazil
c/o Poste Restante
... London (England)

Dear Kishino,
No co-inside-ence (I split 'em in syllables!) that I got you as a pen pal, pal. I tell the Tarots myself but Sis is the tops. She told me good that Queen Fortune's a smiler on me from an old, old country. Gipsy luck! says the Romany, yours truly Jim, when I get a real Injun gel for a pen pal, Kishino Jhangiani, Bandra-side, Bombay! from the land of the pretties, the rag head (turbans, to you), sari for seat covers (seen 'em on the telly!) and holy bilge water! yuk! yuk! and her interest, arts, *musica!* Well, here goes.

ART LARK IN FLORENCE
In Florence, Kishino, where the kid had gotten himself an art scholarship, I really got seeing things. Boy, what a bash this city had had at the art lark!

In the year 1280, in Florence, the kid informed me, it is like you and me. Nothing doing in the art line. Then a *signore,* the name of Giotto, gets going. *Whew!*

He's following a painter, the name of *Fra.* The kid showed me this Angelico's work. This *Fra,* he paints his reds, and he paints his *pales,* and he's doing it all the time. In the 13th century, Kishino gel, this *illustrissimo signor* is mixing his own paints! He's manufacturing the stuff, solo, as good as the machine-mixed! How's he *doing* it! Makes your head go ga, ga!

This *Fra*'s quality is that he's *sweet.* Raphael (another Florentine) is sober. Piero's got space. And Masaccio has none of that, but he's got *drama.* To top 'em all, Michelangelo's got it all, and he's got the *rhetorical gesture!* All kids of Florence!

Well, this Signor Michelangelo paints, or makes stone people, I am not sure, with his *rhetorical gesture.* He's mad keen on the nude male. Botticelli, another painter boy, is mad keen on the nude female. Dressed women upset him. The kid took me along to see the Botticelli piece, *Venus.* Plenty color, and it's telling a story. Two types on the left are blowing hard at a nude female. She's standing on a fan or something, and there are two dressed females in spotted casuals on her right. In the middle, this there nude, is the *center* of the theme. She's Venus, the kid tells me, and her hair is flying, on account of the laws of perspective, because the two types are blowing at her. I cannot make out if she has feet, because there is always a crowd in front of the Botticelli, and all the Adams and Eves are taller than the Romany, luv.

Another Florentine of free dimension is Leonard. Leonard da Vinci's done everything in the science line (discovered submarine navigation, jet planes, fluorescent lighting, the rhythm method, malaria cure) and he can paint the *far-away smile.* No mother's son, Eyetalian or other, can tell what Leonard's models are smiling at! In spite of the centuries of art work, the smiles are anybody's guess. The reason for this maybe, eh, I am telling the kid—and he's listening ter me respectful like—that the *signor's scientific* before he's *artistic,* huh? But the kid adds that he's mystical as well! Don't seem human! With one hand, Kishino, he's painting his childhood sweetheart, Missy Gioconda, and with the other, Len's writing textbooks on friction, motion, how to mine the enemy, in *addition* to what I told yer above. Between him and the *rhetorical gesture signor,* they've got it all!

Then as sure as he's a son of a true Romany, the kid showed me the sculpture. I see the St. George lark by Donna Telli. *Slim!* Well, they've nothing on this Donna. She's got it too. She's sharing the *mass* with Giorgiono, I'm informed, and a brushman by the name of Titian. Yes, Kishino, Mrs Telli's got it too. Finally, I am acquainted with Tintoretto, Jocopo Robusti. He's a former resident of near-Broque, now a near-Florentine, but a real Robusti! The Eyetalian calls him *Little Dyer,* on account of his being a little dyer. Well, this dyer can paint shadow like anything! He's throwing light about, on his model's knees, does the diagonal perspective, like you never saw! It's amazen'.

Florence got it all. In the art lark, she's leading the world. Well worth the *lire* and *centissimi* to go and see her. Ssmashin'.

Overheard by Jim B.:
Dowager: "Florence!"
Domestic: "Yes, mum. Coming!"

Ciao,
Your pal, Jim Brazil

Papaji,
You sacrificed too much, daddy, to send me to college. After two years studying English language, I do not understand what he writes. Would I lie to my own father, papaji?

I took his letter to a big professor of Fine Arts. He gave me a note for you. I do not understand what he has written now.

Note No. 1: This fellow Brazil strikes me as a scoundrel and so-and-so. No culture, obviously. To dub Donatello, one of the most honored names in European art, a signora, a Mrs Telli! It is a wonder that the fellow has not referred to a Frau Angelico!

"Viva l'Italia!" say I. *"Italia, Italia, O tu cui die la Sorte Donatello!"*

I took this to our Latin professor to understand as I don't know what Fine Arts professor says. He only wrote: *Note No. 2: Appending the name Donatello to the quotation, "Italy, O Italy, thou who hast . . ." is a liberty, surely?*

Papaji, do not be angry. Why is he writing like this to my little sister Kishino?

Your elder daughter, Gagi Jhangiani

J. Brazil
c/o Poste Restante
. . . London (England)

Dear Kishino,

I was thinking of Indio, the old, old country, Shalimar, and the pale hands I love, the Taj Mahal, and Shiva! Change yer name, wouldya? Fall for the old line, "Mrs. Jim Brazil," eh, Jhangiani? Boost up the footloose Romany ambassador-at-large to quit his Britannic Niblet and the Dowager, abandon job as a wage-earning lackey, and live off Hindoostan?

Here's something on music, meantime, gel.

MUSIC IS MELOS

It's melos, *viz.*, melody. And every mother's son, and every doll of Eve is born tuned: she's either soprano, or alto: he's tenor (*Figaro! Figaro! Fee-garo!*) or bass. And all musical expression, he's telling me, is sonata (played) or cantata (sung). As to the note: it's either sharp, or flat. The Hindu music, the kid says, differs in the tonal regard. The addition to the players of the monkey, *viz.*, the conductor, is another regard where the Christian music differs from the curry.

In the Christian music, the function of the monkey is to flog the members of the orchestra. ("Not in public, guv! Please, guv!") He *excites* 'em. To *excite* 'em, the monkey uses a *baton.* It is with the *baton,* pal, that he obtains the widest results: from the plain soothing narcotic to kicks, ahem, *ad posteria (et cetera).*

Now, the prime function of the monkey, the kid tells me, used to be to set Tempo. But on the 10th day of April, the year 1820, a monkey by the name of Spohr turned Protestant. For the first time in the history of Musick ("Fateful day! O the fateful day!"), instead of a stick, he uses a *baton*. Since then, monkeys—Toscaninis to Ragtime Gershwins—use the *baton*. Some use it, just: and some—like M. Julliens—use it in style. Julliens conducts Beethoven with a jeweled baton, served him on a silver salver, and he uses white gloves, exclusive like, for the Beethoven jobs. Pending the appearance of a future Protestant, a Spohr, who might use a laser equipment or a loaded pistol, the *baton* remains the all-in-all *regola d' arte* of the monkeys present and the monkeys past.

A monkey depends for his livelihood on the composer, Kishino. If the composer does not compose, the monkey is flung out in the street. He's outa job. Now a composer is an artist. The composer is genuine. To make art, the composer must live dangerously. He's got to borrow, sleep odd, love 'em, and leave 'em, and bash 'em, like a true Romany, 'cos he's *temperamental*, and he's got to have *force*. As a primo artist, he *dictates* to monkeys.

For his *8th*, Mahler *dictates* that 1,000 instrumentalists play his symphony. Under pain of starvation, a monkey must submit. If Mahler's *8th* is played in a concert hall, with a seating capacity of 900, the public must remain outside and 100 members of the orchestra must play standing outside the hall. Asked by an art historian, "Why, this is the absolute *negation* of art, old man! The *masses* old man!"—a certain monkey, with some heat replied, "The masses, old man? The masses can Marx-well go to *asterisk!* This is the *8th!*"

In the dictating line, Bach (pronounced *Buck*, and *h*, as in Bukkhoo Oil Fields), *d*. 1750, is a *force*. Himself the father of twenty, the kid informs me, he had three musical grandfathers, viz., the late Germans Schein, Scheid, and Schutz. To the three of 'em he owed as much as he *could* owe. Another force is G.F. Handel. ("Mind how you handle, you bashing Romany!") This G.F. Handel is *wunderschon* and a *herrlich force*, with Schinkenbrot, very tasty, very sweet. In contrast, as *chic*, is Rimsky-Korsakov. (*Le Coq:* "Chick's *coq*"—get it?) He's *quasi-barbaric* (no offense). In the same line is Comrade Boris Goodenough, with his sonata *Glinka und Ludmilla.* These *forces,* Kishino, gel, form the *sturm und drang* of the Christian music. It reaches the fartherest point *away* from the curry and rice—and the far Eastern, Nippon and the like—in such *pieces d'occasion* as Bizet's *Le Lizy Ann,* Showpan's Polish pianism and the Blue Danube Magyar music of Paprika Liszt. The *echt Deutsch* Beethoven remains *kolossal.* Only when he's behind paying his rent—April it is, like it is today, and I am thinkin' orf yer, Kishino, and the old curry country, Bandraside, Bombay—April, the year 1802, that he puts the mute on the pastoral stuff and his music becomes suffering—on account of his losing his voice and going mute. In contrast to this *force,* Gioacchino Rossini, a monkey himself ("Guillaume, tell! Guillaume, tell! Otherwise, I'll bashya!") is vocal, a true Eyetalian, and he's done the *Saviglia* barber, *Maometto Secondo,* and *La foi! Ma foi!*

> *Overheard by Jim B.:*
> His Nibs: "This isn't cricket, James!"
> Lackey: "Mayhap, it is football?"

> Yours (musically, m'yes),
> Jim Brazil

Papaji,

I showed this to our Librarian. She is herself English. She has written like this. *Note No. 3: I could not find any reference in the umpteen Beethoven biographies, that at any time he lost his voice. Regarding Tempo, the only reference we have is from a book published in 1707, London, and it is as follows: "The Master of Musick in the Opera in Paris had an elbow chair and Desk plac'd on the Stage, where, with the Score in hand, and a Stick in the other, he beat Time, on the Table, put there for the purpose. He made noise greater than the whole Band, on purpose, to be heard by the Performers."*

J. Brazil
c/o Poste Restante
. . . London (England)

Dear Kishino,
Here's a bit more on the *musique!*

THE EXCESSIVE BACH

Who was Parsifal, I asked him.

An old man—replies he—says to his parrot, "They are trying to take you away from me, Percy boy! I'll fight 'em, Percy boy!"

Not Percy, says I. *Parsifal!* Wagner's *Parsifal!* Wagner wrote *Parsifal* and there are today in Germany at least a thousand art historians, I reckon, son, who would give their right arm to know why this Herr Wagner shifted over to Bayreuth, in the Lebanon, Middle East, instead of making music in his native Germany!

Thereupon the kid gets red under the collar, and hopping mad, and sweating something awful, yells words at me. *You crazy S.O.B.!*, and more in that line, *you blank, blank son of a Romany! et cetera*, Kishino, and concludes, ". . . Bayreuth *is* in Germany! That Lebanon place is Beirut, on the Eastern Mediterranean!"

O.K., O.K., kid, I said. German people have an ear for music, like you said. So Bayreuth's in Germany, *O.K.!*

People matter, he says, cooling. In music, especially, a lot depends on the *sensitivity* of people.

What the Oriental, the curry-and-rice man does to music, the kid continues, enlarging, is in the line of the *chant*. He worries a coupla words, for their *euphonic* value (it was my kid who said that!), *sāre-ga-ma-pa-dha-nee-sā!* and climbs down to *sā-re-* . . . and so on.

The chant (above), when developed, becomes folk music, the *euphonic hooza! hooza!* The ultimate basis of all such music is *hooza! hooza!* (Do you understand this, Kishino? I don't and I was afraid of interrupting the kid from fear of exciting him, as he often is, excited, like a lotta cats at a mouse show.)

After the *hooza! hooza!* stage, Kishino, gel, the *chant* becomes song. Take, for example, Comrade Egmont, no, Borodin. Aleksandr Porfirevich Borodin, professor of chemistry, the kid's telling me. He's written *Prince Igor.*

Now, all *song's* self-expression. That's the kid's theory. All *song*-making's autobiography. Unless a musician is stealing another musician's life-story, he's writing up his own life-story. That's the kid's theory.

Accordingly, what's the autobiographical significance in the very choice of the title *Igor* by the said Prof. Borodin? *He* doesn't know, *you* don't know, *I* don't know! *Nobody* knows! (the kid's insisting).

Maybe, I says, the professor was living as a research nomad in Central Asia one time. As a nomad, kido, listen ter me, maybe he kept a donkey; maybe a donkey the name of *Fidor.* As one Central Asian nomad to another Central Asian nomad, maybe this *Fidor* would speak to the nomad Borodin? Maybe in this wise . . . *Hee-ho! Hee-o!* and, therefrom, *Ego! Ee-go!* and finally *I-gor,* mm?

From the stage *song,* the kid continues, ignoring my ideo, music leads to *orchestration.* And *orchestration* leads up to Ludwig van Beethoven. Van Beethoven, in his symphonies, introduces—the kid expands it—woodwinds, horns, trumpets, timpani, the piccolo, the contra-bassoon!

It's terrific, the kid says.

When van Beethoven *orchestration* is fully established, violins guffaw, tubas answer back, contra-bassoons mutter *fortissimo*—wait, kid, I say, till I get this down—joking with timpani, *giggle, giggle, giggle!* from nowhere a trumpet comes in, then an oboe affirms—affirms, objects—*nein, ja!* no, no! yes, yes! too warm, no, *kalt!* Israel in Egypt! *not* in Egypt! *is* in Egypt! basses greet one another, *he'llo! he'llo!* derision from the violins, *shh-rupp!* Fate's knocking at the door! Come in! *Kommen Sie,*

Mein Bruder, and whadyawant? Van Beethoven *am* the 8th! the 9th! *Horch! Horch! Ppst!* Hey, you! *C'est* Emperor! *C'est* Abercrombie! Emperor, and I'll bashya! Abercrombie, and I'll bashya! It's a Turk! Come in, F Major! Make merry, peasants! Ha, ha, ha! Malibran! *lieber* Malibran! Cosima van Bulow! Joy, joy, joy, and all hail! *Ein, zwei, drei!* Kisses to all, and to Herr Liberty! Herr Schiller! Der ode is *schon, und schon! und* extra *schon!* All joy, *ja, mein frau, mein* Comrade!

Whew!

That's Beethoven's *orchestration*, Kishino!

In his 9th, after he goes mute, on account of his having lost his voice, van Beethoven introduces song *mit orchestration—* "*Melisande! Melisande!*" —and this *Bund* up produces *excess* in music, and there are *effects* achieved that are unheard of in the curry *sāre-ga-ma* . . . or in *da-di-aha-da! La-di-aha-da!* and the aforementioned *hooza! hooza!* and the song, *Ego! E-go! I-gor!*

It's like your French butler, Kishino, who tiptoes to yer in the night, wakes ya, and tells ya, "There's a customer to see ya, chum, who's *satanique, irresistible,* and *terrificante!*"

Whatdyaexpect?

But it is in Bach (pronounced *Buck,* and *h,* like in Bukkho Oil Fields), *d.* 1750, also a German, that the entire Christian and the curry music is *exceeded*, done with, and evolved beyond all limits of *chant, song* and *orchestration* of van Beethoven or anybody else.

It's absolutely *Gutterdammerung*, the kid says, using strong language.

Yes Sir, a lot depends on the *sensitivity* of people.

Van Goethe says of Herr Bach, the kid's quoting and I am putting it down forya, ". . . *One seems neither to possess nor to need one's ears, still less eyes or any other sense.*"

In the night, thinking orfya, Jhangiani, and of Bandraside, Bombay—on account of a student type, on a scholarship lark, the name of T.V. Kailasam, B.A. Hons., from Madras, who plays some Indian discs ter me—I was ramping mad with van Goethe!

Is you crazy, van Goethe? *Seems* neither to possess, van Goethe? *Seems* not to *need* ears, van Goethe? How canya *hear* without ears, van Goethe? How canya *see* without eyes, van Goethe? I'm a poor Romany, what's lonely for the old, old country, and his gel, but for two pins I'll bashya, van Goethe! for committing this here bad writing, and *faux pas*, van Goethe! How canya do without *senses*, van Goethe?

> *Overheard by Jim B.:*
> His Nibs: "James, voice me the longest word in German or you are fired."
> Lackey: "Lebensmittelzuschlusseinstellungskommissionsvorsitzenderstellvertreter."

Auf Wiedersehen!
Your pal, Jim

Dear Papaji,
I am crying now. Being in a big university, I cannot help you. I am only a freshman. How can I understand this English? This is also German. Why is he writing this German?

My roommate is in India Government chancellery in Abu Dubai. She is one semester here. She is improving her German language ability. She said she will write down everything. After she went to see her German professor. She has written this. *Note No. 4: I greeted him politely ("Herr Doktor!") and although his manners are always impeachable, even kissing hands, and he did not seem quite himself and wanted Mr. B.'s address so that he could write him a real stinker, I expect, if not make an example of him. He seemed particularly peeved about those bits about Beethoven and Goethe.*

As we were getting nowhere, I said I must go ("Ich muss gehen") and rather sardonically (as P.G. Wodehouse would have put it) he said that I was to give you his love ("Gruessen Sie Fräulein Gagi"), and he added, "Rufen Sie einen Schutzmann und einen Krankenwagen!" (*"Send for a policeman and an ambulance!"*) *and he asked his bearer for* Das Eis *(ice)*.

Papaji, you sacrificed so much for me. I am not able to repay. Why is he writing like this? What is the matter?

Your eldest daughter,
Gagi Jhangiani

J. Brazil
c/o Poste Restante
. . . London (England)

Dear Kishino,
How's about penning a line to a pal, pal?

THE MYSTIQUE OF WASSERS

The kid and I were traversing towards Bonn, Germany, in the tin wagon hitched to His Nibs' ottomobile. Thence onwards to Cologne!

Cologne has the *largest* Gothic cathedral in Northern Europe, the kid informs me.

Who has the *smallest* Gothic cathedral in Northern Europe? Search me, he says.

This city is the original maker of the *Kolnisch Wasser;* the *eau* (French) of Cologne. Situated in the Rhein-Provinz, it is on the Rhine, the *echt Deutsches Wasser* (water, to you!) *par excellence!*

Here the kid pauses and gives me a theory he has about the *Wasser* motif: a sideline he has worked (while he was doing his scholarship lark). G'wan, I am saying, after he gives me an opening, you are dead right! It's a singe! There's no human doings without *Wasser*. Life's not possible without *Wasser*. I agree, kido.

There's more in this than that, Dad, he says. I am arsking him to explain his position in full.

A Herr the kid used to know in Milano, who dealt in hay, optics, guano and petrol by-products—and he was no idealist but plain human, the kid says— used to froth in the mouth and work up a spasm at the very mention of this one particular *Wasser, pere* Rhine! (The nearest namby-pamby reaction, *jawohl,* I am saying, to a hi'cupping Hindu at the very mention of his particular *Wasser, Mater* Ganges *Wasser. Ja,* he says.)

By Bonn and Cologne, there are human doings and goings-on, and there are *Herrs* and their *Fraus,* going about on outings, *kneipen* together and they name such does *ein Familien Ausflug (a family outing* to you, Kishino).

On these *Ausflugs,* they feed on *Brotchen mit* tasty tit-bits, gel, *mit* beer and *Bowle,* the diet of Germany. The *Herrs* and the *Fraus,* they *kneipen* up, and they are great on the family ties, and they are great on their *running Wasser* (note this, luv), the river Rhine.

Arising in Switzerland, the cheese and watch country, this particular *running Wasser,* the Rhine, passes on, touching a place called *Chur* ("*Cher* Monsieur Brazilie, as *vous is late paying the blushing rent, vous* is kicked out!"). It is joined, among others, by a *running Wasser* called (*sic*) *Worms.* ("Worms? What worms? Is you crazy or somepin, Romany?") reaching a hole called the *Zee* (Dutch): the sea of North (*Noord,* in Dutch).

This family-ties feeling—here the kid gives away his theory in full— has something to do with *running Wasser!* Unless a *Wasser* is *running,* there is no *movement,* he asserts, *there is an absence of this family-ties feeling, the get-together, the cosy kneipen ups.*

That's the kid's theory in full, Kishino. Stands to reason. Wouldya go and picnic by a quiescent puddle? I agree with the kid and am willin' to shake hands on it.

Referring to the Zee (Dutch *Wasser*) above, and to the Dutchmen in general, I notice that they are polite in these Netherland *dams:* Amster, Rotter. Always they call a waiter *her ober* (Mr Up). Always *her ober:* never *his,* yuk! yuk!

Van, in Dutch, he tells me, means *from*. And when a Dutch mine hair announced himself at the youth hostel as *Van Doom*, the kid was in no two minds about it, and decided to shift from these *Nether*lands. (Van Doom's first name was Lodewijk: The kid pronounced it as *Load* [heavy *load*] and *wijk* as *wi-Ike* [like "I like Ike!"]. He said that is the correct Dutch naming-the-names pronunciation, Kishino.

We took a ship and crossed the Zee. Abroad, the kid showed me an ideo he had worked out for the final act of an opera he's writing. It goes like this, Kishino, luv:

Street scene: night. On the stage is seen a cottage. Light is seen at the winder of the cottage. There is seen, at the winder, a *mine hair* playing at a piece of string and a yoyo. He is Mr. *Izzy*, the famous Dutch old-timer. As much of him as is seen through the winder shows he's wearing the Frisian costume.) Another *mine hair* approaches the cottage door. He is carrying a watch—the size of an omnibus tyre. He wants *Izzy*, the famous Dutch old-timer, to mend it. It don't tick no more. (It is a cardboard watch with the figures and hands painted on't.)

He unloads the watch—he acts the stage business, wipes his forehead, *etc.*, from exertion. The watch is now leaning against the wall of the cottage.

Mine hair approaches the door of the cottage and delivers a helloa Othello, the Moor, *Knock! Knock! Knock!* triple kick upon it. He means to call upon *Izzy* to open up, somepin dire and urgent, and take delivery of the watch pronto. *Izzy* takes no notice. He is seen at the winder, playing at the piece of string, and a yoyo. *Knock! Knock! Knock!* is repeated.

The door is opened. A hefty *M'frau*, the name of *Lizzy*— daughter of *Izzy*—is at the door. She's *furious!*

The monkey strikes up the band and *mine hair* sings:
Mine hair (pleading):
Izzy! Izzy!
Izzy! Izzy!

M'frau is *furious*! She mocks *mine hair*. She stands akimbo, her hands are shaped as fists, legs astride, a challenging, menacing and a monumental personality—the sheer weight of her!—and she's bent upon preventing *mine hair* from entering the cottage with his watch, and contacting *Izzy*, who's seen at the winder, playing at a piece of string and a yoyo.

M'frau Lizzy (gives out in the highest soprano range, most emotional, and her body—the heavy bosom part in particular—heaves, from great emotion, and she scorns, ridicules, and in derision, mimics *mine hair*):

Izzy!! Izzy!!

Izzy!! Izzy!!

Deeply hurt, *mine hair* clutches at his heart, and gives out a gruesome Pagliacci cry, *"Ha!"* He points at the winder, moreover, and at *Izzy*, who is playing at a piece of string, and a yoyo. He goes down on his knees and implores:

Lizzy! Lizzy! Lizzy! Lizzy!

Izzy, Izzy, Izzy, Izzy!

Lizzy answers (most energetic):

Izzy's busy! Busy's *Izzy!*

Busy, busy! *Izzy, Izzy!*

Mine hair (astounded, says in faltering prose):

What?

Sings (the interrogation):

Izzy busy?

He points at *Izzy*, and at the winder, and pleads somethin' pathetic:

Lizzy, Lizzy!

Lizzy, Lizzy!

There is no resolution of the conflict and they duet their respective lines, and a basso profundo joins 'em. It's *Izzy* and he adds a throaty death march slow, *"Lizzy! Lizzy!"*

Meanwhile, light continues to be seen at the winder, and *Izzy's* seen playing at a piece of string, and a yoyo. As a climax, neon lights go on, and a sign shines upon the cottage, reading in the winking multicolored neons, *Monte de pieta* which is Eyetalian for a pawnshop, the Uncle's, the Shaver's establishment, thereby showing an avant-garde pathos-symbolism. This is further heightened by the appearance on the stage of an *alligator,* who is run amuck, at the sight of which, *Lizzy* and *mine hair* register emotion and have a hair-breadth escape. *Izzy,* still playing the yoyo, but espying the *alligator,* senses the danger and breaks out of the winder and flees through a porthole followed immediately by the reptile who, further roused by *Izzy's* bolt, advances upon the porthole, his tail lashing.

Orchestral sound effect: brakes being applied to a dozen speedsters, to avoid a frightful accident on the track.

Fizz.

(Curtain.)

The kid insists, Kishino, that he wants *real* talent to play his opera, as all the *pleading, beseeching* and *protest,* is to be communicated with mine hair's *"Izzy, Izzy!"* and all the *mocking, obstinacy, obstruction, challenge,* by Lizzy's *"Izzy's busy!"* and finally, he's dead keen on having an actor of wide-world repute to act the non-challant (syllables, gel!), yoyo-playing Izzy, who does not act or sing, except for the last bit of the song and the escape through the porthole, but who is—the kid says—the very *life* of his piece, as he represents the universal forces that oppose, overpower and obstruct mankind.

I could only think of an Australian bird called Joan Sutherland and a lime-juicer the name of Peter Pears (who's no mean tonsil-exerciser, and I said so). The kid assured me that he would think it over, after he has heard 'em on the discs, but Izzy's was the most tricky casting. He wanted a real footlighter. That kid o'mine has a *future!* I have faith in him, Kishino. You should get to know each other, gel.

Overheard by Jim B.:

His Nibs: *"Ist Bonn am Rhein, bitte?"*

Lackey: *"Ja!"*

Aloha! *Lebewohl!*

Jim Brazil

Papaji—daddy,

One more letter from him! Is there any protection for us, papaji? Why not India democratic government do something about this? He is writing to an Indian Hindu girl like this! All we can do is to cry like this? Does he think we are nobody? The librarian has written angrily. She has written he is monstrous. *Note No. 5*, from the librarian. *Ever since my convent school days, I have known some filthy spellers, but this man is the limit!*

The Dutch form of address for a gentleman is Mijnheer, *not "mine hair".*

It is true Rimsky-Korsakov wrote or sired Le Coq d'Or. Coq, *French for cockrel, and* d'or *golden. The composer is referred to as* chic *and later on alluded to as* chick (en), *from Coq, rooster.* This is outrageous!

Boris Godunov *not Goodenough. He has put down* L'Arlesienne *(Bizet, 1842–1912) as Le Lizzy Ann, and Showpan is revolting (for Chopin, 1810–1886).* Paprika Liszt *(1811–1886) is so rude. Nowhere could I find a reference to "Kommen Sie, mein Bruder," a phrase occurring in his Beethoven para. It means, "Come in, my brother." "Former resident of near-Broque" is monstrous, obviously.*

J. Brazil
c/o Poste Restante
. . . London (England)

Dear Kishino,

I have written a malodorous missive to the postmaster, Bandraside, for not delivering your mail. Why no reply, luv? How areya? His nibs has won a cricket match. I said I was going to write an essay (as they say) for you on *The Psycho-Greek in Greece.* He gave me a day off and said nice-like, "Enjoy yourself, James."

THE PSYCHO-GREEK IN GREECE

The Hindu god Indra, the kid informs me, enlarging my savvy, is the same rain-maker Thunderer Zeus, the Greek, the sky-father, and he's complementary to the Greek goddess of corn, one corny Persephone d'Meter (and the kid wasn't tarking about no gas meter, but *the* Meter) who, in the Greek myth, is kidnapped by a character named Pluto (Disney, excuse). And this rape of Persephone d'Meter, the kid continues, being the national myth as well as the *psychosis* of the early Greeks, is the answer to all the *mystery* of Greece.

In Greece are the fauns, the satyrs, and *selene* (the moon)— and in pre-Christian times, the Greek was organizing phallic processions, to which the Greek dominions and colonies contributed representative phalli galore—same as ambassadors, high commissioners and Congressmen who join processions—and all this *mystery,* me boy's informing me, the Greek's organizing on account of this Persephone d'Meter *versus* Pluto lark. And it is the same lark that's at the bottom of the murals the Greek's done, all on account of an amour, betwix' a Greek boy, the name of Dionysus, and his chum one Aphrodite, the Greek.

It is impossible, insists the kid, to fathom the Greek unless you understand this group *psychosis*—Persephone d'Meter taken by one Pluto, Accused/Respondent—and which is responsible for a vandalism, the like of which even the Hun and Tartar-haunted world never knew.

Listen ter me. In the ancient times, the Greek went in for *mysteries*—the symbols and the ritual of which to this minute defy solution. In pre-Christian times, the Greek elite set itself up as Brahmins, experts in all devices of purification, a kinda living human Soaps (and head-and-hat-check boys). And it was this Brahman Greek class who went about putting the fear of this Pluto character into the lay Greek. The class recruited 'em—the lay Greek— initiated 'em by a soak in a river, flogged the females (take a tram to Pompeii murals, Kishino, gel, and see), called 'em *mystai,* till they (the *mystai*) were raised, and lost the

delusion of separate individuality ('ark at the Romany!), and till
every Greek undergoing the *mystai* ritual was *re*-born. ("Back to
life, ye Greeks! The Egypto-Asian immortality is yours, ye
Greeks! Arise, O Greeks!")

It is from such beginnings, Kishino, that the Greek starts
and goes for art, like a true Greek, with his potter's cup; and the
first cup, luv, he's insisting prettily, is molded on Helen's breast.
(Yuk! Yuk! You don't psychoanalyze your Greek. He psycho-
analyzes himself!) Well, from this molded cup the Greek works
up to sculpture, and he conditions his sculpture by rigid rules.
Those rules make his sculpture as no other sculpture on earth,
and he does a *perfect* job of everything he sculptures, the kid
says.

Now, gel, having made *perfect* sculpture, the Greek is up
against his national group *psychosis*—Persephone taken by Pluto
lark, remember—and it is on account of this (the kid's absolutely
final about it) that he *(subconsciously) imposes upon himself the
ultra of ultra super-Greek rule:* a vandalism, the like of which
even the Hun and Tartar-haunted world never knew! Kishino, O
Kishino, he *(subconsciously) bashes* up his own art!

When the kid's viewing Greek architecture, and sculpture,
in Greece, and in the museums, on account of his scholarship,
like I toldya, he's *astounded* to observe that the Greek first makes
perfect jobs, all accordin' to the rules, and then he *bashes* 'em up!

So much so, that in every available specimen seen by him
of Greek architecture and sculpture going, there were left only
pillars, and columns, and broken noses galore, arms, legs, feet,
and the fig-leaves over the phalli and the phalli themselves missing ("Autumn is here again! Fig-leaves are falling!"), stone
grapes smashed up, wings of figures and the shaggy Greek hair
done with, *bashing! bashing!* so much so, Kishino, that—the kid
says—to restore Greek art would make the word *restoration* stink
to high heaven, and become the most potent art-hate in the capi-
tals of Europe, Asia, the Americas!

Consider, gel, before you consider the case for restoration,
the Greek sculpture *Young Hermes*—the Roman *copy* of which,
too, is *bashed* up! No legs, no arms, and the skull missing!

Regard, Jhangiani, before you regard the pleas to the world for
Greek art restoration, the figure *Aphrodite of Cyrene.* Arms missing! First, the Greek makes her *perfect,* accordin' to the rules—
she is rising from the sea, two waves that had hugged her fondly,
tenderly, have rested and are sculptured pretty, she is wringing
her hair and the drops of brine are seen in relief,—and then, *yi!*
yi! yi! the Greek picks up the hammer and, true to his d'Meter
group *psychosis* lark, he goes over his Aphrodite and, like a true
Romany, he *bashes* her up!

> *Overheard by Jim B.:*
> His Nibs (looking down on the missive before I mail it terya):
> "This is Greek to me, Jim!"
> Your pal: "It isn't to a Greek, suh!"
> His Nibs: "Eh, suh?"
> Her Ladyship (disturbed in repose): "Be Quiet!"

Salaam 'aleikum!
Your pal, Jim

For Papaji, from own daughter Gagi,
Note No. 6. My own psychology professor has read this
essay and he told me before giving an opinion, he would *"definitely like to know something more about the 'kid' mentioned in
these pages."*
Do you know who he is?

Gagi

J. Brazil
c/o Poste Restante
. . . London (England)

Dear Kishino,
His Nibs and her Ladyship let me and the kid have tickets
for the opera *Carmen,* done by one Gorgeous Bizet (*t* is silent
on account of Gorgeous being French).

CARMEN AND THE LAD ESCAMILLO

In the First Act which the kid and I are viewing from the pigeon perch, the gallery, Gorgeous shows some skill. The scene's a square in Spain. Guardsmen are standing to the left, a bridge is seen in the background, and there is a cig factory. (*"Yessirrie, Dad!"* I says to the castor-oil artist, the em dee, "I roll 'em and smoke 'em! *Look, no cancer!"*) There is taking place the changing of the guard and in spite of the labor laws—the kid whispers to me—Bizet (*t* is silent) exploits child labor and brings below-the-age French kids on the stage to do a mock changing of the guard: *ta, ta, ta, ta, taa! ta, ta, ta, ta, taa!*

Whilst this's happening, the decent gel of the opera (one Micaela) has a palaver song with one Corporal Morales. (Actually, she is looking for another Corporal, one Don José, the chief character. But I may have lost the thread at this juncture on account of the kid jawing too much information to me.) Whilst the palaver is on, a gay crowd is moving on the stage. *Enter* Captain Zuniga, followed by the chief character, Corporal José, and the dragoons. The guard's changed.

The factory bell goes and the cig gels (*les impudentes*) are on the stage singing and they compare the smoke from a cig (fickle!) to the vows of lovers (fickle!). Meantime, the gay crowd (it is the boys) join 'em with Carmen! Carmen! What about Carmen! Is she fickle, too?

It is at this juncture that the saucy cig girl Carmen enters. Men arsk her when will she love 'em? She responds to 'em in the mezzo-soprano, gives 'em the *Habanera,* and states, Will I love? Maybe yes, mm' yes! Maybe, no! Maybe, tomorrer! Who knows! (She's kinda indefinite, the kid says, concluding.)

Whilst she's rendering it, Corporal Don José, the chief character, is engaged in the stage business of mending a chain. At that juncture, Kishino, in spite of her sentiments, stated above, she tosses an *ersatz* flower at the boy. He takes no notice. Meanwhile, the good gel (the said Micaela) approaches. José takes notice. He duets with her. The decent gel gives him news of his Mom. She's brought a kiss for the Corporal (from his Mom). She delivers it on his forehead. Touchin'. Real touchin', and I go over the burnsides with a modicum of brilliantine from my pocket in memory on my own Matron. (Duchess loved my young side-burns and her glass of beer and stale cake, luv.)

Then drama happens with some *tempo*. There's a fight in the factory! They've struck! Zuniga orders Carmen's arrest! The Corporal (the same as was kissed on the forehead by the decent girl) is inviting Carmen to be seated (so as he might tie up her wrists!). Carmen, at that juncture, sings the *Siguidilla*, signifying I know an *officier*, who's neither a *captain*, nor a *lieutenant* (all in French, luv) but a *Corporal*!

Stop it, José begs. She don't. Meanwhile, Zuniga returns. Orders, orders! Prisoner, march! Carmen marches, renders a line from the *Habanera*, marches up to the bridge, shoves the Corpo-ral, walks away *free*, on account of the Corporal *never having tied up her wrists*!

Consequently, the Corporal surrenders to Captain Zuniga. "I've done it, *mon Capitain!*"

Now the monkey strikes up Don José's song, Bizet's No. 10. The scene's changed. It's Lillias Pastia's inn. Carmen and her friends (one Frasquita and one Mercedes), and *mon Capitain* Zuniga are there (seated). Zuniga informs Carmen that her Cor-poral's free. "*Oke. Bon soir,*" she says to him, in French. Mean-while, a lad by the name of Escamillo is arriving at the inn. (He's a heavily-built runt, and I am noticing this, he has his sideburns rounded at the end like mutton shops, and the ivy's flashing good from liberal touches of tallow and Vaseline.) As he approaches, the monkey gives, in a vast tempo, *To-re-a-dor! To-re-a-dor!*

The runt's singing about bullfights and black eyes. He's struck on Carmen. He approaches her. He's repulsed.

He leaves. (On account of having been repulsed.) Carmen's waiting for her Corporal. With her are two Romany smuggler types, El Romedado and El Dancairo. (That might be El Rama-dan, Romany, and O 'ell! the Dan of Cairo, another Romany, and Bizet's abusing the Romany race, I'm thinkin'.) The two types proposition a smuggling deal to Carmen. She declines, "Cos why?", they arsk. "Cos I'm in love!" she replies.

Meanwhile, her Corporal—on account of whom she won't smuggle—arrives at the inn. She's happy. Accompanying herself on castanets, she dances for him Bizet's No. 11, *La-la-laa! La-la-laa-la!*

Whilst he's appreciating this *La-la-laa-la!* and the castanets, the Retreat's sounded. Hell, he *must* go! A soldier's dooty!

Carmen insists. Stay, *mon ami* (she insists). What's the hurry? She sauces up her persuasion with more tempo, *La-la-laa-la! La-la-la-la!* Cissy, you! (She derides the Corporal.) Meantime, the bugle continues to sound the Retreat. He *must* go! The Corporal's set to *go!* Before moving, however, he produces from his pocket the *ersatz* flower she gave him in the First Act. She's softened and says to him (in French), "Oke, cherry. If you love me, come with me to the Alps." (She wants him to desert the parly-voo outfit and do his bit with the Romany band—the Arabmen I mentioned, Kishino—and smuggle the *verboten*.) While the Corporal's chewed up between dooty and the Alps, *mon Capitain* Zuniga arrives. He *orders* the Corporal to do the double and march auht of it! You heard! It's the Retreat! 'Op it! *Marche, soldat!*

The Corporal don't obey. There's a fight. El Ramadan and Dan of Cairo persuade the Captain to disarm. (Two loaded pistols do the persuading.) The Captain quits, sayin' he finds 'em *irresistible*. (The cultured section of the audience larfs at this wit.) The Act ends with a chorus to Liberty, and *La-la-laa-la! La-la-laa-la!*

Curtain's up. It's the Alps and an unspecified frontier. José, the Corporal, is present (on account of his having beached and joined Carmen). He's singing of his Mom, something pathetic. Carmen tells him, Why don't ya go to yer mama and cook yourself? *Cissy! Cissy!*

At them awful words, the Corporal warns her, "*Vous* better not say that again!" "Kill me, wouldya?" she arsks. "It don't matter," she says. "It's destiny!" (She adds it in the *moderato*.)

Whilst she's giving it to him, her pals Frasquita and Mercedes lay out the cards, same as me and Sis, and examine *their* perishing destiny. In the meanwhile, Carmen continues to sing, and she's singing Bizet's No. 13, where Bizet (*t* is silent) states the futility of avoiding death.

Dan of Cairo interrupts the singing. He arsks them to get going with the contraband. Right at that *moment,* Kishino, the decent gel (Micaela) arrives. She sings. Right at that *very* moment, moreover, there's a hellova shot. The decent gel takes fright, stops singing, and hides.

Actualla, it's the boy José, aforesaid, the chief character. He fired the shot at a stranger, who's no stranger, 'cos he's the lad Escamillo (*To-re-a-dor! To-re-a-dor!*) what was repulsed earlier. He's come, obvious, looking for Carmen. The Corporal and the lad Escamillo start fighting.

Carmen approaches. She—and the two Romany Arabmen—intervene. It's a draw. The lad leaves, singing (in French), "Anyone who loves me may see me at the next bullfight in Seville!" (He throws a glance at Carmen while rendering *anyone* and *who loves.*)

At that Juncture, Kishino, the good gel comes out of hiding and there's an exchange betwix' her and Corporal José mainly about his Maw. The decent gel does the persuading. José decides to go straight, leave Carmen and the Arabmen, and the decent gel's willing to take him back. (The cultured section of the audience applauds this Act).

The last Act of Bizet (*t* is silent). It's a bullfight in Seville. A girl's selling oranges on the stage: *Program! Cigs! Chocolate! Gum! Brassiere!*

There's a grand procession for the lad Escamillo. He's arrived. Carmen's there too. (*"Anyone" "Who loves."*) They duet together. The lad communicates to her that this is *it!* She agrees. It's real *love.* He bids her a temporary adiós. (He leaves her to bear the bull, like the kid says.)

At that juncture, the Corporal arrives. He hasn't shaved or anything and the face foliage's visible from the gallery, where the kid and I are seated, luv. (His Nibs and the Dowager are below, sharing a box with Sir and Lady Bimshaw Stinkers Kt. *et cetera.*) "Come, cherry," he invites her in French. Carmen tells him it's all over. It's destiny. José insists.

She scorns his appeal. Meanwhile, the Spanish boys off stage are yelling, *"Viva Escamillo!"* Carmen's anxious to leave the Corporal and join 'em in cheering the lad. The Corporal arrests her movement. "Do you love the lad?" he demands. *"Oui,"* she says, in French.

The Corporal warns her. She gives it to him proper. *Why don't ya go and have a shave, José?,* in that line of talk. It's terrific, Kishino. What's a Romany to do? The Corporal pleads some more. In response, she takes orf the ring he's given her and, somethin' cruel, tosses it away, missing the front row by inches. (The kid and I are following the ring, from the gallery, with our eyes a-popping.) Whilst the Corporal watches the ring roll, the Spanish boys off stage continue to yell *Viva! Viva!* for the lad. That's too much for the Corporal. Then to make the stated situation worse, the monkey takes it outa him by bashing it away with *To-re-a-dor! To-re-a-dor!* (also in honor of the lad).

Jose can't stand it, and the Romany can't stand it! Why don'tya bash her, Corporal? She's beetya, cookedya, and done-ya! Let her have it, Corporal! Atta boy, chief character José!

It's terrific, Kishino. I'm enjoying every minute of the Act. I'm all worked up, and what with the sizable singing by the lad, and the *Viva* boys earning good money off the stage, and the *La-la-laa-la! La-la-laa-la!* from Carmen, and the castanets all a-rattle, it's too much for the Corporal, too, I can tellya.

He's got a knife. Like a true Romany, he draws it. Carmen falls! It's *over*! It's destiny! It's *moider*! (I go over the lip muff with a modicum of brilliantine and caress the Romany-pride handle-bars.)

The monkey takes a bow.

Overheard by Jim B.:
Dowager: "Bartok Madga, give me a long word in Hungarian, other-wise take a week's notice!"

Domestic: "Yes'm. Megkaposztasitottalanitottatok."
Dowager: "Thank you, Magda."
Domestic: "Yes'm."

Schlafen Sie wohl!
Your pal

Papaji, from your own daughter Gagi,

My English language professor himself sent me to the music critic of our College magazine, also music faculty. He gave me back this last letter and told me to go see somebody or go see the Beatles for all I care. I said to him, "I did not know, sir, they were in Delhi." He shouted for no reason and said he did not say that. He then said he had better things to do than to *"flog some vagabond pronouncing upon a jewel of a French opera."* I made a note and said, "I do not understand, sir." He said he had many burdens to bear. He did not want the problems of an emancipated Indian young woman also. I got angry, Papaji. I told him my father is a widower. He has no sons. He has only two daughters. He has sacrificed too much to send me here to College. I am following my vocation. He said, "Follow it!" I then left quickly because he has no sympathy.

Pitaji, we have been insulted because this man is writing to my own innocent sister like that. You must now tell the government finally.

Gagi

To,
Shri . . .
Member of Parliament,
New Delhi.

Respected sir,

I am sending per registered post the file containing the duplicates of letters from one Shri Jim Brazil and my own university undergraduate daughter's inquiries, with professors' and librarian's notes for perusal and disposal. I reserve the right to release the same to the press if deemed necessary.

Sir, my daughter Miss (Kumari) Kishini Kiriparam Jhangiani, to whom he has written these letters, is aged five years only, and she is very fond of music and also inclined to child art. I firmly believe a mistake was made in programming the computer in New York, N.Y., to whom I had furnished her true particulars, with a fee, being anxious to contact some cosmopolitan children pen pals for her. I have written three letters to the New York mail order house responsible. But they do not reply but only quote on printed paper slip a fee for supplementary information input. I have not sent this fee as they have already made a big mistake.

I need immediately now to have this matter taken up by appropriate official authorities through the medium of your good self to stop this. We are not rich but Indian citizens from a decent family. So as to avoid international misunderstanding, I have sent this file to you, instead of writing to him direct through my lawyer and point out to him the legal consequences. All letters are postmark London. So he is an Englishman and can be an American, although gipsy.

You would not like a man like that to write to your daughter.

Yours in respect,
Kripo Hariram Jhangiani

–21–

Rudyard Kipling's Evaluation of His Own Mother

I have the privilege and high honor to deliver this evening your distinguished society's annual Rudyard Kipling Memorial lecture and thereby make—in the cordial words of your chairman—"a consequential contribution" to your society's ongoing series BARDS IMMORTAL—MASTERS EVER-ENDURING.

May the genial chairman's words prove prophetic! Many-fold! I intend to offer my contribution immediately—without delay!

> If I were hanged on the highest hill,
> Mother o' mine, O mother o' mine!
> I know whose love would follow me still,
> Mother o' mine, O mother o' mine!
>
> If I were drowned in the deepest sea,
> Mother o' mine, O mother o' mine!
> I know whose tears would come down to me,
> Mother o' mine, O mother o' mine!
>
> If I were damned of body and soul,
> I know whose prayers would make me whole,
> Mother o' mine, O mother o' mine!
>
>> Rudyard Kipling

Kipling's proposition is obvious, chairman. He says *if* he were hanged, drowned and damned, *then* (*a*) his mother's love would follow him still, (*b*) his mother's tears would come down to him, and (*c*) his mother's prayers would make him "whole." *If* none of these disasters happened, *then*—he asserts—the above results would not follow. (To assert something is to deny something. To assert it is day is to deny that it is night. Necessarily, though obliquely.)

Let us amplify his argument, by an in-depth analysis.

First, if he were hanged (*contingency*), on the highest hill (*location*), then, he asserts, (he *knows,* he says), love would follow him still. Now, as for the *location,* Kipling, quite clearly, refers to the top of Mt. Everest in Tibet. (The highest hill can be read as the highest mountain—a minor point.)

Now this combination, of the event and the location—being hanged upon Mt. Everest in Tibet—envisages a human agent other than Rudyard Kipling: to wit, a hangman. Because of this all-important factor, we *must* consult the law of probability. The suggestion that a court of a civilized country would condemn a man to be hanged, on the peak of Mt. Everest in Tibet—only recently reached by Sir Edmund Hillary and Sri Tenzing Norgay—and provide, be it noted, at the same time a hangman, with the gear, to carry out the sentence, so that the victim's mother's love could follow him still—he does not predict her physical presence at the hanging but merely the continuous flowing up to him of an emanation of hers, to wit, her love—is, though not an impossibility, an improbability. (By asserting improbables, Kipling falsifies. Yet, one is bound to grant, that since his proposition is not experimentally verifiable, it cannot be proved false. Still, his very foci make his utterance predictably erosive though viable.)

Secondly—let us state the problem—if he were drowned (*contingency*), in the deepest sea (*location*), then he asserts (nay, he says he *knows*), tears would come down to him. He means, obviously, one of the submarine troughs of the Pacific Ocean—the West Pacific—most likely the Mariana Trench, enjoying the measured depth of more than 32,000 feet. (The deepest *sea* can be read as the deepest *ocean*—a minor point.) Now, Mt. Everest in Tibet, allowing for minor adjustments in its height of 29,002 feet, say the experts, could be sunk whole into the Mariana Trench. If Kipling were drowned in the trough, he asserts, then his mother's tears would go down to him.

We can accept this prophecy only if we assign an extra, a supra-physical quality to Mrs Kipling's tears. If her tears were composed of an element so far unknown to man, they might, even in the deepest sea, retain their extra, supra-physical quality, and yet *be identified as tears,* the characteristic physiological and aqueous humour of man.

Let us analogize. If we were to empty an ash tray containing a quarter of a grain of cigarette ash into the sea—any sea—we may assume that the sea would not, thereby, be modified to any *measurable* degree. Whatever might have happened to the quarter of a grain of cigarette ash (although it, or its analogue, or ultimate, might continue to exist as a *Something,* or as an *It,* or as *Another,*[1] or as *fivefold Something*[2]), thereby, therewith, the sea, we may infer, would *not* be modified to any measurable degree. The best guess we can make is that the ash has *extended:* and, although it can be said that the sea is *ashen* to the extent of a quarter of a grain of ash, we might conclude, that the material

---

[1]"The THIS is thus NOT THIS, or as SUBLIMATED, and therewith not nothing, but a definite nothing, or a NOTHING HAVING CONTENT, namely the THIS. . . . The thing is ONE, in itself, reflected; IT IS FOR ITSELF but it is also for ANOTHER: and it is also ANOTHER for itself as IT is for another," Hegel. (Translation quoted in Bertrand Russell's *History of Western Philosophy.*)

The learned audience is urged to reflect on these words of Hegel, and then reflect upon *Something, It* and *Another* in our text.

[2]"Now this completeness is made up as follows. Mind is his Self (husband); speech the wife; breath the child; the eye all worldly wealth, for he finds it with the eye; the ear his divine wealth, for he hears it with the ear. The body *(atman)* is his work, for with the body he works. This is the fivefold sacrifice, for fivefold is the animal, fivefold man, fivefold all whatever. He who knows this, obtains all this." *Brihadaranyaka Upanishad* (translation, Max Muller).

which once occupied space, to contain a quarter of a grain of cigarette ash, is now extended to (the space and) the length and the breadth of the sea. (We assume the sea to be moving and mixing—a minor point.)

We must avoid the issues which rightly belong to high physics and belong, possibly, to the propositions implying the ultimate oneness and the indivisibility of all matter and all emanation whatever. We must avoid, too, all attempts at interpretation from phenomena, the theories of the cosmic (as opposed to the biological) evolutions and devolutions, the Hindu *srishti*s and the *pralaya*s, and the Buddhist view of the universal flux *etc*. We must confine ourselves urgently, for our sake, as well as Kipling's, to the *measurable* alone.

Let us, therefore, stop at chemistry: and, at the *measurables* of chemistry. Recapitulating, the quarter of a grain of cigarette ash exists in the sea and it—chemically conjecturing—is in a possible colloidal state.[3] The sea has, let us note in passing, a *measurable* colloidal state or content. Apart from salt, the sea carries, so far known and discovered, some forty-seven gases, minerals and chemicals. Moreover, below the surface waters— where Kipling's drowning might take place—the sea is stratified. It is difficult for the water of one stratum to mix with the water of another stratum. It has something to do with the specific gravity of water, which varies from stratum to stratum, and it makes an invasion or mixing of waters difficult. All is dark in the deepest sea. There is very little movement—the stratified waters hardly move, in spite of the earthquakes under the sea—and there are no breakers, no waves, no wild horses, no sound.

Now to assert (he says he *knows)*, that a saline aqueous constance, issuing from the human puncta lachrymalis, would

---

[3]The views of certain homeopathic spokesmen, and high-potency men— Hering, Boericke, Kent, Weir *et al.*—might be considered as indirectly relevant to our suggestions concerning the chemistry involved—following the disposal into the sea of a quarter of a grain of cigarette ash.

get propelled—by an agency unspecified and *not* mentioned by Kipling—and perform an office, namely, of going down to a drowning, nay, a *drowned* man—through the stratified sea, without mixing, or being *extended,* and being in a possible colloidal state (as we assumed the quarter of a grain of cigarette ash to be)—and regardless of the depth, the darkness, and the stillness of the deepest sea—that, making all allowance for the licence assumed by Kipling, is both improbable, and impossible, despite Kipling's assertion that he *knows:* although, in fairness to him, it is appreciated that he is scrupulous in pointing out the precise nature of the object in question—to wit, his mother's *tears*—and that he no longer insists upon his mother's *love* which might follow him, still (as he had it first), thereby admitting, albeit unwittingly, but necessarily, though obliquely,[4] that it would be both improbable and impossible for her to let her love follow him still: the deepest sea, obviously—he admits it!—is a more perilous proposition than the highest hill: nonetheless, it is this very precision—his scruples—that is his undoing: and makes his proposition outside the bounds of the possibles. Had he not insisted upon *tears* (which have a physical presence, at any rate a visible physical presence) and asserted instead *love* (which has no physical presence, at any rate no visible presence) he might have brought his proposition—somehow—within the bounds of the possible, though hardly within the limits of the probable.

Lastly—let us state the proposition—should Kipling survive the two tremendous disasters, on Mt. Everest in Tibet, and deep down in the Mariana Trench, West Pacific, on his *own* power, so to speak—because, although in the first instance, love follows him, and in the second, tears go down to him, *he is nowise helped, assisted, or rescued by Mrs. Kipling*—and if, (subsequently), he were to be (further) damned of body and soul, he would be made "whole" (the result prophesied).

---

[4]V. para 1.

This promise, or prediction, assures us, without a qualification or reserve, that Kipling is seized of (he says he *knows)* two certainties: those are (1) the certainty of being in a condition known to himself as *damned of body and soul,* and (2) the (subsequent) certainty of being *made "whole,"* through his mother's prayers. (We assume, on Kipling's assertion, that being "whole" is a state of conscious being which is *contra* the state of conscious being *"damned of body and soul."*) Now this proposition can be entertained only if we further assume (*a*) a non-material Kipling, not only the body but (additionally) the soul—the ultimate Kipling, the irreducible, indivisible Kipling, the *ātma,* and the Overself Kipling—and (*b*) we (as well) assume a non-material, a nebulous world, a gaseous ghost world, wherein the qualified Kipling, now non-material, ultimate, irreducible, indivisible— can exist in a state of *conscious* being known to himself as Kipling non-"whole" (after, let us remind ourselves, he has been consciously *"damned of body and soul"*).

It is in *that* non-material world that Rudyard Kipling would enjoy a state of being prior to being made "whole"—a *semi-* or *supra*-purgatorial state of being, which would persist, assuredly, if his mother did not pray for him, and whereabouts, we might further conjecture, bereft of his mother's prayers, he would remain in a state of *conscious* passivity, inaction and incapacity— waiting for a change, namely, of being made "whole."

Now, all in all, Ladies and Gentlemen, in or outside this institute of learning, we do not *know* this non-material, ultimate, irreducible, indivisible Kipling: we do not *know* this nebulous world of his. But Kipling is certain of both: he tells us he *knows.* This certainty—to say the least—makes the entire proposition personal, or mystic, to Kipling and to Kipling alone. We cannot, in the circumstances, urge upon him (*a*) the test of many meanings of a word (*b*) call upon him for decisive proof and evidence of his *Over-Self* and *Over-World* (*c*) demand from him a statement in accordance with the canons of logic: and that being that, we are left with two alternatives: (1) of meekly accepting his

propositions and predictions and so renounce all empirical testimony and (2) simply let him escape by adjudicating his mother
as yet another inscrutable in art. His claim of certainty—he has
said thrice that he *knows*—so far as we are concerned, makes his
proposition without any objective realism (which we can share
with him). The consequences arising from his statement, in short,
are both improbable, and impossible, for all others but himself.

In Kipling's defense, it might be said that he, being a product of his age and society, merely echoes the beliefs of his age
and society: and does no more. Were he born a Bahutu male
individual of Rwanda-Burundi, he would have enjoyed a Bahutu
of Rwanda-Burundi destiny, and entertained a Bahutu of
Rwanda-Burundi attitude to his mother (and evaluated her accordingly): secondly, it might be said in his favour that he is
sincere. He believes. He *knows*. Now beliefs are often based on
wants (and what the believer wants to believe). Kipling, to be
sure, has a certain opinion of his mother. (An opinion—a minor
point—is necessarily different from the object: the subject of an
opinion). And our opinions, and the inferences, conjectures, con-
clusions drawn from such opinions, are very likely influenced
by our wants, our needs, feelings, fears. Kipling believes his
mother to be the most effective agent for coping with whatever
frightens him most. To make this private opinion and belief
public—to support his altogether subjective estimate of her—he
offers us three manifestly fearful propositions: *viz.*, the *highest
hill* and being *hanged* thereon (obviously, a fearful event), the
deepest sea and being *drowned* into it (obviously, a frightening
event), and being *damned of body and soul* (truly a terrifying
event, should it, unfortunately, come to pass): and although, he
cites experience (he insists he *knows*), he is doing—for want of
a better and a fuller analysis—propaganda for his mother, and
doing no more. His evaluation of her—minus the fearfulness and
her alleged almightiness—simply amounts to saying, "Look,
chaps, what my mamma would do for me!" (or, it might be
shrewder to say, "... *wouldn't* do for me"!). Mt. Everest in

Tibet, the Mariana Trench in West Pacific, and the *damning* of body and soul are the devices of saying it aloud: of boasting, bragging, and giving vent.

He extends a purely personal and indeed an entirely *local* matter—his dependence on Mrs. Kipling—to this unpardonable dimension, and he introduces all this fearfulness—*hanging, drowning, damning*—to say this: "Fellows, I love my mom!" That being so, Gentlemen, he would assuredly depend on her in certain fearful emergencies, regardless of Mrs. Kipling's incapacity to cope with such fearful emergencies, and it is no use our (1) demanding from him decisive proof and evidence concerning his assertion, (2) questioning him about the standard and measure wherewith, and whereby, he would have us accept his assertion, however wild, and (3) asking him to be his age and let go of his mother's apron-strings, because we say so.

He has expressed his belief and he would make no concession to us. We may leave it at that. We may let him assert his mother and leave it at that. We may, if we wish, Chairman, regard his mother as the irrational in Art—that mysterious, the yet *another* inscrutable woman—and this evaluation of an Englishwoman, as yet *another* revision and re-creation of flesh and blood. We must not question how this lady stands as a social unit. We should not even breathe if she is a useful member of the society: (*vide* the once extreme Leninist-Marxist and, quite recently, the Chinese—*post*-Chairman Mao and the party planners—view of the true purpose and function of Art.) We must regard her as unique: and definitely as *another*. We may not—in the States, for instance, admittedly economics-wise—regard her, as you regard other women: as female fiscal units, and *vis-a-vis* the male, complementary fiscal units, or as audited Social Security Federal liabilities and, statistically speaking, no more. Instead, we must take her on trust—accept her on her son's word—as an overall *omnipotent being:* and accept her as such simply, silently, summarily. [It is noted that she is not, even symbolically, the Supernatural Being: and that she prays for him to this

(Extra Cosmic) Supernatural Being. He has chosen not to tell us anything of that (Extra Cosmic) Supernatural Being.]

And we are bound to accept Kipling's trespasses on the natural and man-made laws for two more reasons. First—re-affirming what is almost a *cliché*, Chairman—logic would not discover truth although we might detect untruth by it. It is because Kipling loves, that we cannot subject him to a process of logic. Though he does not say so, he *does* love his mother, Chairman. Now then—need love be logical? That, Sir, is the *crucial*, the *central*—if you like, the *real McCoy*—issue:—use any expressive or eloquent adjective or symbol that you will. That is the issue. Chairman, you can't blame Kipling because he loves. . .

Chairman: "I am not blaming Kipling! I don't blame anybody . . ."

'Preciate it! Nice talking to you. Reiterating, Chairman, you can't blame Kipling because he loves. And speaking for him, in his behalf, we have no earthly right to question Kipling and we must submit and suffer all this fuss about his mother, especially so, because—and since—none of us is asserting his mother. The second inescapable argument—in Kipling's favor, and anticipated, indeed cited by this honoree—*(vid. supra)*—is this: in order to verify his assertion—or, indeed, to *falsify* his assertion—we *must* experiment: and enact a *hanging,* a *drowning,* and a *damning* (of body and soul). That would have us up against the law—the *police!*—even *if* we were able to account for, *id est,* philosophically—in the safety of this temple of learning—the spiritual, the non-material element in his assertion!

Meanwhile—while we face insurmountable difficulties—legal, philosophical and other—Kipling remains certain. He is sure. He *knows.* He would make no concession to us. His mind is made up. In fact, concerning Mrs. Kipling, *qua* mother, *qua* an *omnipotent being,* his mind was made up before he began offering us his conditional *if/then* propositions. (His *if,* be it noted, was joined by the conditioning conjunction *then.*) The very improbabilities of his *ifs* made his *thens* improbable. Yet—recapitulating—we must quietly accept—accept what he asserts—for no other reason than this: we cannot, Chairman, in U.S.A. or elsewhere, anywhere at all, prove him false [*unless* we *hang, drown* and *damn* him, *and* so do on the *highest hill,* into the *deepest sea,* and (subsequently) *damn* him, body and soul, *somewhere unspecified,* whereabouts he foresaw the referred *damning* of his body and soul]. The extreme rigor of this obligation, which he has imposed on us, makes me feel helpless and rightly deserving of your Society's sympathy.

It is an utterly unenviable position he has us in: a bind, professors: a veritable Aswan Dam, let me add. And unless it is further meditated upon by the researchman, the academic, and its, among other, logical sequelae considered as a matter of urgent rational necessity, indeed *national* necessity, thereby, hopefully to ameliorate certain forseeable individual and group traumata—*at least,* howsomever—we may as well capitulate to establishment, submit to Mrs. Kipling & Son, give up, and go home . . .

A Voice: Like he said, we can go home now . . .

(Jubilation)

Order, I say!

(Pandemonium)

You tykes have learnt nothing from the trial of Socrates? Never nothing in the world, huh!

–22–

"... Down with Philosophy!"

A random conversation between two members of the philosophy faculty (for the college archives)

Like you were saying . . . *maestro* . . .

You don't have to call me *maestro*, brother. Still. . . It is this problem of conflict. The point I was making—and hope to develop—is that there is an *obligation* on professional philosophers to shift position and commit themselves to *themselves*. It might be a professional necessity. It arises from the cliché *what is good for the cat is not good for the mouse*.

You are going to say more on this?

Well, I have here the skeleton of a story. It is about a character and a Goan. I should like to make a start with the Goan . . .

You do that.

I wonder if it is relevant though . . .

Everything is relevant in philosophy . . .
Thanx. Well, there is this little Goan living in Goa, a few hours' bus ride from Bombay. Except for the bare a, b, c, very little of his background is known or need be known. What's known of him is (a) that he had a Tamilian wife, from the Tamil country, South India, her name Karupai. I might be mispronouncing the name. Tamil's not my field . . .

Neither mine.

. . . (b) at the age of forty or thereabouts this Goan won a position
for himself as the unpaid and unofficial conductor of the village
orchestra in his village, a village hemmed in between Daman and
Diu . . . *Mon Dieu!* pardon the digression . . . (c) That this Goan
aimed at world fame and no less and, in the interest of his musical
career, he changed his name from Wilfred Maria Pereira to
Wilfrid Peacemaker Pareira. Furthermore, it was as the result of
his meeting with a free-drinking publicity man from Calcutta,
touring Pareira's part of Goa, that the ambitious Wilfrid Peacemaker Pareira decided to go original, and exclusive and—as a
consequence—he gave up his starch and black—he owned a
tuxedo, a dress suit—and devised for himself a quilted mask and
a costume, a combination if ever there was, made to *resemble
exactly a parrot* . . .

A publicity stunt? I get it . . .

He decided to conduct his amateur fiddlers' orchestra of six,
wearing his skin-hugging parrot costume, and he managed to
look an enormous parrot, standing up and conducting . . . Imagine a man covered head to foot in quilted green satin, standing
up, and looking like a huge musically canny parrot, conducting.
Imagine it happening in your neighborhood . . .

O.K. Done.

. . . Thoroughly sensationed, his fiddlers were uneasy for a bit
but they soon got used to Parrot Pareira and so pleased was he
with his pose—there is a beaut French expression for this which
escapes me, pardon the digression—that he decided to keep it
up at home as well . . . Imagine a man covered head to foot in
his green satin parot costume, sitting in a chair facing you—his
protruding beak in red satin raised up purposely—to breakfast,
lunch, and sup his staple—mutton curry and rice, apple jam,
chutnee, and salted beer—and subsequently, so dressed, indulg-
ing in *all* the actions that a husband and a householder is sup-

posed to indulge! Imagine this as something happening to you personally . . .

He wore the costume all the time?

Happens-so, he did. Well, Karupai was chilled and no wonder. But being without *option*—as the commercial classes say, pardon the digression—she soon got used to the way her husband conducted himself at home and abroad although she did not complain about it once. "Darling," she said to him, "I can't see *anything* of you!" Now, this would have gone on for years but for that F—for *fateful*, no offense intended, any of your kids listening on the extension telephone?—day of the month of F, when one of the F—for February—concerts was going on . . . and Parrot Pareira faced his amateur six, conducting Beethoven's 9th, movement F—for the *finale*—whereabouts the girls do the chorus to liberty or joy, the ode being by Schiller—*Shillah!*—pardon the digression. Now there was present, at that precise F moment, in the audience of ten or twelve, a visitor—an exchange student who had a scholarship granted and who was holidaying in Goa. The student was from Samoa.

Samoa.

"*Gimme sum'moa,*" said the little girl, asking for more. Fudge. Accordingly, I gave her some more, excuse the digression . . . And this Samoan had tribal connnotations, and those connotations had the things like totem and taboos and such, connoted into him . . . Absolutely all of us—*U* totem, *me* totem, *he* totem, *she* totem, *we* totem, *they* totem, pardon!—*everyone* at all has tribal connotations. If in doubt, have the goodness to consult the nearest anthropologist. It is common knowledge, moreover, the tribal totems and taboos and such are connected with the things classified *sacred*—which you love and venerate—and the things you *abhor*—loathe and fear. The sacred cow, fur'instance: the sacred crocodile, the sacred monkey, the sacred cat of Egypt are the examples of the first class. With regard to the second, suffice it to say that the exchange scholar from Samoa had one basic for those: *"Kill'um!"* As his tribe venerated the crocodile, and *loathed* the parrot, the likely chant formula—in pidgin—would be . . . Can I sing it for you?

You do that.

This' um croco! No kill' um croco!
This' um parrot! Kill' um parrot!

Thank you kindly.

Not to mensh. Did you you know Chinese coast *lingua franca* Pidgin English—slurred by *pidgin* speakers as *pigeon*—means *business* English? From *busy, to suby,* adverbially, *busily:* hence *business* (*pidgin* or *pigeon*), from Middle English *busi,* variant *bist* . . . Consider *bust.* A business failure is a *bust,* demotion from officer to private is a services *bust, busting* horses is to bestride horses which *much* above-average punchers daren't, and what about *busted* in Mexico or Spain or wherever? There are overtones here. One is *scarcely* aware of these issues!

Scarcely.

Well, as soon as the Samoan saw Parrot Pareira, he came up with something savage and chronic: a *kill' um* attitude. He meant to dispatch—reporting his thoughts—that "goddam parrot" as soon as possible. Needless to say that Wilfried Peacemaker had no notion of an enemy sufficiently heated to execute a murder . . .

What happened?

Pardon the digression, but hear this . . . You share a tribal hate and it converges—condenses—upon an *abhorred* bird. And never in all your born days you expect to see, actually *see* your hate, standing up, *defying* you! and *conducting an orchestra of fiddlers!* Now the chances are—when you *see* it—you would be stirred to your inmost, your utter uttermost, and you would want to *triumph* over the *abhorred* object, your hate, and you could do that by destroying the object, and you would be *clean* . . . no after-effects. And you would *not* suffer from the guilt complex of a so-called sophisticate, or the artist, a Gaugin—is that *how* they pronounce it?—or a van Gogh—the last Dutchman I met, *coughed* it!—because, regard this, you have found a straightforward primitive solution to your problem: and you have *not* done in a man but a "goddam parrot." These acts and results have something to do with the resilience in man, his eternal something or other to *be,* to assert his destiny, to *triumph,* to master his environment, till the last *red sunset* . . . as William Faulkner orated in Stockholm when they were giving him the Nobel Prize. Well, it should suffice—to further this account and to explain, in parentheses, the Samoan innocence—if I emphasized that *that* is what the exhange student was up against although he did not know it: and which business, it is granted—to those belonging to a different law, concept, philosophy, tribal connotation, you, me, fur'instance—might amount to a premeditated murder of Pareira. And it could be, too, in U.N. context, actually an issue of amenity or otherwise between *Goa* and *Samoa* . . . observe the particularly felicitous rhyme. Well, the scene's in the backroom of a boarding house in a village of Goa and the Samoan—in pajamas—is pacing up and down, up again, and down, and he acts as if *possessed*. . . "Something of Dostoevsky's in all of us, m'dear," I said to the old lady of El Paso, helping her to iced tea and a cookie, pardon the digression . . . The Samoan was on the brink of a confrontation, a clash of tribal connotations, not forgetting the Goan's individualism, and he *had* to make a decision. And the result of his decision—one could prophesy, with accuracy—could be either a neurosis manifested as compulsive washing of hands, or acting as if washing hands, being terrified of women sheathed in furs, and of door knockers, planning to migrate to Libya—Rommel and Monty, stream of consciousness!—or escape to Siberia—Russian symbol for exile, hardship, living death, *da,* although they are mining minerals and gold up there!—being the uncompromising prude for all his days, a virtuous Liz—you there, Richard Burton, you listening?—do the rounds of psychoanalysts: *or,* hear this, colleague and sir! act in a *manly* manner and *triumph* over his—

tribally subscribed—*abhorred* object by doing in Parrot Pareira and so escape all psychological ill. He could attain this hugely desirable result by *expressing* himself . . . Pardon, we can't all be *expressing* ourselves or can we? There are not too many of them, are there?—the Joyces, the Pounds, the Eliots? "Cash in on your complexes, kiddo," Freud says to me, when I was having one with him in Vienna. I hollered, *"Nein, Herr Doktor, nein!"* And wouldya believe it, brother, he orders *nine* of 'em for me! Does Freud . . .

Sigmund?

Nyet. Barney, Ph.D. Well, having decided, the Samoan bought that very day an antique Indian lance to execute Parrot Pareira. Be pleased to note that the Samoan was neither for *expressing* himself nor for *repressing* himself. Instead, he decided to act F—for Wm. Faulkner, the *triumphant* human spiritwise—*normal.* To destroy parrots and so to *triumph* was *normal* behavior for his tribe and Pareira was confessed—from choice—a parrot . . . And as he stood, poised to execute a fiddlers' piece, the Samoan approached Pareira from behind . . . and before you say *hey! zitt!* he let fly the lance towards the *wooden-O*—for the source, see Wm. Shakespeare . . . Check it out. As defense, you understand. It's all this *reality* . . . these conflicts, confrontations, clashes, contentions, and the international safety problems, too, although the old lady of El Paso says that all my recent symptoms—including the compulsive trigger to digress—are from these meditations I swathe in and the lack of regular meals . . .

Who is this old lady of El Paso?

Symbolic. Well, *the lance missed Pareira by a tenth of an inch or a millimeter!* . . . "Really, old boy, we *must* do something about this *poz'itive* confusion between the British and the Continental *sisstims! Eggswas*perating, what!" urges Bertrand Russell upon the President of the Swedish Academy, as the said President felicitates and hands him the Nobel Prize . . . Excuse the digression. I am all for a *uniform* system of weights and measures.

The metric, I tell you, would be the *sunset* of the prevailing system . . .

What happens to Pareira?

Well, although the Samoan's *zitt!* missed him, it *ripped off his beak,* exposing his upper lip, and the moth-eaten moustache—a spot of *alopecia areata.* . . . There was a terrific confusion among the audience of ten or twelve. In the confusion—convinced that the parrot was slain, totaled—the Samoan *escaped.* Pareira was shocked—*very!* . . . Bang he goes home! Bang he goes to his den! Bang he falls on his cane chair! Bang he covers his face with his hands! . . . Observe the tempo . . . Karupai dropped her washing with a cry, *"Oh, h*ll!"* and following the oath, she rushed into the den. And she saw and heard the pint-sized, beat-up, no-gooder parot *sob!* . . . Stirred to her depths, she put her arms around him.

What happens now?

Hear and consider this. . . What would you *do* if a Samoan hot-head, unknown to you, and inspired by his tribal connections, should identify his abhorred object with you, make an issue of it, and so promote social relations and good will—according to his lights—by removing one more "goddam parrot"—that's you—from the face of the earth, by *zitt! zoing!* letting off a murderous lance at you—and, as a consequence of such cheerful attitudes—from the splendid isolation, the happy independence of a bird—broken and shaken, drive you into the arms of a woman, absolutely regardless of the not too obvious issue *What is good for Samoa need not be good for Goa?* . . . Well, sooner or later we must face the fact of this built-in hostility, this conflict and confrontation possibility between the Samoans and the Goans.

What do you suggest we do?

Well, philosophy's stood for either the Samoan or the Goan—symbolically considered—till the recent *sunset,* I mean past. . . And, accordingly, it's been concerned with such issues as a world

view, a God view, and character, conduct ... Well, what is
suggested now—colleague, philosopher, friend—is that *that's*
all hooha and old rot and fossil and the professional philosopher—dig the qualification "professional"—should commit himself to nothing, nothing at all, but *himself,* to hold *his* end up, to
ensure *his* viability, and, considering the cat and mouse game, it
is a professional necessity. And to dignify it as a philosphical
necessity, we should spew *words!* Agree, if necessary, with *both*
the Goan and the Samoan on all issues including the justified
attempted murder of the Goan by the Samoan: and, in certain
circumstances, murder by the Goan of the said Samoan. That's
contributing—in a professional capacity—to the pleasure of *both*
the Goan and the Samoan! Not the old philosphy's concern with
principles, with right and wrong, law, order, and all that malar-
key! To hell with that jazz, so long as I'm all right, Jack! This's
a professional *obligation,* and it has something to do, too, with
the resilience of the philosophical man, his eternal something or
other to *be,* to assert his destiny, to *triumph,* to master his environment till the last *red sunset*—Wm. Faulkner said it—and so
escape all ill, including the psychological. And that's no *minor*
gain! How many philosophers aren't—in confidence, strictly *not*
for publication—unbalanced, plain nuts, well, *non compos men-
tis?* Ever carried on an international statistical survey of mental
disease among philosophers, amigo?

No.

You'll be surprised! And now the gentler sex—*ha!*—is muscling
into the profession, more of 'em joining the cause! *Place aux
dames!* Lor', talk about susceptibility to neuroses! Yessiree!
Women *have* it! They *have* it!

What do you suggest we do about it?

The first thing to do about it is to *cede* words—isn't that what
professional philosophy's about—*words? Words* to assert, insist,
urge *this: Down* with philosophy! *Up* philosophers!? That's *it!*
That's the *ticket!* That's *conclusive, terminal, final!* ... Mean-

while, Komrad! every unique untouchable among us *genuine* artists and creative fellows, too, owes a professional duty to the society: and, *therefore,* for sure, the story of Wilfrid P. Pareira— as if they didn't know it, the punks!—*must* have a happy ending. That's professionalism and it is—pardon the digression, as a philospher, a ripe nut, once said about something else—an artistic necessity . . . So-*o* . . . Looking through the tear in the quilted satin parrot mask, and recovering, Karupai says happily to kaput Pareira, "Darling," she says to him, smiling, and adjusting her sari, "at last, I can see *something* of you!" which was perfectly true . . . *Adiós!*

–23–

The Mandatory Interview
with the Dean

Wherefore, *benei* Elohim, the sons of God, lusted after daughters of man and were cast out of heaven. Among the sons of God, untouched by passion, was angel Sapphire, beloved of St. Michael, and called Sapphire because of his beautiful sapphire-blue glow. This angel Sapphire, once upon a time, it is said, experienced an innocent curiosity as he saw emerging, from a pool of water, a child of man in a state of undress. Her entire form glittered blue from the angel's own exalted splendor and she was transformed as if she were an ethereal thing; a holy icon. Awed by her beauty, the angel wished to burn incense to her and so committed, by intent, an act of idolatry. He was thereupon exiled to earth to rue for his offense, with his angelic identity intact, his comprehension clear and Michael's love for him unchanged. All that augured his speedy return to heaven.[1]

As he parted from angels, Sapphire invoked the Lord with, *Dominus illuminatio meo!* Thereupon, Michael's sworn foe, Sa-

---

[1]After he took leave of the heavenly host, led by Michael, the Sapphire-blue angel fell upon the highest mountain peak in continental America. The impact flattened the mountain because of the high status of the fallen. The mountain is currently known as Mt. Tom, western Massachusetts, Connecticut River Valley, a bare shadow of its former glory, its present height being 1,202 feet and no more.

tan, King of the Underworld and Earth, smote his thigh with delight and proclaimed Sapphire as the second highest worthy of his kingdoms and lauded him for his independence of will and for his great gift of subtle and succinct sarcasm. How can the omnipotent Lord be anyone's Light, since he could not prevent his angel's fall into Darkness in a condition of high duress? This reasoning caused saints to seal their ears and the assembled demons to laugh out loud. Then Satan, happy and high-spirited, made an astonishing debut.

He appeared to those assembled as a mighty wolf. This mighty wolf whirled furiously as if hunting down and savaging an invisible thing; arching his back, snarling, leaping, spinning, tumbling, and it was an awe-inspiring dance with no mercy for the prey. Then the wolf stopped and an unbearable silence followed. Soon after, he sat on his haunches, raised his head to the sky, his mouth wide open, and from the void of his belly issued forth this disclosure: "Michael's seraph has fallen, born to me! I am kindled and enlarged! Hear me, the sweet angel, the innocent angel, the most ministering angel is mine, ministered by me! You are stained, abused, scorned, abased, abashed, undone, and remissed, disdained and lacked of your seraph, Michael! Mourn, Michael! Forfeit, forfeit, forfeit, I say! Retire, and rage, rage! Michael! Thy heart is in my manacles, fie, fie, O fie! Michael, Michael, O Michael!"

A great cry of fear and jubilation went up from those of the kingdoms who saw this happen and heard this said.[2]

---

[2]In this writer's sight, Satan has a double, a shadow, and it is the wolf. The wolf is white as precious porcelain and now and then is seen with wings. He has jaws harder than steel and with his claws he is known to tear deep into the earth and his angry howl did once command clouds and made a happy summer's day an awesome night. His rages enlarged, the wolf fasts and then heartily feasts upon those who oppose him. Who is there to say it is not so? Everyone is warned not to incur Satan's displeasure. Do not be a thorn in the wolf's paw, be you man, woman or child. Furthermore, and moreover, this is said for the good of all. *Omit,* both in company and in a dialogue with yourself, voicing slanders against the wolf. In your exorcisms, *desist* from issuing commands,

To do him the honors, in the second debut, named the Parade of Appearances, Satan stood before Sapphire first as a 20th Century pawnbroker, wearing a high collar, narrow lapels, a spotless shirt, a necktie with a sapphire stickpin, a silk handkerchief, striped pants pleated up front, very conservative, with a two sizes too small Stetson on his balding head. Following that manifestation, he appeared as a maharaja, wearing an unearthly sapphire in his turban, accompanied by a harem of maharanis in sapphire blue saris and sapphire tiaras. Then he appeared, for the third time, in a guise of a bearded monk in a brown habit, a leather belt, and sandals, his blond hair gathered up in a ponytail, his ten fingers bedecked with episcopal rings set with sapphires. After these revelations, to add to angel Sapphire's wonder, the four sub-Satans, Satan's Senate Extraordinary, materialized as indomitable stallions and in full regalia: velveted, mantled, tasseled, and sashed, with medals and insignias of the highest Orders. The magnificent animals, as the Dukes of the Realm, moreover, wore collars of fine gold mail, and necklaces of flashing silver and were followed by their Kings of Arms, bearing shields and lances. The company surrounded Sapphire and escorted him forward, the Dukes being so merry and spirited, their hooves pounding and ploughing into the metallic path, and the celebrants, now joined by the flutists, provided for those assembled an unprecedented spectacle, a splendid alternative to any ritual or ceremony, ever devised, on earth or under.

The procession stopped at the College of Projects Building for Sapphire's mandatory interview with the Dean. The sentry, a gigantic brute, was asleep on the steps leading to the high

---

"*Exorciso te! . . .*" and while administering baptisms, *avoid* such abuse as calling it unclean, ". . . *immunde spiritus!*", *etc*. For your own sake and the sake of those you call your own, *resist* the temptation to defame the wolf when you bless water, salt, repast, potions, infants, buildings, ships, wines, *etc*. Inventory *at least* the *size* differential between you and the wolf, Mr. High and Mighty! Bishop, busybody, bellhop, witch or whatever. How dare you flay with invective a supernatural thing, fellow! *Selah! Selah! Selah!*

building. Alerted by the sound and sight of the sub-Satans ushering the blue angel, he raised himself up, stretched his spine, lifted up his shoulders to the height of his cheeks, marched in step and stood to attention. It sounded like a bulldozer accelerated, lumbered forward, and with a roar came to a stop, and every massive part, gear, pulley, piston, chain, and wheel, fell into its place.

The waiting *Aide-de-Camp* briskly saluted and led angel Sapphire to the administration complex and to the Dean.[3]

As the beautiful angel entered, the Dean, wearing an immaculate suit, got up and prostrated himself on the carpet. He ceremoniously trembled and convulsed, to signify awe in the presence of his visitor. After observing these formalities, he crawled on his knees, spoke the litany, stood up, and sat down at his desk. He respectfully gestured to the angel to be seated on the sofa. Conforming to the strict security requirements, straight as an obelisk, the *Aide-de-Camp* stood behind the Dean's desk, to guard the Dean.

The Dean said, "Adonai, it is a great honor to receive in this office the All-Highest's owned son. My felicitations! It is also the All-Highest's command to the Senate Extraordinary that you be given the freedom of this College as Governor of the Realm, enjoying the same powers and privileges as enjoyed by our Sovereign, the All-Highest himself. With that end in view, I will try to acquaint you with the working of the College. There will be absolute frankness between us.

---

[3]The Dean, whom Sapphire was destined to meet, had a singular form, almost twice the size of an exceptionally large man. Additionally, he was bald, not the kind loved by the human female, it is said, the raw head whispering in her ear and dredging up the memory of an unforgettable moment and causing her to giggle uncontrollably. His green eyes and bushy grey mustache were no more anomalous in the human mold than the rest of him. All this added up to an emphatic presence—the presence that made you uncomfortable and, if you lingered, gave you a pain in the middle of your brow, then in the ears, then in the temples, and then all over. To sum up, you are fortunate if you do not see such a shape, not one time, not often, not ever.

"We of this College, by our own admission, are contrary, opposed, counter, at variance, unlike, *recto/verso* and *verso/recto,* depending, and juxtaposed as counterpart to Light, God or whoever. The notion that Light, God or whoever, is constant, eternal, suffers no change, is offensive to reason. It offends the laws of nature.

"We of the Darkness are actually the Light. The very conception of Light is impossible without Darkness. Light is Darkness-dependent, contingent and subordinate. The Prince of Darkness is *pre*-existent, prior to the appearance of all lights, and *post*-disappearance of all lights, he reigns again. He is the Alpha and the Omega, the beginning and the ending, who was and will be and *is.* The All-Highest, the Robbed Crown, the Fallen Throne, is the Supreme Light: *ergo,* in whom all other lights are vested, as they appear and disappear, although his own true form as substratum of Light, God or whoever is occult and unseen.

"However, the College of Projects does not concern itself with philosophy. It deals in human souls. Our Incentives Department, generally speaking, does not cause behavior: not directly. It provides models. Although our ultimate model is the All-Highest himself, the Light of all lights, worthy of veneration and imitation by all, in our dealings with human beings, for maximum results, we have recently introduced the minimum exposure technique.

"In this endeavor, we are backed by the strictest scientific protocol and unique research facilities. My Research Department knows when and where exactly which individual butterfly pupated and which human being mated. Our records can tell you instantly whose piles hurt and whose are about to hurt. The information on the files is of utmost practical value: for instance, a certain change in the chemical/mineral content of ordinary drinking water was effected by my colleagues in Research absolutely avoiding brining: yet, they have successfully simulated a death by drowning in the sea, the conclusion to a deep diver's destiny, although the late athlete was nowhere near the sea. The tests run on the deceased, no friend of this College, included blood chemistry studies, Medscreen 23, and a Heidelberg Gastric Analysis. Negative. That is the state of the art here!

"The All-Highest has been blamed for all travail on earth, sire. The College, by adhering to the minimum exposure policy, now holds up man and his woman as culpable[4] since it is they who choose to imitate our models. Subject to their own inclination, quite briefly, our goal is the damnation of their mortal souls for ever and soon or eventually.

"The minimum exposure program requires of us that we promise the potential victims health, wealth, happiness, progress and an all around improvement. This indulges them. It gratifies their need for hoping, dreaming and aspiring. We yield to the spokesmen for the Western nations who serve soup as the *first* item at a formal dinner. We agree this is a measure of civilization. We defer to the Chinese who serve soup as the *last* item at a formal dinner. We agree that the soup-first practice is lacking in culture and civilized behavior. *Circa* the Middle Ages, this College supported Eastern European brides-to-be in their enterprise to protect their persons by wearing necklaces of garlic buds—genus *Allium*, vernacular, stinkweed. If a bride-to-be remained unmolested by the incubi and the werefolk, to ensure fertility, longevity and marital happiness, we endorsed the formula that she eat the necklace on her wedding night. If I may add, the College, *circa* the 3rd and 4th Centuries, likewise endorsed and, later on, helped legalize the hallucinations of the Desert Fathers, the hermits of Egypt.

"We yield to their pleasure, although we can, unaided by any human agency, simulate and intensify the birth pains *via vercundia*. The College, under the present management, does and will maintain the minimum exposure standards. Now and then a

---

[4]*Fons malorum,* source of all evils. Actually, *fons et origo,* source and origin of evil. A slander and an ignorant attempt to summarize the meta-glectic Intent of the All-Highest and its relations to man, both the lay lout and the preaching man. This is a clarification of the Dean's view of culpability.

few among us succumb to their nature and are hostile. Two of my faculty colleagues were committing a robbery recently. They were engaged in this robbery for sport. We do not need merchandise or money. The victim, a dramatic actor, happened to return to his apartment unexpectedly. He addressed the intruders with a dramatic 'Ah, ha!' and added, 'Burglars, I presume!' For lacking in seriousness, he was struck down with horns and hooves and pitchforks and left for dead. I, personally, do not mind mordant jokes or even mockery. There are tribes, your grace, sons and daughters of Allāh, who curse the All-Highest on rising and again on retiring. I myself have been called 'an unmitigated bastard' to my face by a poet in this very office. We let him leave unharmed. Before the adoption of the low-profile policy, in a similar situation, eight of us would have surrounded the man and read to him the Miranda spiel . . . 'You have the right to remain silent . . .' Meanwhile, our Junior Detail would have been loosening up his gas mains, and his holiday condo *puff!* up in smoke and he and his woman would be left with not a penny to call their own. The insurance, meanwhile again, based on material evidence, would have charged fraud, and now the prosecuting attorneys would be singing to him and his woman, 'You have the right to remain silent . . .' They never learn, sire. The administration and its high officials must appear inoffensive at all times.

"My predecessor used to dispense images of nude women in men's dreams. Our present dream stereotype is always in her underwear, partially clothed, panty hose being mandatory. This is minimum exposure. The Research Department, I may add, has not been able to estimate women fully, the common kind, the nesh, and the luxe. Women are important, sire. Go to any hong and you will find women in charge, though appearing not to be in charge. In their desire to exercise power, they practice minimum exposure techniques.

"We can, of course, assume any form at will. Yet, being incorporeal, we remain, in a sense, virgins. As players, we don't feel the wind blowing behind us. This is an extreme situation. I do not like extreme situations . . ." Looking at the yards-high the living, at home, at your hardware store, supermarket, parking lot, wherever and whenever, and it is allowed to do so with impunity.

"The College was in touch with Albert Einstein before his eyes were closed. Actually, I am the chair of a peace among nations movement named after Einstein. Covertly, we support all warfare, and subversion, mythologies, incomprehension, unacceptable behavior, and conflict between the sexes.

"The College recently recognized and took pride in its Junior Detail, named after the All-Highest. They are our runts who indulge in pranks to pressure, to vex. A young woman says to her husband, on the second anniversary of their wedding, 'Did we forget anything?' 'No. Why?' She says, 'You did not remember!' He says, 'I am sick and tired of your anniversaries and birthdays!' He then upsets the kitchen table, smashing up the crockery and walks out. At the marriage counselor's he admits to his tearful wife, 'I don't know what made me do it!' '. . . Dearly beloved, we are gathered here together. . .' Yes, indeed. We are. This gathering has been provoked by solid labor and expense and a little help from the Junior Detail—the quiet emphasis on the Rose of Jericho and loadstone rubbed with camphor and whiskey, the black nail varnish to make effective the High John and the Sabbatic Goat amulet, and the lily and the heather, guaranteed to generate love and the fancies. On their honeymoon, she asks for suggestions to cook him a *pulav* dinner. Looking at the recipe, he asks, 'What do you *exclude?*' While she is lost for an answer, he says, 'What the hell is this Louisiana type hot sauce doing here?' He then kicks open the door and walks out. He, too, says, 'I don't know what made me do it!' However, our Research found that excluding items and ingredients from the recipe was actually a serious argument about money—a demand on her to curb her ostentatious concern with cooking and so conserve money. He had scorned, too, as extravagant, the modest menu for their wedding breakfast—canned consommé, cold cuts, tossed salad, the remains of the wedding cake and coffee. Persistent insistence on saving money, and so decisively interfering with the will of the victim, is an effective means of causing disenchantment and conflict between married couples. In a certain extreme case, Adonai, a woman has been inspired to spite her man by swearing to cultivate hair and to abstain from shaving her armpits for ten years as her Lent. This gave him a hard time, enough to make him go through the ceiling, as they say.

"A bridegroom, flanked by his best man, is facing a frocked clergyman. The two and the congregation await the bride, who is to be slowly walked down the aisle on the arm of her father. It is he who is in the process of losing a daughter and '. . . giveth this woman.' It is then that one of our minimum exposure runts urgently whispers to the groom, *'Your pants are on fire!'* and to the bride, the maid of honor, the bridesmaids and the flower girls, *'Your panties are on fire!'* *'Look out!'* *'Nylon!'* *'Polyester!'* *'Flammable!'* We have taped the reaction. In the ensuing commotion, actually an uprising against the church's consecrated peace, the bride's father, a construction man, who had recently experienced arson from the competition, responding to *'Hey, mister, fire!'* is heard shouting to the officiating minister, *'Mind the circuit breaker!'* *'The two-by-fours!'* *'Watch it!'* *'Watch it!'* However, the really rousing hue and cry comes from the pew and is furnished by the bride's mother. One of the veteran doctors of the College, yielding to an impulse, had stirred up a slumbering mouse, accelerated it up her ankle and sent it racing towards her foundation garments. Her somewhat vigorous gymnastics, including a high leap through the air, and her *circa* French Revolution hat with the brim above her brow turned up high to high heaven, were acknowledged by one and all . . . They were shooting photos too! She had promised her daughter a 'wonderful wedding' . . .

"Oh, dear! What a shindy!" The Dean slapped the top of his head and rocked with boisterous laughter, his enormous swivel chair rocking with him. He wiped a tear from his eye, and restraining himself, said, "Pardon, your grace. I was carried away . . . How did all this happen? To explain this successful sacrilegious kaput, and muting of the church organ, too, *tah dah!* we put two and two together. Among us, dearly beloved, gathered here in this holy kibbutz, a rotten shame! had intruded the Dean's Junior Detail, and fee-faw-fum! Take care now, sir or madam!

"The College inspired a man to compare his beloved female's slender waist to an ant's. An earlier version of the poem, offered to her with a thermos of chilled wine and a freshly harvested rose, had compared the luxuriant curls falling on her brow to the abundant curls of a pampered lamb, seeing the world through the turbid and twisted veil of unclipped wool. It was that poet's etheric double who, while his body lay in bed, confronted me in this office. The College has invisible arrows for astral bodies and we can stretch anyone's silver cord to infinity. We let him go.

"If I may add, a good many women's nightmares originate from us. I have found most women of sixty-five and better, in their dreams, for reasons not quite known to us, prefer not to be called by their real names, but answer to such names as Kimberly, Denise, Geraldine, Maxine, Doris, and *Tracy!* It is an absolute mystery to me.

"The College has taken due cognizance of man's flight to the moon, which constitutes, in our view, an abortive attempt to escape from the All-Highest's authority on earth and under. This operation is *ultra vires,* and may merit punitive action, the moon being well within the All-Highest's contentious jurisdiction, if man, his legitimate quarry, happens to set foot on it.

"We are honored, sire, by your visit. I deeply regret two omissions in the protocol. The College has a legitimate and recognized opposition. The present leader of the opposition, the transvestite, my rival in the next election for dean, was not introduced to your grace. The administration, depending on the principle of freedom of choice, has accepted his entire wardrobe, and the accessories. But recently the campus police have issued as many as five citations to him for dresses that have been considered too daring. I have on my table a notarized complaint against him for sporting a too revealing gown. We are not the bourgeoisie. But we enroll from the bourgeoisie. We need to *appear* as bourgeoisie; with its class mores, morality and so forth. I am fully aware that the most popular course on the campus is the transvestite's *The Female Dress* (graphics and sketches based on *Gray's Anatomy*). My own seminar, *cogito: ergo sum,* in spite of the full budget advertising, has not attracted a single student-participant. Yet, however, the college must draw the line somewhere. The transvestite recently gave an exhibition, *Women of the Amazon Forests,* with himself as an *Amazon Adam,* a cameo participant. Sire, need I add that the women in the Amazon forests environment are *au naturel?* There was a *riot.* He was suspended from appearing in public for a year. The next election for the office of Dean is scheduled next month. We win. We fight this one on moral grounds.

"The College of Projects, further, regrets the absence of security detail on your grace's arrival. However, every inch of the campus ground is guarded. It is, of necessity, a covert operation, under the command of Toro, the Chief of Security.

"Your grace, we neglect security at our peril. Only a day before your felicitous arrival, I myself was molested by the theology don from Oxford. He was hiding behind a tree. And he aimed a cowardly, if I may say so, *karate* chop at the back of my neck. After the near-fatal blow, he held me in a Hindustani hold, after the manner of the boa and the python. My own training and practice, sire, is straightforward, above board attack, *go! go! go!,* no sneaking, the adversaries both visible and ready to give and to take, as in an honest free-for-all street fight.

"I managed to pry myself loose from his hold and ran for the Humanities Building, the Oxford man following and gaining. He got me from behind, his arms around my buttocks—this is a technical lock—and we tangled. Sire, there will be no secrets between us, including those buried in the *top secret* file for our eyes only: the Chief of the Security Detail is *incognito,* disguised as a farm animal. The All-Highest Himself, endowed her, named her Toro, and later on, for meritorious service, dignified her Emerita (Dame Toro, of Academe). Her song, after an Italian

air, *Dame Toro, cara mia!* Her absolute virtue is the gentle look
that requests no reaction or response. This is the inoffensive and
gentle cow, unknown, unnoticed, who roams the campus
grounds, and while the don and I were battling to win the day,
each for each, Dame Toro was stretched on the grass, enjoying
a light slumber. We tumbled and fell on her, head on! I am large,
sire. What followed is beyond description! We barely escaped
with our lives! Two Volkswagens parked outside the Humanities
Building were smashed out of shape, and there were several
windows opened to investigate the alarming din, then shut, and
there was considerable property damage. We had known *power!*
It was as if we had tumbled over the All-Highest Himself and
dared to ruffle up his beard, and *roused* him! The Researchers
who questioned me closely for the record, noted that for two
weeks after the contact with power, actually one of her rear
hooves, I could not communicate: my sole response was the
same for all inquiries, situations, a simple one word: *'Dirigo!'*[5]
The Researchers concluded that my unutterable, unnamed experience was the *ecstasy, mystic union,* the *two are one,* 'I am that'
to attain which men and women fast, observe celibacy, mortify
the flesh, seek solitude in caves and caverns.

"The overpowering experience made me forget the don.
Only a moment before my *ecstasy,* I wanted to dispatch him into
the earth *hic jacet sepultus* and let the earth take him, bone and
brawn, to be fertilizer and let the bountiful earth make returns
abundantly of fruit, grain, greens, for the good of the tiller and
the farmer. We don't clean up, no taking care of what was once
a man, a colleague, now a grave! The Researchers noted that the
don, as he was assisted crawling on all fours from under the
rubble, announced he would resign. He said, too, 'I turned down

---

[5]"I direct!" "I guide!" A severe and traumatic blow is known to open up the
faculties. It is possible the Dean clairvoyantly read the letters of the motto of
Maine, U.S.A. It might have been, on the other hand, an out-of-body experience. This is written for the good of all.

an offer for Vice-Chancellorship of a colonial university for *this!'* He told the chair of the Research, 'I warn you bastards! I will tell all! This is not a cow, dammit! Wait for my autobiography!'

"I can assure you, sire, Dame Toro's eyes were on you all the time during your visit, the Chief of Security at your service! *Pronto!* At the ready, aye!"

Amazed, the angel asked if everything the Dean had said was true.

"Adonai, Adonai! What is the truth? Who speaks the truth? Do *I* speak the truth? *Never,* and that's the truth! Having confessed, I *deny* it! *Now* did I lie! What do you think, sire?"

It was then that the seraph gave his blessings to the Dean and the receding blue disappeared in the swirling darkness. That very instant the beautiful angel was welcomed back in heaven. The Dean assumed seraph Sapphire's sudden departure was occasioned by a summons from the All-Highest. He considered the blessings pronounced upon him an unfortunate retrograde habit, quite unbecoming to a Governor of the Realm and the son and heir of the All-Highest. He turned towards the *Aide-de-Camp,* and sharing his thought with him, said, "This is a matter for the Dukes or the All-Highest Himself, Jonathan." He added, after reflection, "It is not for us sons of bitches to reason why."

granite ceiling, the Dean reflected for a few moments. "Some-times, sire," he resumed, "I wonder if all this is worthwhile! As virgins, we are committed, compromised, but at no time consum-mated. I did promise you absolute frankness . . . However, per-sonally, I am more interested in skills, and in exercise of skills, than in results. Nonetheless, if we are to research women fully, we must know them carnally and as ourselves and not as players. I have spoken as a committed technocrat, of course.

"This College recently gathered a dozen disabled senior citi-zens from a nursing home, helped them dress up in overalls, oversized tweed caps, sweaters, wing collars and long scarves, and persuaded them to perform a precision crutch dance down-town—to the delight of our folk and those downtown. I prefer a coerced dance to an outright effort to render them defunct, *sic transit!* It is they, being dispirited, who should freely wish for the hereafter in the All-Highest's care. Meanwhile, we encourage them to live and try harder. 'You can do it!' 'Up! Up!' *'Enjoy!'* 'You need to get out and meet people, Kathy!' 'You are only sixty years young!' 'You need an alternative to nursing home living!' 'There's a real world out there!' We give them zest. 'Hey, Yancy, you want pretty girls to say "yes" to you, don't you? You are not trying! Put some muscle in it!' 'Having your way again, are you, Joyce? This is no picnic! Get with the pro-gram! Move; unless you want a knitting needle in you!' 'Hi, Shirley, me darlin'!' 'You are coughing something awful, Jeff . . . Have a cigar, one for later.' If they are defeatist, we send them off on vacation, to get away from it all, sleep in bags, camp out and be bitten red and blue by gnats, mosquitoes, mites and other creation, and no indoor plumbing. Most are lucky to be back alive and spared the farmer's shotgun for invasion of pri-vacy, of fishing rights, indecent exposure and using his acreage as the facilities.

"Our policy for the dead is no longer what it was. My predecessor's order was specific: Disturb the dead! Currently, we tolerate a soul which refuses to remain asleep and sing with the choir silent and wishes to make *postmortem* connection with

10